THE IMAGE IN THE
VIEWSCREEN SHIMMERED . . .

With the familiar distortion effect of a starship decloaking, the attacker hung before the Xawe starship *Gift of Flight*. Major Kira's heart pounded as, hours away, she watched the sensor feed from the Xawe bridge.

The ship the Xawe faced was a hulking, ungainly shape studded with angular projections. A Klingon hull, Kira thought, and those look like Cardassian phaser emplacements. Most of the hull was bare metal. Only the central projection, rising up out of the center of the hull like a tower, was painted: a solar face—grim, unsmiling, humanoid—looked out from the towering metal.

The ship fired then, a massive phaser bolt that streaked toward the Xawe ship. Kira flinched in spite of herself as light momentarily filled the screen. And then the screen went blank. . . .

Look for STAR TREK Fiction from Pocket Books

Star Trek: The Original Series

Star Trek: The Next Generation

Star Trek: Deep Space Nine

STAR TREK

DEEP SPACE NINE®

PROUD HELIOS

Melissa Scott

POCKET BOOKS

New York   London   Toronto   Sydney   Tokyo   Singapore

POCKET BOOKS, a division of Simon & Schuster Inc.
1230 Avenue of the Americas, New York, NY 10020

This book is published by Pocket Books, a division of Simon & Schuster Inc., under exclusive license from Paramount Pictures.

ISBN: 0-671-88390-9

First Pocket Books printing February 1995

10 9 8 7 6 5 4 3 2 1

POCKET and colophon are registered trademarks of Simon & Schuster Inc.

Printed in the U.S.A.

PROUD HELIOS

PROLOGUE

THE SHIP SWUNG SLOWLY in its hidden orbit, matching the
course of the local moon, shadowed by that greater shadow.
Power output had been pared to the bone, only the cloaking
device fully operational; within the armored hull, in the
crew's quarters and on the dimly lit bridge, the air was stale,
and cold. The captain bent, intent, over the tabletop sensor
display, watching the lights that were the Cardassian battle
fleet as it swept through the system. He had timed their
passage carefully, aligned his own orbit to keep his ship
perfectly concealed from their sensors. As long as the
cloaking device worked—and it would, or he would know
why—they were safe; even so, he kept his eyes on the screen,
and his crew huddled in the forward section of the bridge,
giving him a wide berth, until the last Cardassian ship had
shrunk to a mere pinpoint on the screen. Only then did he
lean back, working his shoulders—the long wait, and the
unacknowledged tension, had tired his back—and motioned to his first officer, waiting at the command console.

"Bring us back on line."

The first officer nodded, her hands already busy on the controls, and there was a sound like a sigh as life-support whirred back up to full capacity. The lights flickered on a moment later, and the navigator leaned back in his chair, rubbing his hands together against the cold. "Course, sir?"

The captain looked at him for a long moment, long enough to make the navigator shudder, certain he'd gone too far, and then the captain turned away, crossed to the plotting table. At his gesture, the first officer rose to her feet and came to join him, stood respectfully silent at his elbow until he deigned to speak.

"We've made the Cardassian reaches a little hot for us," he said, and the first officer gave a slight, ironic smile in answer.

"Ten ships in as many months," she said. "It has attracted attention."

The captain returned the smile, but his eyes were on the plotting table. "Traffic in the Bajor Sector has increased significantly in the past year."

"The wormhole," the first officer answered, and shrugged. "Everyone wants to be in on the opening of the Gamma Quadrant."

"So do I," the captain said.

The first officer frowned. "That's Federation space—"

"I know," the captain said, and the first officer went abruptly silent, braced for the explosion. To her surprise, it never came. "But here and here—" The captain's hand reached out and into the illusion of space re-created on the plotting table, drew a pair of intersecting lines just on the Cardassian side of the invisible border between Cardassian and Federation space. "I've been analyzing local traffic. The border isn't well defined, a lot of Federation shipping slips over into Cardassian space here—one might call it a shortcut, I suppose. But we can take them there, and still remain in Cardassian space."

The first officer studied the image for a moment, her face carefully neutral in the reflected light. "The Cardassians will still be hunting us. May I remind you that Gul Dukat wants your head and several other parts of your anatomy served to him on a gilded tray?"

The captain laughed. "They haven't caught us yet."

"They haven't really tried." The first officer looked for a moment as though she wanted to bite back the words, but the captain laughed again, and she relaxed slightly. "And the Federation?"

The captain touched keys on the edge of the plotting table, conjured up a new image, a star system, and then, at its edge, a shape like some strange sea creature, a disk within a ring that held three curved pylons. "Their presence hardly matters. There are no starships in the vicinity, no planetary bases. A single space station—what can it do, to stop us—to stop *Helios?*"

He walked away to stand over the navigator's shoulder, gave him the course and watched the Andorian key it in. The first officer stared for a moment longer at the plotting table, and the space station displayed above it, then shook her head, and turned away. The image remained, rotating almost imperceptibly against the illusory starfield.

CHAPTER
1

COMMANDER BENJAMIN SISKO stared in some bemusement at the report flashing on his desk screen. He wasn't sure that he'd seen that particular set of Cardassian characters before, or the scrolling band of—was it really decoration?—that seemed to accompany it, but the message from his own software was perfectly clear, and one he couldn't remember seeing since he had taken command of *Deep Space Nine*. His schedule, for the next four hours, until the end of his working day, was completely clear. He considered it for a moment, thinking of baseball, of an afternoon game played in the holosuite, and pushed himself to his feet. He went to the office door and looked out and down, already framing his request to Dax—she would understand his need to take a brief rest, to spend some unscheduled time with Jake, and maybe keep him away from that blasted Nog—and stopped abruptly, staring down into Ops. The space was all but deserted, only a single Bajoran technician busy at the engineering station. Sisko's face drew into a sudden frown.

5

And not that busy, either: if he wasn't very much mistaken, there was a game, one of Quark's sleight-of-hand games, playing on the technician's screen. Neither Dax nor O'Brien was anywhere in sight.

Sisko's frown deepened, and he came down the short flight of steps into Ops. The Bajoran technician heard his footsteps and turned hastily, one hand fumbling with the controls to abort his game. Sisko drew breath to point out the Bajoran's error—one did not play video games on duty, not on Sisko's watch—when the turbolift rose into Ops, and the science officer emerged. Sisko looked at her, at the sudden, spontaneous smile that formed on Jadzia Dax's face as she recognized what had happened, and was not amused.

"And where the hell is everyone?" he asked.

"Chief O'Brien is on the Promenade working on the modifications to Garak's tailoring equipment, Major Kira is escorting some visiting Bajorans on a tour of the station, and I—" Dax's smile widened even further, became at once good-humored and conspiratorial. "I have been playing truant, Benjamin. I confess. I've been borrowing computer time for a project, and I stopped in to check on its progress." She did not sound in the least repentant.

Sisko sighed, and admitted to himself that he was angry primarily because his crew had beaten him to the punch. Still, this was no way to run a space station—and if he himself was succumbing to temptation, it was definitely time to shake things up a bit. "I think we need to talk, Dax," he said, and turned back up the stairs to his office. Dax followed him, still smiling slightly.

Sisko seated himself behind his desk, waited until Dax had seated herself opposite him. "We're getting slack," he said, and saw Dax's smile widen.

"I'm not sure that that's the problem, Benjamin," the Trill answered. "Or even a problem. The fact that we've finally got the station running at something close to Starfleet standards seems to me to be something of a cause for celebration."

"And I agree," Sisko said. "In principle, anyway. But I'm not pleased to come out of my office and find Ops deserted, and the one tech still on duty playing video games." Dax was watching him steadily, an all too familiar expression in her dark eyes, and for an instant Sisko thought he could see the ghost of the former host looking out from behind the mask of Jadzia's face. It was at times like this that he understood, not just intellectually, but emotionally too, that Dax was truly three hundred years old, and alien—and, he admitted silently, a good and honest friend. "And, yes, I suppose I'm annoyed because I would have liked to take the afternoon off myself."

"I can take over for you, Benjamin," Dax said. Her expression didn't change, but Sisko thought he heard a fleeting note of approval in her voice.

Sisko hesitated, tempted—it had been a long time, too long, since he'd felt that things were enough under control even to contemplate taking an unscheduled holiday—but shook his head, not bothering to hide his regret. "I know. And I appreciate the offer. But there are still a few things I need to do."

"Such as?"

"The Bajoran delegation," Sisko answered promptly. "And I'd like to see how far ahead O'Brien is with the repair schedule. And—" He smiled suddenly, the expression lighting up his rather somber face. "And I intend to draft a notice to all station personnel, to remind them of the procedures that are to be followed if they have to leave their stations. It really won't do, Dax. We can't afford to get careless."

"I do agree, Benjamin." Dax tilted her head to one side, the mottling on her temple just below the hairline suddenly vivid in the office's lights. "I don't like to suggest it, but I

7

suppose we should consider running some surprise exercises."

"If I had suggested that," Sisko said, "you would have called it malice."

Dax nodded, not quite suppressing her smile. "That's why I suggested it."

Sisko grinned, acknowledging the point. "I admit, I'm not eager to do it—I've been enjoying the peace and quiet as much as anyone aboard. My God, this will be the first time since Starfleet took over that we've had the leisure even to think of relaxing. But we can't afford to get slack."

"Shall I—"

Sisko shook his head. "No, I'll take care of it, Dax. If I'm going to break up everyone else's rest, I should at least have the grace to do the work myself."

"As you wish, Commander." Dax levered herself easily out of her chair. "I'll leave you to it, then."

"Thank you, Lieutenant," Sisko began, but his words were interrupted by the sudden shrilling of an alarm in Ops. "What—?" He froze for a fraction of a second, automatically assessing—not environmental failure, not hull damage, not a threat to the reactors—and then thrust himself away from his desk. The technician was already at the communications console, all business now, video game forgotten, his hands delicate on the controls.

"What is it?" Sisko demanded, and came down the short flight of stairs to stare over the technician's shoulder. The Bajoran looked up for a second, acknowledging Sisko's presence, but his attention returned instantly to his controls.

"Commander, I'm picking up a subspace distress call, very faint. I'm trying to boost the pickup."

"I'll take it through my console," Dax said, and the technician nodded, willingly relinquishing the controls.

Sisko watched just long enough to be sure that Dax had taken over, and stepped to the intercom. "Go to yellow alert. Major Kira, report to Ops at once. Chief O'Brien, report to Ops at once." He looked back at the multiple screens. "Well, Dax?"

"It's a distress call, all right," Dax answered, her eyes fixed on her screen. "Not automated—and not Federation, I'm fairly sure. I'm trying to get a clean signal to put it on the main viewscreen."

Sisko nodded, knowing better than to press her further, no matter how much he wanted to, and the turbolift rose into sight, carrying the chief of operations.

"Trouble, sir?" O'Brien asked, and took his place at the engineering console.

"We're receiving a distress call from an unidentified ship," Sisko said. O'Brien nodded, but Sisko was pleased to see that he kept his eyes on the station controls, automatically checking system status. It was a small thing, but one of the reasons he was glad to have O'Brien on board.

"Where is it? Can the runabouts reach it, do you think?" O'Brien asked.

Sisko looked at Dax. "We don't know yet, Chief—"

"I have it, sir," Dax interrupted. "I've routed it through the tactical scanners to boost the signal."

"Put it on the main screen," Sisko ordered. Behind him, he heard the turbolift hiss softly, but did not turn his head as Kira took her place at the operations table. He fixed his eyes on the main screen instead, staring as the image slowly swam into focus. It was streaked with static, but the picture was plain enough: an alien, an amphibian by the look of him—her?—with mud-colored skin and half a dozen fleshy barbels at the corners of its wide, lipless mouth, looked back at him from the bridge of an unfamiliar starship. From the arrangement of the consoles, and the unmatched gear of the crew people visible behind the speaker, Sisko guessed that it was not a military ship, but he didn't recognize the makers.

"—ship *Gift of Flight*," the alien who spoke—he or she

did not belong to any of the species Sisko knew by sight—was saying. "We are under attack from an unknown vessel, request any assistance possible. I repeat, we are under attack and require assistance."

"Can you open a channel to the ship?" Sisko asked.

O'Brien answered, "Aye, sir. I'm working on it."

Sisko nodded. "Dax, can you identify him?"

"Yes, Commander." Dax touched keys, brought a file onto her working screen. "According to the computer, he's a Xawe—they're an independent race, with a couple of colonies on the Cardassian border of this sector. Xawen hasn't joined the Federation yet, though there are perennial negotiations."

"I've never heard of them," Kira said.

"The Xawe keep pretty much to themselves," Dax answered. "They don't engage in much commerce, but when they do . . ." She looked at Sisko, her face very serious.

Sisko nodded. "But when they do, their ships are heavily laden. And rich pickings. I remember them now." In the background, the Xawe captain's voice droned on, repeating his appeal. "See if you can get a fix on the ship, Dax. O'Brien, have you got a channel open yet?"

"No—yes, sir." O'Brien looked down at his console. "Open now."

Sisko faced the screen image, locking eyes with the Xawe captain. "This is Commander Benjamin Sisko, in command of the Federation space station *Deep Space Nine*. We are receiving your distress call, how may we be of assistance?"

"A space station—?" The Xawe's barbels writhed, a gesture that Sisko could only read as anger and despair. The Universal Translator added the same tones to the hoarse voice. "We are under attack, Commander, we need military assistance."

"What's your position?" Sisko asked, and the Xawe's barbels twisted again.

"I am not familiar with Federation mapping conventions—"

"I have a fix on them, sir," Dax interrupted. "There's no sign of another ship in the area."

"We have you on our sensors, Captain," Sisko said, in what he hoped would be a reassuring tone, and looked at Dax. "Well, where are they?"

"They're just inside the Federation's borders," the science officer answered. She touched controls, and a two-dimensional map appeared, superimposed on the lower corner of the main screen.

Sisko studied it, said aloud, "Captain, what's your top speed?"

"We can make warp five if we have to," the Xawe answered. The barbels curled inward, and the translator tinged his voice with grim humor. "We are doing warp five now."

Sisko nodded. "Still no sign of the other ship?" he asked.

Dax shook her head. "But if it's cloaked—"

Which would mean the attacker's a Klingon, Sisko thought, or maybe a Romulan. Or someone who trades with them. He shook the thought away as unproductive, fixed his eyes on the screen. "Captain, come to course—" He looked down at his own console, touched keys to slave his screen to the map on the main viewer. "—one-nine-six mark fourteen. That puts you on the most direct route for the station. Proceed at your best speed—"

"Warp five," the Xawe interjected.

"That'll still take him six hours," Kira whispered, as much to herself as to any of the others. Sisko glanced at her, startled, to see her eyes locked on the Xawe's image, her mobile face set in an expression almost of anguish.

"We don't have that much time, Commander," the Xawe said. He looked down at his console, out of sight below the edge of the viewscreen, and his barbels twitched again. "We will proceed as you suggest, course one-nine-six mark fourteen, but we are only lightly armed. If the ship attacks again, we will surely be disabled."

In the background, Sisko could see the crew moving to obey the new orders, could see red lights flicker across one console—engineering, perhaps?—before one of the other Xawe did something to the control board and the red faded again. "I understand, Captain," Sisko said. *I understand only too well, I've been in your shoes, and I never want to be there again, or to see anyone else faced with those choices*—He clamped down hard on those memories. They weren't important now; what was important was to find out what he could about this invisible attacker, so he could save other ships, if not *Gift of Flight*. He said, faintly surprised to find his voice so steady, "What information can you give us about your attacker, Captain—?"

"I understand," the Xawe said, and Sisko was suddenly perfectly sure that he did. "I—my name is Arrishan fin'Yrach, and my ship is called *Gift of Flight*. Remember us to Xawen if all goes ill."

"I will," Sisko said. *But I'll be damned if I'll give up without a fight. Too bad the* Defiant *is at Utopia Planitia for repairs.*

Again, the Xawe seemed to read his thoughts. The barbels curled again, and fin'Yrach said, "I'm afraid I don't have much data on our attacker, Commander. The ship is large, and travels cloaked; our sensors cannot follow it at all. We came under fire as we crossed the border into the Bajor Sector, photon torpedoes and phasers both—very powerful phasers. We took evasive action, fired three of our own torpedoes, and ran. The ship disappeared again, but it is following. We have seen it uncloak half a dozen times, and we have been fired on repeatedly. We are continuing evasive action."

"Right." Sisko looked at Dax. "Any sign of the attacking ship?"

"No, sir." Dax shook her head for emphasis, still watching her screens. "Not even a sensor shadow."

Sisko looked back at the screen, then down at his own console, the first hint of a plan beginning to take shape in his mind. "Fin'Yrach, what's your cargo?"

There was a little silence, almost a hesitation, before the Xawe answered. "Why do you want to know?"

"Can you tell me, please?" Sisko bit back his impatience, willing the Xawe to answer. After a moment, fin'Yrach's barbels drooped, and the translator relayed a sigh.

"We are carrying the taxes and the ceremonial tithe from Anabasi—our richest colony world—to Xawen itself. We carry letters of credit, and three thousand bars of gold-pressed latinum. And handicrafts of the planet."

"Three thousand?" Sisko repeated. He heard O'Brien whistle, looked toward the engineering station to see the younger man staring openmouthed.

"I wonder what they mean by handicrafts," the engineer muttered.

Dax said, "Sir, Xawen is particularly noted for its manufacture of computer equipment, which they treat as an art form—"

"All right," Sisko said again. "Major Kira. I want you to take the *Ganges,* and rendezvous with *Gift of Flight*—a Federation presence may be enough to scare off this mysterious attacker, now that they're in Federation space."

"Yes, sir." Kira nodded sharply, touched her communicator to contact the docking bay.

Sisko touched the intercom controls. "Dr. Bashir."

To his surprise, the young doctor answered at once. "Infirmary. Bashir here."

"Doctor, we have a ship under attack, a Xawen ship, and

I'm sending a runabout to intercept and offer assistance. Put together a medical kit that can go into the runabout—and I need it immediately."

"Yes, sir." Bashir's voice did not change. "Um, sir, these are the amphibious Xawe?"

Sisko suppressed a surge of unreasonable annoyance. *I don't mind him being right all the time, what I mind is him rubbing my nose in it.* He said, "That's right, Doctor. Immediately, if you please."

"Yes, sir." There was a little pause, but Bashir didn't cut the connection. "Sir, request permission to join the runabout crew."

"Bashir, you're a doctor, not a combat pilot—" Sisko stopped, took a deep breath.

Bashir said, "Yes, sir. But if their ship comes under further attack, there may be wounded, and I'm best qualified to provide frontline treatment. I'm more familiar with my own equipment than anyone else is, too."

And that was true, Sisko admitted. Bashir was young, inexperienced, but as far as medical training went, he was one of the best Sisko had ever worked with. "All right, Doctor," he said. "Bring your equipment to the docking bay—you're going aboard *Ganges.*"

"Thank you, sir," Bashir answered, and cut the connection.

"Sir, the docking crew reports that *Ganges* is ready for preflight," Kira reported.

"Very well," Sisko said. He gestured for O'Brien to reopen the channel to the Xawe ship. "Captian fin'Yrach, how many people are in your crew?"

The Xawe's barbels twitched. "We carry a crew of fourteen."

Sisko allowed himself a sigh of relief. It would be a tight squeeze, but the *Ganges* could carry them. "We're sending an armed runabout to rendezvous with your ship. Keep to course one-nine-six mark fourteen—your most direct line to us—as much as you can. We'll be tracking you from the station as well."

The Xawe dipped his head in acknowledgment. "Thank you, Commander. We will proceed as ordered."

"Sisko out." Sisko motioned for O'Brien to shut down communications, looked away to find Dax watching him with a slight frown. "Well, Lieutenant?"

His tone was forbidding, and intended to be so, but Dax ignored it. "Benjamin, fin'Yrach has already said that *Gift of Flight* was outgunned by this—this pirate. Our runabouts aren't well enough armed to make much of a difference."

"I know." Sisko was aware of Kira watching him, waiting for further orders. The Bajoran was already fond of lost causes, too fond in his opinion, and it was to her he spoke. "Major, I don't expect you to fight the attacker—in fact, I'm ordering you to avoid a firefight if you possibly can. My main concern is *Gift of Flight*'s crew. Your primary mission is to get them to safety. If you can bluff the attacker now that he's in Federation territory, well and good, but my main concern is fin'Yrach and his people."

"Yes, sir," Kira said. She stood braced for an instant, then burst out, "Sir, Bashir's a doctor—"

"Precisely," Sisko said, riding over whatever objection she might have made. "You may need one."

Kira took a deep breath, nodded once. "Yes, sir."

"Then let's get on with it, Major," Sisko said. "And good luck."

Major Kira Nerys made her way through the corridors of the habitat ring to the service bay where the *Ganges* was docked. The airlock at the station end of the docking tube hissed open for her, and she hurried down the dimly lit corridor, the airlock rolling closed again behind her. The second lock opened, and she stepped into the runabout's crowded cockpit. Three of O'Brien's technicians—fellow Bajorans, all of them; none of them familiar—were busy at the various stations, working on the preflight checks. One of them—the senior, Kira assumed, a tall man with a receding hairline and a concerned frown that looked permanent—looked up from his work and came to meet her, snagging a dataclip as he came.

"Major Kira. We've finished bringing *Ganges* on line, and we're about halfway through the preflights." He held out the dataclip, and Kira took it, mutely. "The phasers and shields are all fully operational, but I wanted to remind you that you only have two microtorpedoes aboard. We could load another one, but that would take time—"

"How much time?" Kira asked, scanning the dataclip's miniature screen. As promised, everything seemed to be in order, but it would be nice to have more to fight with than just the runabout's standard equipment.

"Another hour, at least," the technician answered.

And that really was too much time. Kira shook her head, forced a fleeting smile. "Thanks anyway, I think I'll pass. When will we be ready to launch?"

"As soon—" The technician interrupted himself as one of the others turned away from the last console, tucking her dataclip back into a belt pouch. "You can begin the pilot's preflight now, Major."

That was the last step before launch. Kira nodded. "Thanks," she said again, and flung herself into the tiny command chair. The boards lit at her touch, and she ran her hands over the controls, initiating the final check sequence. She heard the airlock open and close again behind her, assumed it was the technicians leaving, and did not look up until she heard someone clear his throat behind her.

"Excuse me, Major? Where should I stow my equipment?"

Bashir, Kira thought. *Sisko would have to send Bashir.* She understood why he was there, knew he was needed, would be better with the wounded than anyone else aboard the station—*but if there aren't any wounded,* she thought, *if I pull this off without a fight, I am personally going to have words with Sisko when I return.* She put that thought aside—she didn't mean it, anyway—and said, "Somewhere accessible, Doctor."

"Yes, I know," Bashir said, in the politely reasonable voice she found most annoying. "But where are you planning to put the Xawe when we bring them aboard?"

It was not, Kira admitted silently, an unreasonable question. *And I don't have an answer yet.* She looked down at her controls, playing for time, and the communicator crackled.

"Major Kira."

It was Sisko's voice, rich and assured, and Kira took a breath to calm herself. "Kira here, sir. Dr. Bashir's aboard, and I'm pursuing the final preflight. We should be ready to launch in ten minutes."

"Good." Sisko paused, and Kira could hear indistinct voices in the background, but couldn't spare a glance at the smaller viewscreen to see what was going on. "Dax has the plans for the Xawe ship—it's a standard freighter, a Federation hull—to upload to you, just in case the transporters aren't working and you have to take them off directly. She suggests you leave your ventral airlock clear for emergency use; it should be easier to mate to their airlocks."

"Very good, sir," Kira said. "Standing by to download."

"Downloading," Dax answered, and lights flared on a secondary console.

Kira turned to Bashir, and was surprised to see that the doctor had already finished tucking his equipment into hull-mounted storage compartments. He had left the approaches to the transporter and the ventral airlock completely clear. He was wrestling a final piece of equipment—some kind of a scanner, Kira thought—into place beside a pull-down emergency bunk, mating its cords to the runabout's power supply.

"It's a hydrator," he said, sounding almost cheerful. "The Xawe are prone to dehydration. They don't have a very efficient circulatory system, and they require a great deal of moisture from the air as well as from their drinking system. This should help keep them from going into anhydric shock."

"Oh." Kira looked back at her boards, saw that the download was complete, and turned her attention to the preflights still flickering through her systems. They were almost finished, and even as she watched, the last indicator bar went from yellow to green.

"Can I help with anything?" Bashir asked, and took his place in the copilot's chair without waiting for an invitation.

Yes, by keeping quiet, Kira thought, but curbed her own tongue. He was also Starfleet, and that meant, of necessity, he knew how to fly a runabout. The little ships were easier to handle with a two-person crew. "Open a channel to Ops," she said instead, and to her surprise, Bashir obeyed instantly.

"Channel's open, Major."

"Kira here. We're ready to launch."

"This is Sisko." The commander's voice was very calm, a deep, soothing resonance that no longer deceived Kira. "You may launch when ready, Major."

"Keying the elevator," Kira said. The runabout shivered as the docking tube withdrew, and then there was a soft rumble of machinery, more felt than heard, as the elevator began to move, lifting the runabout to the surface of the station. The hold light flashed red on her main screen, and stayed red even after the elevator shuddered to a halt.

"Put the scanners through to the main viewscreen," she said, and Bashir obeyed without comment. The screen lit, displaying the outer skin of the habitat ring as it curved away from the runabout. To the left, the core of the station rose in massive terraces, a warning light blinking from Ops at the very top of the station; to the right, the upper docking pylon loomed at the top of the screen, more lights blinking from its tip.

"*Ganges,* you are clear to launch," Sisko's voice said, from the speakers. "And good luck, Major."

"Thank you, sir," Kira said, and took a firm grip on the controls. "Launching now."

Ganges was light to her touch, responsive to her controls. Kira eased the runabout free of the pad, then threaded her way past the upper docking pylons. "We've cleared the station," she announced, and was not surprised when Sisko answered.

"You're cleared for impulse power, Major. Our sensors show that the *Gift of Flight* is maintaining a more or less constant heading, still on course one-nine-six mark fourteen. Backtrack along that line until your sensors pick up the ship."

Kira glanced at Bashir, who shook his head. "I don't show any sign of it."

He seemed to have the sensors aligned correctly. Kira said, "We're not picking them up yet, Commander. You'll have to talk us in, at least until we're in sensor range."

"Acknowledged, *Ganges,*" Sisko said. "Dax will keep you on course."

"Thank you, sir," Kira said. She was oddly glad it was Dax who would be guiding them; she liked the Trill. "Going to impulse now," she said, and triggered the engines. The station seemed to drop abruptly away as the runabout picked up speed, all internal sense of motion banished by the inertial damping system. Kira smiled, watching the stars' apparent motion, and brought the runabout onto its proper course.

"Who do you think is out there, Major?" Bashir said suddenly.

Kira looked at him in surprise. It was hard, she thought, to know how to answer a question like that: it was too tempting to be literal, and tell him, "The Xawe and a pirate," when she needed to stay on at least civil terms with him for the duration of their journey.

"I mean," Bashir elaborated, "who do you think is attacking?"

"I figured," Kira said. She had been wondering that herself, wondering if it was some new Cardassian ploy—but the Cardassians didn't have the cloaking device. "I don't know. There's not really enough data to make a guess."

"Do you think it could be the Cardassians?" Bashir went on.

"*Gift of Flight* said the ship was cloaked," Kira said. "Cardassians don't have the cloaking device." *Yet,* a small voice whispered in her mind. *They don't have it yet.* And if the Cardassians did have the cloaking device, they would certainly use it, she thought, and probably in just this fashion, trying it out on defenseless merchant ships first, and then proceeding against their enemy's warships and planets. . . . "I don't know," she said again, hoping to silence the internal voice. "We just can't tell."

"*Ganges.*" That was Dax's voice, and Kira seized gratefully on the interruption.

"*Ganges* here. What's up, Dax?"

"Another transmission from *Gift of Flight,*" the Trill answered, and her voice was grim. "The attacker has fired on them again. They've taken evasive action, but they're still on the same approximate heading. I suggest you proceed at maximum speed."

"Acknowledged," Kira said. "Bashir, stand by for warp drive."

"Yes, sir," Bashir said. "Major, did we get a look at the attacker?"

Kira darted an annoyed glance at him—she hated it when he got his questions in first—and said, "Dax?"

"Nothing immediately identifiable," Dax answered. "I got some readings, but the ship cloaked itself again almost immediately. We'll be running them through the computers to see if we can pick up anything on enhancement. *Gift of Flight* reports no direct damage, but the captain says their engines are beginning to feel the strain."

"Damn." Kira shook herself. "Thanks, Dax." She looked at Bashir. "Warp four, Doctor."

"Yes, sir," Bashir said, and the stars hazed briefly in the viewscreen. "Warp four."

Kira leaned back in the command chair, watching the numbers shift on her screens. Everything was operating at peak efficiency, all systems green, but she wondered, suddenly, if it would be enough. Whatever was out there—and it felt Cardassian, somehow, the sort of thing they would do—it was a potentially dangerous enemy, and the runabouts were never meant to be warships. *But you stood up against the Cardassians with less than this,* she reminded herself. *You can do it again.*

Dax watched her multiple screens carefully, emptying her mind of everything except the point of light that was the enhanced image of the Xawe ship, and the cross that marked the last sighting of the attacker. Paler lines and symbols overlaid the map of space, indicating both physical features and the invisible, political distinctions. *Gift of Flight* was inside the Federation's borders now, but not by much; at the

projected rendezvous point, *Ganges* would be coming per-
ilously close to the space claimed by the Cardassians. And
that was always dangerous, particularly when Kira was
concerned. Kira had every reason to hate the Cardassians,
and she lacked the temperament—the years of experience,
of training and of healing—that would let her step back
from a challenge, weigh all the implications before she
acted. It was, Dax admitted silently, one of the Bajoran's
most appealing traits. The corners of her mouth lifted in a
faint, fond smile, and she brought herself back to her work.
In the long-range screen, *Gift of Flight* was clearly visible, a
bright pinpoint of light against the schematic chart of the
border; on a second, smaller screen, *Gift of Flight's* course
curved in to meet *Ganges's* approach.

"Any further signs of the attacker?" Sisko asked, his deep
voice rumbling from a point just above and behind her
shoulder, and Dax glanced up without surprise. She and
Sisko tended to think in parallel; it was one of the reasons
she had been glad of this assignment.

"Not yet." She touched her control board, displayed a
blue cross above and to the left of *Gift of Flight's* course.
"This was its location when it fired on *Gift of Flight;* if it
continues on its apparent heading at that point—" She
drew a ghostly line that paralleled the Xawe's course.
"—this will be its course. However . . ."

She paused, and Sisko said, finishing her thought, "You
can't tell much that's useful from one sighting. Dammit,
why don't they show themselves?"

"I'm not picking up wave emissions," Dax said, answering the thought rather than the words. "Not at this range."

Sisko nodded. "Do the computers make anything from
the enhancements?"

Dax shook her head again. "It's large, or at least very
massive, but that's about all I've been able to determine."

"How large?"

"From one-third to one-half the size of a Galaxy-class starship," Dax answered. "I can't be more precise at this point."

"One-third to one-half—" Sisko broke off, frowning. That made it nearly as large as his own lost *Saratoga*. A hostile ship that size would almost have to be heavily armed, and provided with a power plant to match its mass, which meant that Kira was heading into more danger than she, or he, had bargained for. He controlled his instinctive response with a firmness born of long practice. He had long ago learned that his first response to any situation was always the active one; it often worked, but more often it paid him to wait a moment longer, and see what other options were available. Dax's data wasn't firm yet, any more than her course projection could be more than a guess at the stranger's intent. "Or it could simply be very massive," he said, repeating Dax's words. "Heavily armored, maybe?"

Dax nodded. "That's the other possible interpretation of these readings. The computer won't decide between them; they're both considered to have a thirty percent probability of being the correct assessment."

"And which do you think is right, Lieutenant?"

Dax took a breath, buying time for her answer—she couldn't be sure, not with the scanty data—and new lights exploded on her screen. She swung to face her screen, hands already dancing across her controls, and saw a new presence fade into existence, a sensor trace that was already all too familiar. "They're back, Benjamin," she said. "They're firing again."

"Can you get a fix on them?" Sisko demanded. He leaned forward, hands braced on her console, his gaze riveted to the screens as though he could force the alien ship to identify itself by sheer force of will.

Dax didn't answer, too busy with her controls, letting the computer handle the secondary tasks, but directing the main probe herself, tuning the Cardassian sensors as tightly as she could. A series of telltales went from orange to green, indicating that the system had acquired its target, and she thought for a moment that she might have them, but then the lights winked out, and the alien ship vanished completely from her screens. She ran her hands across the controls again, but knew already that it was in vain. "I've lost them. They've recloaked."

"Sir," O'Brien said. "*Gift of Flight* reports that the attacker has fired on them again. They took one hit, no damage, and are taking evasive action."

"Acknowledge," Sisko said, and schooled his voice to betray none of the frustration he felt, observing this battle from a distance. "Dax?"

"This was the attacker's position when it fired," Dax said. A second bright blue cross appeared on her screen, and she traced a line joining the two positions. It matched the projected course almost perfectly, and she felt a small, guilty thrill of pride. "I have a preliminary estimate of their speed and course, based on direct observation and on elapsed time." Her hands were working as she spoke, conjuring numbers from the computers. "You're not going to like this, Benjamin."

"Try me."

"If the attacker stays on this course and speed, he will overhaul *Gift of Flight* a full eighteen minutes before *Ganges* reaches transporter range."

"Damn." Sisko stared at the screen, the intersecting courses, and the numbers that scrolled beneath them. The Xawe ship had already reported that it was making its best speed, and fin'Yrach's engineers would be doing everything in their power to coax a few more ergs of power out of their

24

engines. But *Ganges*— "O'Brien, open a channel to Major Kira."

"Aye, sir."

An instant later, Kira's voice crackled from the speakers, her thin face vivid in the main viewscreen. "Kira here, Commander."

"The attacking ship has fired again," Sisko said. There was no time for preliminaries, and, of all his officers, Kira was least in need of them. "We managed to get a good fix on their position, and a course projection. At present speeds, you're going to be about eighteen minutes late to your rendezvous."

There was a little silence, and O'Brien cleared his throat. "Sir—"

Kira interrupted before he could finish. "It must be possible to push these runabouts a little, sir. Isn't there an emergency factor?"

"Sir," O'Brien said again. "She'll make warp four-point-seven if you push her."

"For how long?" Sisko asked, and gave a bleak smile as he saw the realization strike Kira. The Bajoran, at least, hadn't quite thought through all the implications of emergency power.

O'Brien fiddled with his controls, running a quick series of calculations. "Long enough," he said, after a moment. "You can reach the rendezvous and make it back to the station before any appreciable strain sets in."

"Permission to go to emergency power," Kira said instantly. "Sir."

Sisko looked at Dax, who nodded slowly. "That increase will bring *Ganges* into transporter range ten minutes before the attacker overhauls *Gift of Flight*. If, of course, the attacker maintains its present course and speed."

"Sir," Kira said again.

"Do it, Major," Sisko said.

"Acknowledged," Kira answered, the relief plain in her expressive face before her image vanished from the screen. Numbers shifted in Dax's screens, reflecting the increased speed.

"I can confirm the revised projection," Dax said softly. *"Ganges* will reach *Gift of Flight* first."

If the attacker maintains its present speed, Sisko thought. *And they'd have to be fools to do so—it will be obvious what we've done.* But then, the cloaked ship was unusually massive, Dax had said; maybe that would restrict their speed, too. Not for the first time, he wished for a proper starship, or at least that a starship were stationed in this sector. He stared at Dax's screens, and then up at the main viewscreen, where the intersecting courses wove across dull black. *Nothing yet,* he thought. *Maybe, just maybe, fin'Yrach will be one of the lucky ones.*

"Commander," Dax said, and Sisko turned to her instantly. "I'm picking up wave emissions now, faint but definite. I think—I'm sure it's the attacker."

"Put it on the screen," Sisko said, and instantly a pale blue wedge appeared, tracing a line very close to the course Dax had predicted. "Speed?"

Dax shook her head. "I'm not—no, I have it now." Her voice was suddenly very tired. "Warp seven-point-five-three, Benjamin. They'll overtake *Gift of Flight* with nearly thirty minutes to spare."

"Damn," Sisko said again. He stared at the image in the viewscreen, his mind frantically juggling numbers even though he knew that the laws of celestial mechanics had already defeated him.

"Commander," O'Brien said. *"Ganges* is hailing us."

"Put it on the main screen," Sisko said. "Yes, Major?"

Kira's face appeared again, her expression taut with an agonized fury. "Commander, we have *Gift of Flight* on the sensors now, and what looks like a wave source at extreme range, bearing down on us at seven-point-five."

"I know, Major." In spite of himself, Sisko sounded immensely tired, and knew it.

"Is there any way we can get more speed out of this thing?" Kira looked as though she wanted to hit something, was restraining herself only with an enormous effort.

"Mr. O'Brien?" Sisko spoke without hope, already certain of the answer.

The engineer shook his head slowly. "No." As if he felt Kira's stare accusing him, he burst out, "It's a machine, it has limits—"

"Yes," Sisko said, cutting him off, but the abrupt voice was not without compassion. He had faced this situation before, or ones so like it as to make no difference, the absolute knowledge that there was nothing one could do to prevent a disaster, and that all one could hope to do was to salvage something from the wreckage. He had faced disaster directly, too, and that memory was ashes in his mouth, so that he had to clear his throat before he spoke again. "Mr. O'Brien, see if you can raise *Gift of Flight.*"

"Yes, sir," O'Brien said, his voice restored to its normal state. He worried his controls, repeated the movements, and shook his head. "Sir, they're not responding."

"They may have taken damage," Kira said. "Let me try."

"Wait," Sisko said. "Major, you can't reach *Gift of Flight* before the attacker overtakes it, but you may be able to rescue her people. Tell fin'Yrach to abandon ship—they must have lifepods of some sort. With any luck, the attacker

27

will be more interested in the cargo than the crew, and you can pick them up once the attacker has cleared the area."

"And if they aren't?" Kira demanded, but it was more pro forma than anything. He was right, and she knew it.

"If they aren't," Sisko said, grimly, "it won't make any difference."

Kira nodded. "Yes, sir," she said. "Kira out."

CHAPTER
2

Kira reached across the console to slam her hand down on the communications controls, silencing her link with DS9. Bashir flinched back, startled, but, to her regret, made no comment. The gesture had done nothing to relieve her frustration; she would have been glad of an excuse to rage at him—and that, she reminded herself, was counterproductive, bad leadership. It had been bad leadership in the resistance, and she had conquered it then; she would not succumb to that temptation now.

"Isn't there something we can do?" Bashir asked.

Kira glared at him—*you were here with me, you heard O'Brien*—but heard her own anger in the younger man's voice. "If you can think of anything, Doctor, I'm open to suggestions."

Bashir looked away, but not before she had seen raw pain in his eyes. It was an expression she recognized all too well, had seen before each time she had had to take new recruits out against the Cardassians, that moment when you knew absolutely and for certain that no decision would be a good one, that no matter what you did, someone was going to die for it. Bashir, she thought, striving for her old dislike, was coming to that realization a little late. That was all. And Sisko's plan was the only chance they had of saving the *Xawe* crew. She braced herself to impart the bad news, and nodded to Bashir.

"Open a channel to *Gift of Flight.*"

"Yes, Major."

He sounded definitely subdued, but there was no time to worry about that. The viewscreen lit, and displayed an erratic image, the colors slightly adrift, the edges of objects faintly blurred. Fin'Yrach peered out at her.

"This is the Federation runabout?"

"Yes." There was no point, Kira thought, in trying to explain political subtleties now. "I'm Major Kira, commanding. Captain, we have your attacker in our sensors now, and it will overtake you before we can reach an intercept point. We're running at our absolute maximum now. Can you increase speed at all?"

The Xawe looked back over his shoulder, the barbels twisting as he turned, and there was a musical hum of conversation that the translator did not process. "My engineer says we are already at warp five-point-two. She will try to gain more speed, but she is not confident."

Kira bit back a curse. "All right." *It probably wasn't much of a chance anyway.* "My commander suggests that you stand by to abandon ship. If you take to your lifepods, the attacker may ignore you. We should be able to pick you up safely once we reach your position."

Fin'Yrach's barbels contorted, drawing up into tiny clenched knots, then relaxed. "We have responsibility to our people for this cargo."

"Damn the cargo," Kira began, and bit off the rest of her

words. "Captain, your lives are surely equally important to your people—"

Fin'Yrach shook his head, the barbels writhing. "There are consequences. I cannot commit to this without discussion." He turned away, cutting sound but not visuals.

"Fine," Kira said, to the mud-colored back. *But don't take too long,* she added silently. *We none of us have that much time.* "How long does the computer say they have left?"

Bashir studied his readouts. "If the attacker maintains its present heading and speed, they'll be in close range in seventy-nine minutes—and they'll be in transporter range in ninety."

Kira sighed. Close range was the range at which the attacker's weaponry would definitely overwhelm *Gift of Flight*'s shields; there was a good chance that a persistent attack would damage the Xawe ship long before that point.

"Major," Bashir said. "It occurs to me that the attacker has no reason to spare the lifepods. The Cardassians have a reputation for ruthlessness in such matters."

"I know." Kira controlled the urge to snap at him, to remind him that she had experienced Cardassian "ruthlessness" at first hand. He wasn't doing badly, so far; he deserved at least the consideration she would have shown a new recruit. "First, we don't know that the attacker is Cardassian. Second, we don't know the attacker's real intent. If it's only after the cargo, there's no reason to attack the crew—they must know we're in contact with the ship, so there's no need to hide evidence."

In the viewscreen, the silent image, two Xawe huddled close over a console, barbels twisting in what was obviously a secondary level of communication, jumped abruptly. The Xawe staggered, and one of the two turned abruptly to a different console, where a third Xawe struggled with controls. Streaks of static coursed across the screen, briefly obscuring the image.

"They've been hit," Bashir said, and Kira was startled by the desolation in his voice.

"Wait and see what the damage is." She could see lights flickering on her own console, indicating a transmission from the station, but did not acknowledge it, waiting instead for fin'Yrach. A few moments later, the Xawe captain turned away from his officers and moved slowly forward until his image filled the viewscreen again.

"Federation runabout, I am forced to report that we have received a direct hit on our engineering section." At the corners of his mouth, the barbels hung stiff and still; the translator's voice was too controlled, full of unvoiced pain. "My engineering crew is dead. We are reduced to impulse power, and I see no hope of escape. We have therefore decided to fight."

"Fight?" Bashir repeated, and Kira waved him to silence.

"Captain, we're still—" She looked down at the course plot, checking the numbers a final time. "—we're still more than two hundred minutes from your present position, and we're lightly armed at best. You can't hope to hold them off until we get there. I suggest you prepare to abandon ship."

"No," fin'Yrach said, and the translated voice was filled with sorrow. "It is our obligation, to Anabasi and to Xawen. We will keep transmitting as long as possible, so that you can record all information about this pirate."

"If they're pirates, they want only your cargo," Kira said, through clenched teeth. "Let them have it, save your lives."

"It is a matter of responsibility," fin'Yrach answered. Improbably, his barbels twitched again, curling into something Kira interpreted as a smile. "Remember us to Xawen."

"Captain—" Kira stopped as the image vanished, and was replaced by an empty starscape. Unfamiliar symbols flickered at the bottom of the screen, wriggling past like the Xawe's barbels.

"We're receiving a direct feed from their sensor lens," Bashir said. "I'm recording everything."

"Good," Kira said, and reached across him to acknowledge the transmission from DS9. "Kira here."

"Major." Sisko's voice held a blend of concern and anger. "Why didn't you respond?"

"Sorry, sir," Kira said, and knew she didn't sound particularly repentant. She stared down at Sisko's face, framed in a secondary viewscreen. "We've just received a transmission from *Gift of Flight*. They suffered a direct hit on their engines, and are reduced to impulse power."

Sisko blinked, but made no other movement. "Yes, our sensors picked up a sudden drop from warp," he said. "We haven't been able to raise them. Tell Captain fin'Yrach that his people are to abandon ship."

Kira shook her head. "I already told fin'Yrach that, sir. He says they're going to fight."

Sisko's eyes narrowed. "Can't you talk him out of it? He doesn't stand a chance—none of them do, not in a firefight."

"I tried," Kira said. "They've channeled all their sensor input through to us, we're recording it now. He's cut all other transmissions."

"All right, Major." Sisko took a deep breath. "Proceed at all possible speed to rendezvous with *Gift of Flight*. If they do manage to make a fight of it, there may be survivors. Bring them back, Major, any way you can."

"Yes, sir." Kira hesitated. "If there's anything left to bring back." She closed the channel before Sisko could answer. She was aware of Bashir watching her, eyes wide, his expression torn between protest at her treatment of a superior and reluctant agreement. She made herself ignore him, brought the intercept numbers onto her working screen, and ran the calculations again, just in case she had overlooked something. The answer flashed back almost at once: exactly the same, nothing overlooked. *Ganges* would reach *Gift of Flight*—or whatever would be left of it— nearly two hours after the attacker overhauled it, far too late to do anything except pick up the pieces.

Bashir said, "My God. It's—" His voice trailed off, and he shook his head, swallowing whatever else he would have said. "I'm going to check my equipment," he said, in a choked, unfamiliar voice. "Excuse me, Major."

Kira let him go, heard the soft chirps of a datapadd as he moved around the main compartment, but did not look back. She could give him at least that much privacy: she knew what he would have said—*It's unfair, it's not right*— and she understood all too well the helpless anger. Maybe it was good for him, would do him good to see that the Federation doesn't win all the time, she told herself, but the thought was perfunctory, the old anger missing. The only person to be blamed here was the attacker, whether it was Cardassian or something else. *And I promise you,* she vowed silently, her eyes fixed on the empty screen, the blank starscape that was the image from *Gift of Flight*'s sensors. *I promise you, fin'Yrach, we'll get whoever did this. I'll save your people, any of them that survive, and I will see this killer ship utterly destroyed.*

Bashir returned to his place some minutes later. Kira glanced once in his direction, and looked away, but not before she'd seen the angry scowl. *Good,* she thought, *you'll need that anger, it'll give you the edge you need.* She said, "What are the current positions?"

Bashir scowled at her, but controlled whatever he would have said. "I'm putting them on your screen, Major. The attacker is just coming into standard phaser range."

The ex-resistance fighter nodded in grudging approval— Bashir was doing his job, and better than she had expected him to—but she said only, "Can you get a better fix on the attacker?"

"All I have to work with is the wave emissions," Bashir answered. "They are—very imprecise, Major. This is the best I can do."

Kira sighed. The viewscreen still showed empty space, the unreadable Xawe characters still flickering past at high speed. The minutes ticked by, slow agony. *The ship's in range,* she thought, *why don't they attack?* She knew the answer perfectly well, of course—the attacker, whoever it was, wanted to be certain of inflicting as much damage as possible on its first salvo, to put *Gift of Flight* out of commission quickly so that they could loot at their leisure —but the knowledge didn't make the waiting any easier. She kept imagining the scene on the *Gift of Flight*'s bridge, fin'Yrach and his people gathered there, perhaps to try and orchestrate repairs, perhaps hoarding their power to make their hopeless retaliation as effective as possible, perhaps preparing for near-certain death in some unimaginable way. It was too painful, too much a reminder of her own past, of similar situations that she had miraculously, guiltily, survived, and she put the image firmly from her mind.

"Dr. Bashir—"

She never knew what she would have said to break the silence. The image in the viewscreen shimmered then, the familiar distortion effect of a starship uncloaking, and, quite suddenly, the attacker hung before them, caught in the Xawe ship's sensors. Even without anything to give it scale, it looked huge, the hulking, ungainly shape studded with angular projections—*a Klingon hull,* Kira thought, striving for perspective, *and those look like Cardassian phaser emplacements, but the rest of it . . .* The ship looked as though it had been cobbled together from a dozen different technologies, without regard to aesthetics, or perhaps according to an alien, brutalist sense of form and function. Most of the hull was bare metal, or painted only in pale grey primer, fresh welds showing stark against the dulled background. Only the central projection, rising up out of the center of the hull like a tower—the bridge? Kira thought—was painted, a solar face, grim, unsmiling, humanoid, looking out from the towering metal.

"Not Cardassian," Kira whispered, and didn't know she'd spoken aloud until Bashir looked at her.

The ship fired then, a massive phaser bolt streaking toward them, toward *Gift of Flight,* and Kira flinched in spite of herself as light momentarily filled the screen. And then the screen went blank, was replaced by an innocuous image of the local starfield.

"See if you can raise them," Kira said, dry-mouthed.

"I'm trying," Bashir answered. "Major, there's no response."

No, there wouldn't be, Kira thought. "Keep trying," she said aloud, and Bashir nodded.

"I still have a sensor reading," he said. "The hull's still intact—maybe it just took out their communications."

Kira looked at him, and saw her own hopeless anger reflected in Bashir's eyes. "Maybe," she said, and saw Bashir's gaze falter. "Open a channel to the station."

"Yes, Major."

Sisko's image appeared in the main screen a moment later, looking reassuringly solid. "Yes, *Ganges?*"

"*Gift of Flight*'s taken another hit," Kira said, baldly. "We've lost their transmission."

"Do you still have them in sensor contact?"

"Yes, sir," Kira answered. "So far."

"All right." Sisko's eyes narrowed, as though he were calculating. "Continue as planned, Major, there may still be survivors. But do not, I repeat, do not attempt to engage the pirate. Your concern is for *Gift of Flight*'s crew, not with pursuing the enemy."

Kira bit her lip, but had to admit that Sisko was right, this time. "Yes, Commander."

"One thing more," Sisko said, and his expression in the viewscreen seemed to bore through to her very soul. "You have the recordings from *Gift of Flight*'s sensors?"

Kira looked at Bashir, who nodded and patted his console. "They're all here, Major."

"We have them," Kira said.

"I want you to send the data back to DS9 immediately," Sisko said. "Dr. Bashir, Lieutenant Dax will give you the transfer settings."

"Yes, sir," Bashir said, and a secondary screen flashed the numbers. "I have the settings locked in," he reported a moment later. "I'm ready to transmit."

"Go ahead, Doctor," Dax's cool voice said, and Bashir touched a key.

"Transmitting now."

Seconds ticked by, then minutes. Kira glanced covertly at Bashir's console, wondering when the transfer would end, but couldn't read his screens from her angle. It seemed to take forever, longer perhaps because she understood all too clearly why it was important to make the transfer now: if *Ganges* did not survive, at least all the data they had collected would reach DS9.

"Transfer complete," Dax said at last. "Thank you, Doctor."

"Good, Major," Sisko said, cutting off any answer the doctor might have made. "I want you to keep an open line to us, all data to be passed directly to us from now on. Is that clear?"

"Yes, Commander," Kira said again. *All too clear.* She looked at Bashir, who nodded.

"I've got a direct line set up, Major, using the same settings as before."

"I heard that," Sisko said. "All right, Major, carry on—and good luck. Sisko out."

"Thank you, sir," Kira said, and didn't know if she'd been heard. She sighed, leaned back in her chair. There was nothing more she could do, except wait. Sisko had their data, would have anything else they discovered almost as soon as they collected it themselves. "It's a wise precaution," she said aloud, and Bashir looked at her with a wry smile.

"I rather hope it's an unnecessary one," he said.

Kira returned the smile. "So do I, Doctor, so do I."

Sisko stared for a long moment at the empty screen, then forced himself to turn away, ignoring the numbers that still scrolled across the bottom of the screen. Over two hours before *Ganges* could reach *Gift of Flight*'s last reported position, two long hours during which the attacking ship could take the Xawe freighter apart at their leisure. The attack had been too thorough, pursued with too much ruthlessness, to make it likely that the mystery ship's commander would leave survivors to betray him. He turned away from the screen, from that thought, and went to stand behind Dax at the science console.

"Anything significant from *Gift of Flight*'s transmission?" he asked.

Dax shook her head slowly, not looking away from her multiple screens. "It's too soon to tell, Benjamin. There's a lot of information there, but it takes time for even our computers to analyze that much data." She touched controls, brought something indistinct onto her screen. "I can run the visual image for you, if you'd like."

Sisko sighed, bracing himself. "Put it on the main screen." He looked around Ops, at O'Brien and the Bajoran technicians still busy at their places. "All of you, take a look at this. This is the tape from *Gift of Flight* via the *Ganges*. If you recognize anything about the attacker, I want to know it."

There was a murmur of agreement, cut off instantly as the starfield with its border of Xawe characters filled the main viewscreens. The silence deepened as the stars hung there, all eyes fixed on the screen, and then the image shimmered. A starship hung there, unpainted hull vivid against the stars, the grim solar face glaring from the tower that should be the bridge. Weapons mounts sprouted from every possible angle—Sisko, eyes narrowing, counted four projections that should be phaser mounts on just one of the down-curved, backswept wings—and the hull was laced with what appeared to be sensor points. And then the ship fired, a ball of light that grew and filled the screen, until the image vanished, to be replaced by a different starscape.

Into the quiet, Dax said, "The computers are working on a full analysis, Commander."

"Thank you, Lieutenant," Sisko said, and shook himself back to the business at hand. There was no time, yet, to mourn *Gift of Flight*'s destruction; that would come later, after they had dealt with the destroyer. He made himself look around Ops, making eye contact with each of his people. The Bajorans looked shaken—most of them would have their own memories of war to deal with, he reminded himself—and O'Brien looked grimly outraged. "Well, gentlemen?"

The Bajorans stirred, glancing at one another, but said nothing. O'Brien cleared his throat. "It looks to me like a Klingon hull," he said, "an attack cruiser, maybe, but it's not a Klingon configuration, not with that tower of a bridge. I can tell you more once I've had a chance to go over the enhanced tapes."

Sisko nodded. "Could it be Cardassian?"

O'Brien shook his head. "It doesn't look like anything the Federation's ever seen from them."

One of the Bajorans said softly, "I was a prisoner on a war hulk for a year, Commander, and then forced labor at the yards on Ballimae. I never saw a ship like that."

"The computer doesn't have a match for that ship in our main databanks," Dax said. "I'm searching the secondary libraries now. If I don't find anything, I'd like to extend the search to Bajor's records."

"Permission granted," Sisko said. "Chief, I want you to help Dax go over the tapes, see what you can find out about this ship. I'm particularly interested in its offensive capabilities, and any weaknesses you can see in its structure."

O'Brien nodded, clearly pleased. "Aye, sir, I'll get on it right away."

"Also, Dax—" Sisko paused for an instant, ordering his thoughts. "Contact Starfleet, and see if any similar episodes have been reported in this sector. And I want a report on any other complaints made to Starfleet—anything from direct attack on shipping to commercial dirty tricks. This thing can't have come out of nowhere."

"Yes, Commander," Dax said. "It will take some time to collate those records."

"As soon as you can, Lieutenant," Sisko said. There wasn't much else they could do, at least not until *Ganges* returned, with or without survivors. And Starfleet had to be informed. Even though he knew, rationally, that he had done everything he could do, Sisko still found himself reviewing what he could have done instead, as though he might still find some way he could have saved *Gift of Flight*. And that, he told himself, would never do. It was a waste of time, just another way to put off a task he found unpleasant. He squared his shoulders, and turned toward his office, forcing himself to begin putting his thoughts in order.

"Inform me at once if there's any word from *Ganges* or *Gift of Flight*," he said. "I'll be in my office. O'Brien, patch me through to Starfleet Command, on a direct link."

"Aye, sir," the engineer answered.

Sisko was aware, as he turned away, of Dax's sympathetic gaze, but he did not dare meet the Trill's eyes. Dax knew him too well, or had known him, in an earlier host; Dax would know exactly what drove him now. And while that had been possible to accept from Curzon Dax, who had been physically older, wiser, a trusted mentor, Sisko still found it hard to accept that knowledge in Jadzia Dax. It was getting easier, he told himself, as the office door closed behind him. As he got to know Dax again, he was getting used to the new host form, and was coming to terms with that wisdom that sat so oddly in a young and beautiful body. But, he still occasionally shied away from Dax's ease with all aspects of their old friendship, and felt guilty about his own unease. Luckily, he thought, as the communications menu appeared on his working screen, Dax seemed not to notice —or, more likely, the Trill had been through this transition often enough to be able to make allowances for human behavior.

Sisko sighed, and put that problem aside for later consideration. O'Brien had done his job: a standby notice filled the working screen, warning that a channel to Starfleet was ready, and that someone was ready to receive his message. He took a deep breath, and touched the screen to open the channel.

"This is Commander Benjamin Sisko, Federation space station *Deep Space Nine*. I have to report an unprovoked attack on a Xawe merchant ship in our sector. . . ."

Ganges moved cautiously toward *Gift of Flight*'s last reported position, speed cut to warp two, sensors at full stretch. Julian Bashir strained his eyes, staring into empty screens, and wished for the first time that he had paid as much attention in the required military intelligence courses as he had in his medical studies. He had a good memory, but the material he had been expected to learn was no more than rudimentary—it was not a doctor's job to deal with things like starship identification; even in an emergency, his duties would be expected to lie elsewhere—and for the first time he felt a surge of indignation. He could have memorized the information, that was not a problem; what had failed him was his training, and that was an unexpected betrayal.

And then, quite suddenly, numbers shifted at the bottom of one of the two screens. In the same instant, the computer painted a shadowy haze across the other screen, a core of pale yellow light surrounded by a wider, spreading sphere of blue. "Major!" he said, and ran his hands over the controls, feeding the input directly to the runabout's relatively limited computers. "I'm picking up something now."

"Well?" Kira demanded. "What is it?" Her voice sharpened abruptly. "The attacker?"

Bashir spared her a pained glance—the Bajoran seemed sometimes to go out of her way to think the worst of him—but said only, "No, I think it's debris—the sensors show a core of metallic fragments surrounded by an energy shadow. The shadow is spreading—it matches the results of a matter-antimatter blowout."

"Confirmed," the runabout's computer said, in its emotionless voice. "Further analysis suggests that the energy shadow is a result of the deliberate destruction of a Federation-derived warp drive system."

Gift of Flight," Kira said.

"I'm afraid so," Bashir said. "It's centered on their last position." He ran his hands across the controls again, seeking the largest fragments he could find, and shook his head. "Major, the hull, and everything else, seems to have been completely shattered. I'm not finding any pieces larger than a meter across."

"The bastards," Kira said, and slammed a fist against her console. "Those utter bastards. They didn't need to do that, not if they were after the cargo, they could've left the ship intact—" She broke off abruptly, and Bashir heard the intake of breath as she got herself under control again. "No sign of the attacker?"

Bashir shook his head. "I've ordered the computer to scan for the wave emissions I picked up earlier, and for any other sign of a cloaked ship, but so far there's nothing out there. I think they're long gone, Major. What would they stay around for?"

Kira didn't answer, her thin face intent, eyes on her navigational screens. "What about lifepods?"

"I'm not picking up any emergency beacons," Bashir said. "We may not be in range yet. . . ." He heard his own voice falter, remembering another lecture, and felt that last hope drain away. Emergency beacons, the kind of emergency transmitters installed in lifepods, were variations on standard subspace radio, designed to be heard over interstellar distances. They were well within range of any standard beacon; if there were survivors, they would surely be signaling by now. "They could have non-Federation lifepods," he went on. "Or maybe they're afraid of bringing the attacker back down on them?"

It sounded feeble even as he said it, and he wasn't surprised when Kira didn't answer. She was frowning at her navigation screens, and Bashir risked a direct question. "How long before we reach their position?"

"We'll be in the debris cloud in ten minutes," Kira answered. "Another ten minutes to its center."

Bashir looked at his own screens, willing a blip to appear,

some indication that someone had survived. He glanced over his shoulder in spite of himself, at the equipment he had brought aboard so eagerly. I could have helped them, he thought, I had everything they needed—if only we'd been able to get here in time.

"Open a channel to the station," Kira ordered, and Bashir pulled himself out of his thoughts.

"Yes, Major." He called up another screen, touched the proper controls. "Channel's open."

"This is Dax," the Trill's voice said almost at once, and the familiar and beautiful face appeared in the main viewscreen. "What is it, *Ganges?*"

"We're approaching *Gift of Flight*'s last position," Kira said. "And all I'm finding is rubble."

Bashir winced, as much at her flat tone as at the words, and a new face appeared in the screen.

"Sisko here. Any sign of survivors, Major?"

"No, sir." Kira shook her head for emphasis. "Not so far, anyway."

"And the attacker?"

"Vanished." Kira took a deep breath. "Commander, I want to proceed into the debris cloud, just in case their lifepods were damaged, or they're afraid to make a distress signal. If we scan thoroughly, we may pick up something."

"I doubt that, Major," Sisko said, and Bashir drew breath to protest. "However," Sisko went on, "I agree that you should perform a complete scan of the debris cloud and any surrounding energy shadow, see if you can pick up any traces of the attacker's weapons and offensive styles. But keep an eye out for the attacker. If you see any sign of it, you're to abort the scan and get out of there. Head directly for DS9. Is that understood?"

"Yes, Commander," Kira said.

"Good. Sisko out."

Bashir let out the breath he'd been holding. He hadn't expected Sisko to refuse permission—not Sisko, not with his past—but he hadn't realized how much he'd dreaded the possibility.

Kira said, "Stand by to run a full three-hundred-sixty-degree scan, Doctor. I'm taking the ship to the center of the cloud, and then I'll run a square search until we reach the edge of the debris."

"Standard procedure," Bashir said. That was one thing he did know. Kira scowled at him, and he wondered, not for the first time, why the Bajoran was so short-tempered.

"Let me know when we've reached the center," Kira said.

Bashir nodded, and turned his attention to the boards that controlled the runabout's sensor rig. He fiddled with the controls, invoking an optimization routine, then fine-tuning one section after another until he was sure that the machines would pick up any sign of organic life or organized power. The energy shadow would block some of that, of course, but *Ganges'* sensors were the best the Federation could offer— A light flared on his panel, and he said, "We're in the center of the cloud, Major. It matches *Gift of Flight*'s last reported position."

"No, really," Kira snarled. "All right, run a full scan from here."

"Yes, sir," Bashir said, and stopped abruptly as a thought struck him. "Major, if we shut down all unnecessary activities, I can get a better picture of the debris field— particularly any low-level power usage, such as a damaged lifepod."

Kira gave him another of her fulminating looks, but nodded. "All right, Doctor. Let's try it."

Her hands danced across her controls, and the familiar faint vibration that had filled Bashir's bones since he'd come aboard the *Ganges* faded to an almost subliminal level. It was unnerving, like the absolute silence he had once experienced alone in a cave during his Starfleet training, and he had to force himself to begin the scan. "Mostly duranium and tritanium," he said, his voice sounding very loud in his own ears. "The composition's consistent with a Federation-designed hull. Also a number of composites—also consistent with the internal fittings of a starship. Also—" He swallowed hard, recognizing what the readouts meant, and his memory presented him with a tissue sample he had seen in one of his pathology classes. It had come from a human, a miner, killed in a cave-in in the Miranuri Asteroid Belt; he could see it now, all too clearly, the cellular structure irrevocably exploded, tissues frozen almost as quickly as they'd died, locked in the instant of their destruction. He shut off the image with the skill of long practice—one did not become a doctor without learning to control one's imagination—and blocked out, too, the picture of what those readings meant. "Also organic material."

"Bits of bodies, you mean," Kira said. Her mobile features twisted with revulsion.

"Very small pieces," Bashir said. "None of them can be much larger than, oh, two hundred cubic centimeters." He glanced at Kira, gauging her response—he found his analysis obscurely comforting, but he couldn't be sure how the Bajoran would respond. "They must have died very quickly, Major. The pirate must have destroyed the ship in a single attack—I wonder if they set charges, or if they used a torpedo?"

"I don't suppose it matters very much," Kira said. She looked down at her controls, took a deep breath. "Is the scan complete, Doctor?"

"Yes." Bashir ran his hands over his controls again just to be sure. "Yes, it is. So far, there's no sign of energy output anywhere."

"Then I'm beginning the search pattern," Kira said.

"Keep your eyes open for any energy output anywhere—it could be the pirate, as well as a lifepod."

"Yes, Major," Bashir said. "But I don't think there is any."

"Keep looking," Kira said, through clenched teeth.

"Yes, Major," Bashir said again, and felt the tremor as Kira brought *Ganges*' systems back on line. In the viewscreen, the image shifted slightly, and suddenly he understood what he was seeing. What he had taken for a bright starscape suddenly seemed to move against a background of apparently fixed stars, and he realized that he was looking at the broken bits of the Xawe ship. They seemed to sparkle in the screen, a drift of light against the stars, painfully pretty, like a theatrical effect. And somewhere in that haze of glittering metallic fiber were the bits of organic material—the only remains of *Gift of Flight*'s crew—that were too unreflective, too small to show among the brilliance. It wasn't fair—this was what he had joined Starfleet to prevent—and he swallowed hard, not sure if he was fighting tears or bile.

"Why?" he said abruptly, and half hoped Kira hadn't heard. To his surprise, however, the Bajoran gave him a half-smile that was almost compassionate.

"This is how some people fight," she said. "Like Cardassians. The only thing you can do is fight back. And never forget your dead."

Bashir nodded, not knowing what else to do—he wanted to protest, to insist that there must be, there must have been, something else they could have done, but he knew perfectly well that there had been nothing—and turned his attention to the sensor readouts as though by sheer force of will he could conjure a survivor. He kept his eyes fixed on his readouts as *Ganges* moved through the complex pattern of their search, making sure that every fractional sliver of the debris field was scanned and accounted for.

When they had finished, *Ganges* had returned to the center of the still-spreading sphere of wreckage. Bashir opened his mouth to ask if they should repeat the scan, but Kira reached across his panel to open a channel to *Deep Space Nine*.

"Kira to base."

"Dax here," the Trill answered, almost instantly. "Any— news?"

She had been going to say "survivors," Bashir realized, and felt a chill run down his spine.

"Nothing new," Kira said, her voice tightly controlled. "No sign of any survivors. Permission to repeat the scan."

"Denied." That was Sisko, stepping briskly into the image in the viewscreen. "Unless the first one wasn't adequate—"

"It was," Kira said, involuntarily, and grimaced as she realized what she'd done.

"—then there's no need to repeat it, Major. Return to the station at your best speed."

"But, sir—" Kira began.

In the screen, Sisko shook his head. "There's nothing more you can do, Major. And we need the data you've collected. Return to DS9."

Bashir looked sideways, to see Kira's lips compressed in a thin line. Sisko was right, he knew, but there was a part of him that agreed with Kira, that wanted to make one more futile scan. He was suddenly glad it was Kira's decision, not his.

"Very well, Commander," Kira said. "We're on our way."

The look on her face was still in Sisko's mind five hours later. He stared at the datapadds littering the operations table without really seeing their bright displays, already too familiar with the bare bones of their contents. Whatever the ship was, it was strong enough and fast enough to have destroyed *Gift of Flight* with about as much effort as it would take for him to swat a fly. "How long until *Ganges* returns?" he asked, and Dax looked up from her console.

"Twenty-eight minutes, if they maintain warp four."

Sisko nodded. "Good. How is the analysis of those tapes coming?"

O'Brien said, "I haven't had enough time to go into this in detail, sir, but there are some interesting indications when you analyze the image closely. I think the attacker had already been in a fight, sir."

"Put it on the main viewer," Sisko said.

"Yes, sir." O'Brien touched controls, then stood frowning up at the image. "You see, there, and there, on the starboard wing?" A dot of light appeared, illuminating the sections, which swelled to fill the screen. The grey metal of the hull was streaked with darker lines, like soot from a fire. "There's carbon scoring, and indications of phaser damage—which would have to be from shots that got through their shields, mind you. And then here—" He adjusted the image, rotated it sideways, so that the ragged edge of the port wing filled the screen. At that magnification, the image was a little blurred, and Sisko frowned, unsure what he was seeing. "Right there," O'Brien went on, "it looks to me as though there was some kind of a mounting point—maybe for a weapon, or a sensor cone, it could be either—but whatever was linked there was torn away. If you look very closely, you can see what looks to be conduit hanging from the opening."

Sisko squinted at the image. He could just make out a pair of hair-thin lines, one gently curved, the other twisted like a corkscrew, faintly outlined against the dark background. "Can you get an enhanced image?"

"That is enhanced," O'Brien answered.

"I see." Sisko looked again, but the image obstinately refused to become clearer.

"I've got the computers chasing down that possibility," O'Brien said. "I told them to assume that there are signs of damage, and to give me an interpretation of all markings consistent with that assumption. It might just explain why they had to destroy *Gift of Flight* like that."

"Oh?"

"Yes, sir," O'Brien said. "If I were commanding a ship in that sector, and I'd sustained any serious damage—and I think, assuming this is damage that we're seeing, there has to be worse inside the hull—well, there aren't many places you can go for repairs. Even regular merchant ships are a long way from help out there; you'd have to go halfway to Aden in the Cardassian sector before you'd find a halfway decently equipped starbase. Not that you'd want to deal with them."

"Unless you were a Cardassian," Sisko said, half to himself. "But if you weren't . . ." He nodded to O'Brien. "I see your point, Chief."

"The easiest way to get spare parts for repairs is to take them from another ship," O'Brien said, with a twist of the lips that might have been a smile.

"And then destroy the other ship," Sisko said, "so that your enemies can't tell what you took, or how badly you were damaged."

"Except," O'Brien said, with a quick look at Dax, "we may be able to tell."

"If the attacker took anything out of the engineering section," Dax said, "it should affect the energy shadow left after *Gift of Flight* exploded."

"Assuming, of course, they took major parts," O'Brien added. "But you wouldn't pull an attack like this for anything minor. Not this close to the Federation border."

"That makes sense," Sisko said. "Keep on it, O'Brien. I want to know as soon as your analysis turns up anything new."

"Yes, sir," O'Brien said, and Sisko turned his attention to Dax.

"What about similar attacks? Are there any in records?"

"Yes," Dax answered, "actually, quite a few. I'll put them on the viewer."

Sisko blinked as the screen filled with text. "How many are there?"

"In the past five years," Dax said, "over fifty ships have been attacked in this sector. Now, some of those—" The names disappeared from the list as she spoke. "—are minor, hijackings, rough handling, in-transit harassment, and most of those involve Ferengi ships."

"Normal business practice," Sisko said, and saw O'Brien grin.

Dax's smile was more demure. "I'm afraid so. However, the rest of the incidents on this list—forty-two attacks in all—are almost certainly related."

"Forty-two separate attacks on shipping," Sisko said. "Why hasn't this been reported? Why weren't we warned?"

"I admit, that surprised me too," Dax said. "However, not all the attacks resulted in the loss of a ship—at least a dozen were fired on, but got away—and most of the ships that were attacked were not from the Federation. Primarily the victims have been Cardassians and Ferengi; Starfleet learned about them through secondhand sources."

"That's interesting," Sisko said. "Does that mean this attacker is avoiding the Federation?"

"Very possibly," Dax answered. "Nearly all the attacks took place on the Cardassian side of the border, and this is the first such attack in which *Helios* did not break off when its victim crossed into Federation space."

"Helios?" O'Brien asked.

"There are unconfirmed reports that that's what the attacking ship calls itself," Dax said. "And the name is consistent with the hull markings we saw."

"So why," Sisko murmured, "why has *Helios* chosen to come into the Federation this time?"

"If it's damaged," O'Brien began, and one of the Bajoran technicians interrupted him.

"Excuse me, Commander Sisko. *Ganges* has just docked."

"Excellent," Sisko said. "Tell Major Kira to begin downloading all data from the debris field, and then she and Dr. Bashir are to report to Ops at once."

"Yes, Commander," the Bajoran said, and a moment later Sisko heard her soft voice relaying his commands.

Sisko looked back at O'Brien. "You were saying, Chief?"

"If *Helios* is damaged," O'Brien said, "someone must have damaged it. Do you think the Cardassians are after them?"

"There's some question as to whether or not *Helios* is a Cardassian ship," Dax interjected. "Starfleet Intelligence indicates that, though the Cardassians are believed to have lost ships to *Helios*'s attacks, there are rumors that suggest *Helios* is being backed by the Cardassian government."

Sisko considered the possibilities, staring up at the list of names that filled the viewer's screen. They would need to add one more after today. "See if you can get Starfleet to clarify that," he said, and Dax nodded. The turbolift hissed then, and its cab rose into sight, carrying Kira and Bashir.

"This was a disaster," Kira said, and flung herself out of the cab. "Commander, we have to do something about this. Get a Federation patrol craft out there, a cruiser, something like that."

Sisko suppressed a grin—Kira was never anything less than wholehearted in her reactions—and said, "That had occurred to me, Major. I've already requested that Starfleet send a ship to investigate."

"Good," Kira said. "But we should warn other traffic in the area, tell shipping to stay clear of this sector until we can track down this ship and destroy it."

"This isn't the first attack in this area," Sisko said, with as much patience as he could muster. *"Helios* has apparently taken out at least forty-two ships in the past five years." Kira started to say something else, and he went on talking, raising his voice a little to carry over whatever she might have said. "Lieutenant Dax has a report on all those attacks, and Starfleet's response and analysis, when you want it, Major."

Kira closed her mouth, took a quick breath. "I'd like that."

Dax handed her the datapadd without a word, but her smile was distinctly amused. Sisko suppressed his own grin, and said, "Now. I want everything you can tell me about *Gift of Flight*'s destruction."

Kira looked suddenly very tired, the ready anger draining away. "I don't know what we can tell you that won't be in the computer."

"Even so," Sisko said, and gestured for them to take their places at the table.

Kira sighed, looked at Bashir, and seated herself beside O'Brien. Bashir followed suit, moving with uncharacteristic clumsiness. Sisko glanced warily at him—this was the longest he'd ever heard the doctor keep silent—and Bashir managed a wincing smile, but still said nothing.

"After the pirate—*Helios,* you called it?—took out *Gift of Flight*'s engineering section, we kept them on the screen for about another two hours," Kira went on. "Direct transmission stopped long before that, of course; we estimate that the attacker was in transporter range fifty-one minutes after we lost that image, and *Gift of Flight* disappeared from our screens thirty-eight minutes after that. We reached her last portion thirty-one minutes later, and there was nothing left but pieces, fragments. That whole volume was full of them, like an asteroid field in miniature." Her voice trailed off, as though she'd just realized what she had said.

Sisko said, "Go on, Major."

"There's nothing more to say," Kira snapped. "The ship was blown to pieces, the whole crew was dead. And I'd like to get my hands on the bastards who did it."

"So would we all," Sisko said.

"I think," Bashir said slowly, "I mean, from what we saw, the readings we got, the ship was destroyed in a single explosion, an explosion big enough to break the hull into very small pieces."

"And the crew?" Sisko asked, though he suspected that he already knew the answer.

"I think they were on board when the explosion happened," Bashir said. "Or their bodies were. It's possible they were killed first, and just left there."

"I can't say I find that very comforting," O'Brien muttered, just audibly enough. Bashir glanced at him, perplexed and a little hurt, and Kira scowled.

"Comforting or not, it is evidence. And it shows how these pirates fight."

Well, well, Sisko thought. *I never expected to see that in my lifetime, not Kira defending Bashir.* He kept his expression neutral, and said, "I think that's all for now, gentlemen. Major, Dr. Bashir, I suggest you get some rest. You've done well."

Kira just nodded, but Bashir said, "Thank you, Commander, I—"

Kira laid a hand on his shoulder. "Julian," she said firmly. "There's something I learned long ago that I think it's time you discovered. You need a drink."

Bashir blinked at her for a moment, and then nodded, his face transformed by his sudden, engaging smile. "Oh. Yes. Thank you, Major. I appreciate—"

"Come on, then," Kira said, and propelled him firmly into the turbolift.

As they disappeared from sight, Sisko allowed himself a

grin, but it faded quickly. "I'll be in my office," he said, to the compartment at large, and turned away.

"Benjamin." Dax's soft voice stopped him at the foot of the stairs. "This isn't over, is it?"

Sisko looked at her for a long moment. "No, Lieutenant," he said at last. "I doubt it is." If *Helios* really was damaged, if it had attacked *Gift of Flight* to steal parts for repairs, if it was moving into the Federation for the first time . . . If, if, if: the uncertainties mocked him. But he, and all the station, had to be prepared for the worst. Dax nodded silently, her beautiful face very grave, as though she'd read his thoughts. Sisko straightened his shoulders with an effort. Hard to believe that, only a few hours ago, he had been looking at an empty schedule. He snorted to himself, acknowledging the realities of Starfleet service, and went on up the stairs and into his office.

CHAPTER
3

IT WAS MORNING by DS9's arbitrary schedule of day and night, early morning by most people's standards, but Odo was already busy in the security office, reviewing the report Sisko had given him the night before. His mouth tightened as he read, and remembered the assignment Sisko had added. *Check the ships in dock,* the commander had said, *see if anyone has had any untoward adventures getting here. See if they've seen anything at all that might have a bearing on this pirate.* Odo snorted, looking at the image displayed on the datapadd's tiny screen. If any of the traders currently docked at DS9 had seen anything like that on their way in, they would have run screaming straight to Sisko's office to demand that the Federation protect them from the monster ship. Still, it was an order, and Odo was scrupulous about obeying direct orders. Then his rather thin lips curved into a slow, and not entirely pleasant, smile. It would at least give him a good excuse for taking another look at the Ferengi trader—the ship's name translated to something like

"Sticky-Fingers"—that had arrived two days before, ostensibly with a shipment of holotapes for Quark. Odo did not in the least believe that story—holotapes were cheap, and easily manufactured even on DS9, certainly not worth the expense of importing them from outside the Bajor system—and he would be delighted to take another look at the Ferengi ship, and its cargo.

He called up a list of the other ships in the docking ring, noting four others that had skirted Cardassian space on their way to the station, and then checked the ships scheduled to arrive during the current twenty-four-hour period. Three were due, two Bajorans and a Azhaeri tramp, the *Shannar,* that came and went on a rough six-week schedule. It passed through the possible sector, and Odo made a note to speak to its captain as well. And it was due to dock in forty minutes, if it kept to its flight plan. *If it does,* Odo thought, *it will be the first time since I became security officer here*. Still, the latest display screen claimed that *Shannar* would dock as scheduled, and a quick scan of the dock monitors showed a technical crew busy in the docking port, preparing for her arrival. Odo snorted again, comprehensive disdain, and started for the docking ring.

The ship called *Sticky-Fingers* was mated to docking port eight, and Odo took the long way around, emerging into the cargo bays on level twenty-two to the consternation of a trio of Ferengi crewmen who were lounging outside the main hatch. A cargo sled stood at the foot of the ramp, piled high with transport cylinders, and Odo allowed himself a moment of deep satisfaction. This time, Quark had made a definite mistake. The largest of the three Ferengi sprang into action as the constable approached, leaping forward to block Odo's path, while the one closest to the ship edged back up the ramp.

Odo smiled impartially at the fawning Ferengi and at the

one easing back up the ramp. "No need to announce me. I can find my way."

"Ah, perhaps I should go with you," the Ferengi said, and rubbed his hands together nervously. "You could get lost; Ferengi ships are nonstandard. You could encounter, oh, all sorts of things."

The smaller Ferengi at his elbow added helpfully, "Open wires, open floorplates—"

The first Ferengi silenced him with a look. Odo looked down at them, considering. They were clearly not going to get out of his way willingly, and he didn't enjoy the use of physical force; besides, he hadn't actually expected them to let him on board again without a customs warrant. "I'm here to speak to Quark," he said.

The two Ferengi exchanged a quick look, and then the larger one spoke again. "He's not here, I'm so sorry. You should try back at his place, but I doubt he's awake this early."

"He had better be," Odo said, with a grim smile. "That's his seal on those cargo pods, and I don't recall his export declaration listing a second outgoing shipment."

"I'm sure there's some misunderstanding," the larger Ferengi began, the smaller one nodding madly in agreement at his side.

"Is there a problem, Constable?" That was Quark, appearing suddenly in *Sticky-Fingers'* hatch.

"I'm not sure," Odo answered. "You should be more careful, Quark, your own people didn't know where you were. They told me you were at your—establishment."

"Imagine that," Quark said, and gave the crewmen a sour look. Then he straightened, clasped his hands together, and started down the ramp with what passed for a bright smile. It showed most of his pointed teeth, and Odo, who had seen the act before, was even less than usually impressed.

"Now," Quark said, "what's the trouble, Constable?"

"This," Odo said, and gestured to the double grav-sled piled high with the slim silver cylinders of cargo packed for transsector shipment. "According to the documents you filed yesterday, you had a single shipment of fifty cylinders of *gravis* departing on this ship. Fifty cylinders were loaded yesterday, and yet I find at least another fifty waiting. That is a problem, Quark."

"Actually," Quark began. "Actually, my plans have changed somewhat since yesterday, Constable. It seems I'm able to ship rather more than I'd anticipated—unexpected profits, smaller losses, that sort of thing. So I've revised my intentions. Surely it's not against the law to change one's mind?"

"Certainly not," Odo said. "However, it is against the law to evade the export duty."

Quark's smile sagged visibly, but he recovered himself in an instant. "Evade? Constable, you malign me."

"I doubt it."

Quark contrived to look wounded, showing more teeth in the process. "I was on my way to file the necessary documents."

"And pay the duty?" Odo asked.

"Of course." Quark drew himself up to his full height. "I deeply resent the suggestion that I would deliberately avoid paying my fair share." He glanced at Odo's unyielding expression, and shrugged. "Any more than any other Ferengi would."

"Of course," Odo said, and allowed himself a small, satisfied smile. "But just to avoid any further—misunderstandings . . ."

Quark sighed. "Pay up?"

"Let's just say I want to save you from yourself," Odo answered, and touched his communicator. "Odo to Security. I want a man sent to cargo bay twenty-six at once." He waited for the acknowledgment, and looked down at Quark.

"My deputy will see that you have everything in order before you take those cylinders aboard."

"How unnecessarily generous of you, Constable," Quark said.

"Not at all." Odo paused. "Oh, there is one other thing."

"Yes?" In spite of himself, there was a note of hope in Quark's voice—in the old days, under the Cardassian regime, a comment like that had been an invitation to offer a bribe—and Odo sighed.

"You should know me better than that by now, Quark. It concerns your friend the captain's journey to the station."

"Yes?" Quark sounded wary, and Odo wondered if the other Ferengi had been up to something, or if Quark was being cautious on general principles.

"There have been reports of an attack on a Xawe ship on the Cardassian border. Commander Sisko is quite concerned, and wants me to ask all the captains who've transited that sector if they encountered anything unusual on the journey."

"What sort of an attack?" Quark asked.

"Fatal," Odo answered. "The ship, and her crew, were completely destroyed."

Quark gave him a sour look. "I can tell you right now that Idris didn't run into anything like that. Or see anything, for that matter. If he had, he'd have charged me double."

It was no more than Odo had expected. He waited until he'd seen his deputy, a thin, hard-faced Bajoran, installed at the foot of the *Sticky-Fingers'* cargo ramp, and then glanced at the nearest chronometer. The *Shannar* should have docked by now; he might as well see if her captain had, for the first time in Odo's memory, kept to his schedule. To his surprise, the customs team was at docking port six already, busy at the open hatch that led into the ship's cargo area, and he stopped beside the Bajoran in charge.

"Are you quite sure this is the *Shannar?*"

The Bajoran grinned—he knew *Shannar* all too well—but answered promptly. "Yes, sir, it's *Shannar* all right. I'd know that wreck anywhere. My guess is, the captain's drunk—or maybe sober for the first time."

Or afraid? Odo thought, his attention sharpening. It would take something as serious as fear of imminent destruction to make Radath Keiy hurry. "I want to talk to Captain Keiy," he said aloud, and the Bajoran nodded.

"Certainly, Constable. Oh, and there's a passenger on board."

"For Bajor?" Odo asked. That was still the most common destination, though more and more people were using DS9 as a way station on the journey through the wormhole. To his surprise, the Bajoran shook his head.

"No. And not heading for the Gamma Quadrant, either. Her end destination is DS9."

"Hah." Odo took the datapadd the man extended to him, scanned the tiny characters that filled the screen. The traveler—a Trehanna, a species he didn't know, but that he vaguely thought was humanoid—was indeed scheduled to leave *Shannar* at DS9, and had booked a room in the transients' quarters. "I will want to talk to her, as well." There was no real reason for it, except curiosity—but she had boarded *Shannar* in the sector where *Helios* had been sighted, Odo saw. She might know something, or have heard something, anything, about the mysterious ship.

"She's in receiving now," the Bajoran said. "If you hurry, you may catch her there."

"Thank you," Odo said. "Tell Captain Keiy that I will want to speak with him."

"I'll tell him to contact your office," the Bajoran promised, and Odo turned away.

The receiving station was at the end of the nearest crossover bridge, about a four-minute walk from docking port six. It was a small, sterile place, filled with blued light, and bright display screens—scanners, data-stores, passive and active alarms—banded the walls. A Starfleet ensign, one of the most junior of Sisko's people, was fumbling with the controls of the main console as she tried not to stare at the figure waiting patiently in the column of light from the medical scanner. It had to be the unknown Trehanna, Odo knew, but its shape—*her* shape, Odo reminded himself—was completely hidden under a voluminous dark-green veil. It covered her from head to foot, trailing a little on the floor so that it prevented even so much as a glimpse of her toe; only her eyes were visible, as she turned to face the newcomer, through a narrow slit in the heavy fabric. The ensign gave an exclamation of disgust.

"I'm sorry, ma'am—my lady, I mean—but you have to stand still until the scan is finished."

"I'm sorry," the Trehanna answered. Her voice was low, and very clear despite the muffling fabric. "Please forgive me. I will be still now."

"Thank you," the ensign muttered. "I'm starting the scan again."

"Do you need assistance, Ensign Zhou?" Odo asked, and the young woman gave him a look compounded of gratitude and irritation.

"Not exactly, Constable, but it'd be nice if you'd run her papers through the computers."

"Of course." Odo took the silver disk from the console, and fed it into a universal dataport. The format was nonstandard, and definitely not Federation; Odo grimaced at that—it was all but impossible to keep track of all the petty planets that fringed the Federation, or their paperwork—but ran the matching program. It took a moment for the computer to respond, but then the screen filled with data. According to the search, the Trehanna was from Yrigar on Trehan, and was known as Diaadul, widow of Innaris; beneath the letters was a series of bars that represented retinal and palmprint scans. Odo's eyebrows rose at that, and he said aloud, "No hologram?"

Zhou looked at him oddly, but said nothing. She looked at her console instead, and said, "All right, ma'am—my lady. The scan's complete, you're medically cleared for entry."

"Thank you, Ensign." One hand emerged from a slit in the veiling, a long-fingered, delicate hand that seemed too fragile to carry the heavy rings that banded four of the six fingers, or the stacks of bracelets that encircled her thin wrist. "Is that all?"

"Uh, no, my lady." Zhou looked at Odo. "We still have to verify your identity."

"Oh?" Diaadul's veiled head turned from side to side, as though she was studying the two officers.

"I'll take care of it, Ensign." Odo said. "If you'll step this way, madam." He gestured for her to step up onto the platform that stood in front of the ident machines. "Are you familiar with the procedure?"

Diaadul shook her head again. "I'm sorry. I haven't been off Trehan before. What must I do?"

Odo took a long look at the muffled shape in its trailing veils. "We need to verify that you are the person named on your ID disk. If you would lay your hand on this tablet, here, and look into the scanner—" He touched the hooded lens.

Diaadul stepped forward cautiously, laid her hand on the cool slab of the palmprint reader, and leaned forward until her veiled forehead rested on the edge of the lens. "Just so?"

"One moment." Odo fed her passport into the readers, waited for the machine to give its verdict. Instead, the scanner beeped at him, and displayed an error message. "No, madam, not like that. You will see a blue light at the center of the scanner. Focus your right eye on that dot."

"Ah." Diaadul shifted, obviously trying to see more clearly, and then freed her left hand to adjust the veil's eye slit. "I think—not, not quite." She wriggled again.

"You would find it easier if you removed your outer garment," Odo said, with some asperity.

Diaadul drew back in shock, her hands vanishing into the folds of the veil. "Oh, no!"

"The scanner can't function through layers of cloth," Odo said. It was a statement of the obvious, but the Trehanna seemed unable to grasp the concept.

"I may not," Diaadul said. "Forgive me, but I am a Trehanna and a noblewoman, and I may not show my face to anyone except my lawful husband, now sadly deceased."

"It's a custom," Zhou said quietly, and Odo shot her an irritated look. But he had learned some time ago that when humans or their close cousins invoked "custom" there was little point in arguing with them, no matter how foolish or impractical the custom might seem to more rational peoples.

"Very well," he said. "We'll have to see what we can do. If you would try again, madam?"

Diaadul leaned forward meekly. "I think I have it now," she said, after a moment.

Odo snorted, but pressed the buttons again. This time, the machine flashed its "scan complete" symbol, and a moment later, "identity confirmed." Odo sighed. "All right, Diaadul—"

"Lady Diaadul," the Trehanna interrupted, soft-voiced. "If it pleases you."

"Whether it pleases me or not is irrelevant," Odo said, "if that's the proper form of address." Diaadul made an odd movement, a swaying, dipping motion that Odo realized must be some kind of formal acknowledgment. "Lady Diaadul, then. Your passport checks out."

"Welcome to DS9," Zhou said.

"Thank you," Diaadul said. She stepped away from the scanners, gathering her veil around her once again.

"Are you here for business or pleasure?" Odo asked.

Diaadul seemed to stiffen under the concealing draperies, and Odo wondered what peculiar taboo he had violated this time. Then the Trehanna's shoulders drooped slightly, and she said, in a subdued voice, "Business, sir. I am here to complete arrangements begun by my late husband, the Lord Innaris."

"I see," Odo said. *Actually,* he thought, *I don't see at all. How can anyone do business wrapped up like that? Or maybe it's an advantage having others not able to see her face.*

"I hope it goes well," Zhou said. She looked down at her screen. "I'll have your luggage sent to your cabin—that's on level seventeen of the habitat ring."

"Thank you," Diaadul said. She looked from one to the other. "Perhaps—My lord had dealings with a merchant here, whom I must contact. If it's not too much trouble, perhaps one of you could direct me to one called Quark?"

Odo blinked once. "Madam—my lady. Quark is well known to me in my professional capacity—and I am the Chief of Security for this station. I would advise against doing any kind of business with Quark, under any circumstances."

"Oh?" Diaadul's voice was sweetly innocent. "But I must. It's my duty, as my husband's relict, to finish this last business of his as he would have done it."

"I doubt you could," Odo said. "Forgive me, but you seem somewhat—unused—to business dealings. Quark will have no compunction about taking full advantage of your inexperience, and, not to put too fine a point on it, he would enjoy cheating you of everything you own. You'd be taking a considerable risk in dealing with him."

"Oh." Diaadul's eyes widened for a moment behind the veil. They were quite green, Odo saw, slit-pupilled and inhuman, but the sort of color that some of the younger human males praised ecstatically. Bashir had once lectured him for ten minutes on the particular attraction of green eyes, before he had noticed that Dax's eyes were blue. Then Diaadul shook her head decisively. "No. Thank you very much for your warning, Constable, and I will certainly keep it in mind, but I have to do as my husband wished. That is my duty."

"Let me escort you to your quarters," Odo said. "I can tell you some things that may change your mind."

"That's very kind of you," Diaadul said, "but I am under obligation. I have to complete my husband's arrangement with Quark."

Odo walked her through the maze of corridors and turbolifts, reciting the litany of Quark's more egregious exploits. Diaadul listened attentively, one hand clutching her veil to keep it out of the rolling hatchways, her eyes widening again. Odo began to hope she might be willing to listen to him—it was bad enough for Quark to cheat his fellow merchants, who knew both how to play the game and how to play their opponents; to impose on such an obvious innocent was far worse, and must be prevented—but when they paused outside her assigned quarters, Diaadul shook her head again.

"You've been very kind, Constable, more kind than you needed to be, and I am grateful." She held out both hands, the heavy bangles clattering, and Odo, uncertain of the gesture, took her hands in his.

"And I promise you I will be careful," Diaadul went on. "But you must believe me, I have no choice in this. Though I thank you for the warning." She laid her hand against the doorplate, and disappeared into her new quarters.

Odo stood for a moment, staring after her in baffled anger. He considered pounding on the intercom, demanding that she let him in, listen to him—but she had listened, very politely, and was as stubborn as before. And that was a very human trait, for all that Trehanna were not, strictly speaking, humans. There was nothing he could do to stop her, if she was determined to make her own errors, short of locking her in the security office until she changed her mind. And, though it might make a pleasant fantasy, it would never do. He shook his head, and turned away, heading for the connecting tunnel and the turbolift to the Promenade. But there was one thing of which he felt quite certain: the moment she realized just how much she had lost, she would come running, and then it would be his job to recover it.

He emerged onto the Promenade in a less than pleasant mood, and his temper was not improved at the sight of the *Shannar*'s captain sitting patiently in the outer lobby of the security office. Radath Keiy was a Farruna, large even for his large species, and his bulk seemed to fill most of the available space.

"I was told you wanted to see me, Constable?"

"That's right," Odo said. "I have some questions to ask."

Keiy blinked once, slowly, the nictitating membranes veiling his golden eyes a half second before the eyelids came down, and Odo was meanly pleased by that sign of nervousness. "However I can be of service, Constable . . ."

"Come into my office," Odo said, and led the way into the inner room. The Farruna took up even more space there, a hulking, grey-skinned reptile who seemed unable for a moment to find room for the massive tail that served to counterbalance his heavy body. "Do sit down."

Keiy looked at the available chairs. "With all respect, Constable, I think I'd better stand."

"Suit yourself, Captain," Odo answered. He took his own place behind the desk, and flipped on a working screen. "As I said, I have some questions to ask you, same as I've been asking of all the ships' masters who've come through the border sectors in the last week. Do you mind if I record your answers?"

Keiy blinked again, but shook his head. "No."

"Good." Odo smiled without teeth, knowing that the

expression disconcerted the Farruna. "A ship has been destroyed in Federation space, by something that came out of Cardassian territory. We—Commander Sisko—is deeply concerned, and has asked me to find out if you, or anyone you know, has been attacked, or seen any signs of a pirate's activities."

The nictitating membranes trembled in Keiy's eyes, making him look momentarily blind, but he shook his head again. "I can't help you there, Constable. We had a fine voyage, better than ever. We didn't see anything unusual, nothing at all."

"And none of your friends, your colleagues, have seen anything?" Odo asked.

"Not that they've told me," Keiy answered. "There hasn't been any gossip—except the usual talk about the Ferengi, of course."

"Of course," Odo said. He studied the Farruna for a moment longer. Keiy seemed nervous, but there could be any number of reasons for that, from his involvement in a badly planned smuggling scheme three years before to a general discomfort with legal authority. The Farruna looked back at him, grey face utterly without expression. "If you hear any talk about a pirate ship, I would appreciate your telling me. It's reputed to go by the name of *Helios*."

"*Helios*," Keiy said, on an odd note, like an indrawn breath. "No, I don't know any ship by that name."

"Are you quite sure?"

Keiy shook his head again, showing teeth in his determination. "Never heard of it."

"Very well," Odo said. "That was all I wanted to know."

"Than may I go, Constable? I have a ship to see to." Keiy lifted himself off his tail without waiting for an answer.

"Of course," Odo said, and watched the Farruna maneuver himself carefully through the doorway. Keiy had not told him everything, of that he felt certain, but he couldn't pinpoint the evasion. He ran the Farruna's words through his memory again, but the vague impression refused to become more precise. He shook his head, and turned his attention to the next captain on the list.

Sisko stared at the latest report that filled his desktop screen, wishing that O'Brien and Dax had been less thorough. Unfortunately, there wasn't much doubt about their results. *Helios* was an enormously powerful warship, even damaged; if that was lurking in the Cardassian shipping lanes, or, worse still, heading into the Federation, even Starfleet would have its work cut out to contain the menace. And yet, and yet . . . He tapped one finger on the edge of the display, not quite ready to move on to the next screen. If a ship this big, this aggressive, had been active in the border sectors, why hadn't the Federation heard rumors of it before now? Why hadn't it moved into Federation space before this?

The door chime sounded, and he looked up, to see Odo signaling for admittance. Sisko touched the button to admit the constable, not sorry for the interruption, and Odo shouldered his way into the office. There was always something a little jerky about his movements, as though he were not yet fully comfortable with the shape he wore. Or maybe, Sisko thought, as he gestured for the other to take a seat, maybe it takes more practice than I could ever imagine to learn to manage a humanoid shape.

"What can I do for you, Constable?" he asked. Instinctively, he ran down the list of possible disasters that would fall under Odo's jurisdiction—conspiracy, terrorism, smuggling, even Bajoran quarrels escalating into a full-blown feud—but none of those seemed to match the rather perplexed expression on Odo's face. Of course, Sisko thought, it's hard to be sure what he means by any given expression. It's worse than a foreign language, almost impossible to read a face that "speaks" with an accent.

"You asked me to talk to the starship captains currently docked to the station," Odo said. As always, his voice was gruff, almost harsh, and Sisko wondered again how much of that was due to the alien shape. "I've done so, and I have my report."

Which you didn't need to make in person, Sisko thought, and waited. When it became clear that Odo didn't intend to continue, he said, "All right. I'm listening."

Odo laid a dataclip on the desktop. "The details are there," he said, "but, in summary, there's nothing. No one here at present will say that they know anything about this mystery ship. They haven't seen or heard of it, not even as a rumor."

Sisko raised an eyebrow at that. "Starfleet records report, what, forty-two attacks. And no one's heard anything?"

"No." Odo's mouth curved into an unmistakably sour smile. "That they'll admit to, anyway."

"And do you believe them?" Sisko asked.

"I'm not certain," Odo said. "Commander, I've interviewed seven captains of assorted skills and reputations, and all of them claim to have heard nothing more than the usual rumors of rough trade practices. The Ferengi were, of course, willing to sell me any story I'd buy, but I'd have to discount most of what they said. And, while we're speaking of the Ferengi . . ."

"You have another complaint against Quark." In spite of his best intentions, Sisko sounded resigned, and Odo gave him a sharp glance.

"With all due respect, Commander, it is my job to stop anyone from evading station's law. I can't help it that Quark is the most egregious offender on the station."

"I know." Sisko sighed. "It's just—"

"He amuses you," Odo said. "And he provides some useful services. I'm aware of that, I assure you. But the fact remains that I caught him trying to slip an extra fifty cargo containers of *gravis* onto the *Sticky-Fingers* this morning."

"Fifty!" Sisko shook his head. "Even for Quark, that's excessive."

"Quite." Odo smiled. "However, the situation has been dealt with. He has agreed to pay the necessary fees, and I have a man stationed in the hatch to make sure he does so."

"Excellent," Sisko said, and meant it. "That was well handled, Odo."

"Thank you."

Sisko lifted an eyebrow again. The shapeshifter sounded preoccupied, as though for once he was uncertain of a situation. Before he could say anything, however, Odo cleared his throat.

"There was one other matter."

"Yes?"

"There was a passenger on the *Shannar* when she arrived."

"I heard something about that," Sisko said. A mysteriously veiled woman, the station grapevine had reported; he had overheard one of the Bajorans saying something about a princess, while her compatriot shook her head, insisting the stranger was some kind of spy.

"I gather that the station is talking already," Odo said, sourly.

Sisko grinned. "I've heard everything from a Tuareg in drag to a runaway princess," he said frankly, "with the Bajorans voting—no surprises—for her to be a Cardassian spy. What is she, and where's she headed?"

"Nowhere," Odo said. "Or, more precisely, she was coming here." He reached into his coveralls, and produced a second dataclip. "I've included her passport records and verification, not that there's much information on them.

Her name is Diaadul, widow of Innaris—Lady Diaadul is her title—and she's a Trehanna. Apparently, it's customary for their women to go veiled."

"So what brings her here?" Sisko asked.

"Apparently it's also their custom for the widow to finish her late husband's business affairs," Odo said. "I checked the library computers. It seems to be a religious duty of some sort." He glowered at Sisko. "And that's what I'm concerned about. Lord Innaris seems to have had some sort of deal going with Quark."

"I see," Sisko said.

"With all due respect, Commander, I'm not sure that you do," Odo said. "Diaadul is grossly inexperienced. The Trehanna believe that it's inappropriate for women to concern themselves with trade or finance, and she seems to follow their customs pretty closely. By her own admission, she's never been off Trehan before—she could barely work the scanners in the immigration section. I have no desire to see her cheated by Quark."

Sisko eyed his constable warily. He had never heard Odo so passionate about anyone before—no, he thought, not passionate, but protective. She must be quite something, the Lady Diaadul, if she could find the protective streak in Odo so quickly. "I assume you've already warned her of Quark's reputation."

"Of course. She insists she has to carry out her late husband's wishes." Odo leaned forward slightly. "I would like your permission, Commander, to do whatever's necessary to protect her."

Sisko sighed. He could understand Odo's position. It would be impossible for Quark, or any Ferengi, given their cultural biases, not to cheat when confronted with an inexperienced trading partner. Quark might well complain that she was hardly worth the effort, but that wouldn't stop him from robbing her. And it was the station's responsibility to look after transients' interests as well as their own. "All right," he said aloud. "But bear in mind that Quark hasn't actually done anything yet."

Odo looked briefly affronted. "I had planned to keep Diaadul under loose surveillance until she meets with Quark, and observe their meeting if I could. I hope that meets with your approval?"

Sisko nodded. "I think it's an excellent idea." He hoped he didn't sound too relieved: Odo's intensity could sometimes lead him into schemes that were problematic under Federation law. "Keep me informed."

"Of course, Commander," Odo said, and pushed himself to his feet. "You have my report. I don't want to trouble you further."

"Not at all," Sisko said. "Thank you."

Odo nodded again, sharply, and turned away. Sisko watched the door close behind him, and wondered, not for the first time, precisely where the shapeshifter's loyalties lay. It was not that he distrusted Odo—far from it; Odo had proved himself already to be completely worthy of trust— but he occasionally worried that Odo's commitment to his own ideal of justice might someday conflict with the more mundane considerations of law. Odo was adamant in his convictions—perhaps he had to be, Sisko thought. Perhaps that abstraction was the one solid fact in an otherwise all-too-mutable life. After all, what else could a shapeshifter instinctively trust as solid, but an ideal?

Odo rode the turbolifts back down toward the Promenade, wondering how best to set a watch on the Trehanna woman. It would not be easy—mechanical surveillance was not always reliable, and he was already badly understaffed. He would probably have to rely on a daemon in the computer, set it to record Diaadul's computer usage and entrances and exits from her quarters. He was deep in his plans as he stepped off the turbolift onto the Promenade's main level, and nearly tripped over O'Brien, on his hands and knees beside the open shaft of the second turbolift.

"Careful, Constable," O'Brien said, disgustingly cheerful, and Odo gave him a withering glance.

"Perhaps if you weren't in the middle of the corridor, I wouldn't need to be."

"Sorry," O'Brien said, without sincerity. "Oh, Constable?"

Odo turned back reluctantly. "Yes?"

"That woman, that Tre—Tre-whatever-it-was, the one who came in on the *Shannar*. She was just by here, asking the way to Quark's place."

"Was she, now?" Odo said, softly.

"Yeah." O'Brien stood up, wiping the pale gold lubrication onto his uniform. "You might want to look in on her. She seemed awfully, I don't know, naive to be going in there by herself."

Odo glared at him, and mastered himself with an effort. O'Brien did not, could not, know that Odo had spent the last thirty minutes worrying about Diaadul's business. "What a clever idea," he said. O'Brien started to frown, looking at once insulted and a little hurt, and Odo relented. "The thought had already occurred to me, Chief," he said.

"Oh. Well, sorry," O'Brien said.

"But thank you for the information," Odo said, and turned away. This was the chance he had been looking for, the chance not only to protect Diaadul, but—with any luck at all—a chance finally to catch Quark in the middle of something unmistakably illegal. He had long ago investigated all the corridors and passages that gave onto Quark's establishment, as well as the ventilation and water supply systems. He had even memorized the layout of the centimeters-wide conduit housing that carried the lines that supplied Quark's machinery with power, and his computers with data, just in case one of those passages could take him into some otherwise inaccessible part of the Ferengi's space. This time, though ... He frowned, and paused at the mouth of a narrow access tunnel. This time, the ventilation system should provide as much access as he needed; the conduit housing gave more direct access, but the available space was small enough to push him to his absolute limits. He moved slowly down the narrow tunnel, scanning the engineer's symbols engraved on the walls with an ease that would have surprised O'Brien, and paused at last beside a hatch marked with warning notes in both Cardassian and newer Federation characters. It was locked, of course, and security-sealed, but Odo produced a slim cylinder from a pocket, and fed it into the port. A moment later, the hatch sagged open as the lock released itself. Odo smiled, tucked the cylinder away, and lifted the hatch a scant dozen centimeters, enough to give him clearance, in an altered form, but not enough to attract O'Brien's instant notice. He glanced over his shoulder to be sure he was still unobserved, then exhaled sharply, concentrating.

He felt the internal loosening as taut-held form eased, became liquid, mobile, felt the familiar giddy pleasure as his body contorted, turning in on itself in a series of smooth curves and partial spheres, and then re-formed in an instant in the shape of an *ashikhan,* a Bajoran land spider twenty centimeters long. He stretched his new legs, adjusting to the needs of controlling all eight of them—six for travel, two for rudimentary manipulation—and heard his new shell click softly against the floorplates. That was not something he had counted on; he tilted his head to one side to listen, and tapped again. The noise was perceptible, but not obtrusive: with any luck at all, it would be drowned in the general hubbub that always filled Quark's establishment. And if it wasn't, Odo thought, with an inward grin, Quark would be more likely to call O'Brien to fix a loose connector sleeve than to suspect an observer. He extended a gripping claw, and saw, in the dully reflective surface, a pale brown creature like a cross between a crab and a spider reaching out to him. Double eyestalks rose above his tiny head—the *ashikhan's* brain was located in the center of its body, well protected by its heavy carapace—and the magnetic buds, used to track prey in the utter darkness of the seaside caverns, were tightly furled above the true eyes. He smiled to himself, pleased with his handiwork, and eased the hatch back another few centimeters.

He made his way through the familiar network of the ventilation system, the claws at the ends of his walking legs fully extended to keep his balance on the smooth surface. The buds worked perfectly, the reward of constant practice, outlining the shapes of the ducts and baffles in shades of golden grey. The constantly moving air whistled past him, its pitch changing every time he tilted his head, but it was not fast enough to be more than an annoyance. As he passed the ducts that led to the main club, he could hear the usual hum of voices, conversations rising and falling like the tides of Bajor's seas, but he ignored them, following the familiar markers deep into the heart of Quark's establishment.

He stopped at last at a familiar duct—he had marked this one before, a splotch of high-iron paint that glowed like a beacon in his changed "sight"—and tilted his head to listen. He could hear voices approaching, Quark's familiar tones without distinguishable words, and he edged closer to the grille that covered the opening. Quark's main office was empty, indistinct, painted in shades of grey and gold, and he frowned to himself, and opened his true eyes, furling the magnetic buds at the same time. The scene sprang into sudden relief, the bright colors a momentary shock after the monotones. Quark stood just inside the door, hands clasped

—to keep from rubbing them in glee, Odo thought—as he bowed Diaadul into the brightly lit space.

"Delighted to be of service to any lady," the Ferengi was saying, "and doubly so when I've had such good fortune in my dealings with your husband. I hope you'll allow me to take a kinsman's privilege in advising your investments, as I advised the good Lord Innaris in his."

Diaadul bowed slightly, her veils held tight around her.

"If I may say so," Quark went on, closing the door behind them, "it's a great shame you Trehanna still adhere to so unflattering a custom. Women—women are like jewels, like flowers, and should be seen. It makes business so much more pleasant—"

Diaadul's hand shot out from among the concealing folds, her bracelets clashing, and caught the Ferengi by his throat. Quark jerked back, trying to pull away, but her long fingers held him fast. She lifted him then, pulling him up onto his toes and then holding him for an instant suspended in midair, before she dropped him briskly onto the carpet.

"We have business," she said. "Get on with it."

"Of course, madam—my lady," Quark said. One hand stole to his throat, rubbed hastily at the places where her fingers had pinched. "Let's go into my other office."

"Excellent," Diaadul murmured. She waited, her hands once again folded demurely into her veil, while Quark manipulated something on his main control console. A moment later, a section of paneling slid back, and Quark gestured, bowing, for Diaadul to precede him. She nodded once, and sailed past into the hidden room.

Had he been able, Odo would have growled with frustration. The ventilators for Quark's second office—the *private* private office, in the Ferengi's own words—were on a separate air shaft. He would have to retrace his steps, go all the way back to the junction with the main tunnel, before he could enter the section of the system that fed air to Quark's inner sanctum. But there was no avoiding the necessity. He scrabbled backward, rear claws gripping, until he emerged into the larger main tunnel where he could turn around, and retraced his steps as quickly as he could. At the main shaft, the air flowing through the system was strong enough to force him to crouch low to the ground, head tucked in and eyestalks retracted, using his walking claws to pull himself along. It took him almost five minutes to cover as many meters, but at last he reached the junction, where a smaller shaft split off from the main tunnel. This one, too, was marked in his own familiar symbols, and he dived into it gratefully, glad to be out of the wind. He scrambled over and under the baffles that cut the force of the wind—typical inefficient Cardassian technology, he thought, send everything out at full power and pull off what you need, damping it down at the end point—and then hurried down the long tunnel toward Quark's final office.

The grille at the end of the shaft was dark. Odo paused for a fraction of a second, furious—if he had been able, he would have cursed long and loudly—but then training and nature reasserted itself. He continued up to the grille, swiveling his true eyes on the ends of their stalks to make sure that the room really was empty and that nothing useful had been left behind. The magnetic buds confirmed what sight had told him: not only was the room empty, but the computer terminals had been shut down completely. And that, Odo thought, was that. He had done his best to protect the Trehanna woman, and he had failed. Or, more precisely, he had failed to witness her interview with Quark. From her behavior, she might not need as much protection as he had thought. Odo paused for a moment, still sitting at the mouth of the ventilator, and wondered what he should do. This was not typical Trehanna behavior, at least according to the information he had gotten from the library computer; on the other hand, Trehan was a strict aristocracy, and it was just possible that she had been reacting to a slight to her status. *Possible, but not,* he thought, *not quite right. I think I should report this to Sisko. Perhaps he can explain this behavior better than I.* Patiently, he began to extricate himself from the system, retracing his steps back toward the still-open hatch.

CHAPTER
4

GUL DIJMAS STARED AT his private display screen, schooling his face to an appropriately grim lack of expression. The muted noise of the command chamber filled the air around him, but he ignored it with the ease of long practice, his eyes fixed on the problem filling his screen. The arrangement of the game pieces soothed him, offering a mathematical complexity that mocked and mirrored the problem that waited beyond the hull of his ship. It was a shame, he thought, vaguely, his hand hovering over the image of the multisquared board, that the solution to his other problem wasn't as amenable to analysis. He touched the red vizier, shifted it four diagonal squares, and smiled as the black monarch dissolved in illusory flames. The Cardassian version of chess was complex, owed much to the Klingon version of the game, and to the Bajoran variations; if Dijmas had his way, it would soon owe something to the Federation's game as well. His hand hovered over the controls, over the image of the burning monarch, ready to advance to the next problem, but he shook himself, shut down the program instead. The ship's computer had never been designed to play chess, not at his level, and it certainly had never been programmed to provide him with suitable problems, especially ones derived from the Federation's version of chess. He brought his own problems with him, a tape of a hundred games and situations, and rationed it strictly, eking it out so that it would last most of the voyage.

And he was still no closer to the solution of his most pressing problem. He touched keys, slaving his private display to the sensorman's console, and saw the technician's shoulders stiffen as he realized his captain was watching.

"No reports, sir," the technician—Tobor, his name was —announced, and Dijmas sighed.

"Keep scanning."

"Sir."

Dijmas leaned back in the command chair, watching the strings of symbols course across his screen, and wondered again if Gul Dukat had led them on a wild-goose chase. There was no sign of *Helios* in the barren system, and no place for it to hide, either, with only a couple of rockballs and three gas giants orbiting a nondescript orange star— there wasn't even an asteroid belt to hide the perturbations of a cloaking device. There had been no sign of *Helios* since the *Avenger* had fired on the pirate a day and a half ago. It had been pure luck that they spotted her that time, anyway —only the gods-who-are-not knew why *Helios* had decloaked, there in the middle of nowhere. Perhaps she'd been interested in the merchanter one of the flotilla ships had glimpsed briefly, but that ship had been too small, and too far off, to have been worth *Helios*'s time. Whatever the cause, they couldn't expect that good luck again.

"Fleet status report," he said, to no one in particular, and a technician leaped to obey. "Put it on my screen."

He saw the sensorman relax as the slave link was broken, but ignored him, fixed his eyes instead on the image in his screen. It showed a schematic image of the star system, shown as if one were looking down at the star's northern pole, with the dead planets picked out in pale yellow, and the ships of the squadron indicated in bright blue. *Avenger,* the fastest of the scouts, had reached the far side of the system, was cruising just inside the outermost planet's orbit; the others had spread out in a pincer movement, the heavy cruiser *Reprisal* moving clockwise, supported by the frigate *Vindicator,* while the flagship, *Onslaught,* moved counter-clockwise, little *Counterblast* trailing in her wake. His own *Heartless* remained stationed at the base of the pincers—the pivot point, if one wanted to be poetic. Standard tactics, effective tactics, he thought—if there was anything there.

"Sir," the communications technician said. "Message from the flag."

"Put it on my screen." Dijmas repressed a sigh as Gul Dukat's familiar face filled his display board, schooled himself to perfect obedience. "Sir. *Heartless* hears you."

"Good." Even in the screen's imperfect reproduction, Dijmas could see his superior's eyes narrow. "Your report, Dijmas?"

"Nothing, sir," Dijmas answered, in his most emotionless voice. "We have not picked up any signs of a ship, its gravity shadow, or wave emissions from a cloaking device."

"Then perhaps you should reevaluate the efficiency of your crew," Dukat said. *"Helios* was seen entering the system. She can't have left without our observing her."

"No, sir." *But she wasn't seen,* Dijmas thought. *All we had was a shadow, it could have been a decoy, or just a bad reading. If I were* Helios's *captain, I'd be long gone from here.*

"There is one further order that I want to give personal-ly," Dukat went on, eye ridges contorting. *"Helios* is to be taken if possible—not destroyed. Have your boarding party on standby."

Dijmas felt his own eye ridges twitch. "Very good, sir," he answered, automatically. "But, sir—"

"Are you questioning my orders, Dijmas?"

"No, sir." Across the command chamber, Dijmas could see his second-in-command, Merid, staring worriedly at him, and hastily rephrased his question. "I'm concerned about *Helios,* however. She outguns all of us except *Onslaught.*"

"I am aware of that," Dukat said. His tone changed, became faintly contemptuous. "You won't be attacking alone, Dijmas. Be assured of that."

Dijmas bit back his instinctive anger—he was no coward —and said, "Then we will be making coordinated attacks, sir?" It was a loaded question, and he saw Merid's eyes widen slightly. The squadron's last attempt at a coordinated attack on *Helios* had failed miserably, not least because *Onslaught* had rushed the attack.

Dukat's entire face seemed to tighten, as though he was holding in a shout of rage. "You have a great deal of responsibility in this, Dijmas," he said at last. *"Heartless* will be the pivot of the attack."

"I thank you for the privilege," Dijmas answered, conventionally, and saw Dukat's fleeting sneer.

"Have your boarding party on standby," Dukat repeated. *"Onslaught* out."

Dijmas touched the key that blanked his screen, looked up to find Merid still staring at him. "Place the boarding party on standby," he said, "and pass the word that the crew may stand down to condition yellow."

"Sir." Merid bent low over his own console, relaying the orders, and then came to stand beside the captain's position. "Sir," he said, voice carefully lowered to be sure none of the bridge crew would overhear, "condition yellow?"

Dijmas could almost hear the rest of the question, the question even Merid didn't quite dare voice directly: *Condition yellow—standby, not full alert—when the enemy might appear at any moment? When Gul Dukat might inspect at any moment?* He smiled, knowing the expression went wry, and said, "The men need to eat, Merid. We've been at alert for six hours."

"We can eat at stations," Merid said.

"But not well," Dijmas answered. "Not well enough to keep everyone at full readiness, anyway. Have Chief-of-Supply organize ration-bearers, make sure everyone gets a decent meal. The crew can eat in shifts—let blue watch eat first."

Blue watch was the elite crew. Merid nodded, though he still looked uncertain. "I'll see to it, Captain."

Dijmas nodded, turned his attention back to the main display screen. In its depths, the unnamed sun glowed deeply yellow, its color enhanced rather than dimmed by the filters. A dark speck lay against its face: the innermost planet, little more than a ball of rock. The other planets were invisible, but they were just as dead—as space itself was dead here, Dijmas thought. *Helios* had certainly escaped. But if it had, how had it gotten past the squadron's sensors? He shook his head, still staring at the screen. And if it had not, where could it be hiding?

Cytryn Jarriel gave a final worried pat to the jury-rigged monitor that controlled the Metaphasic Shield, and straightened, glancing around *Helios*'s bridge. All but one of the viewscreens were dark, and the single working screen showed a featureless haze of radiation, the interference of the sun's corona that hid the ship. They were blind, inside the sun's fire, but they were also invisible to the Cardassian sensors—or so he hoped. The strain gauges, external systems monitors deployed hastily across the bridge to keep track of the damage, all showed no change from the previous hour. And that, at least, was something: ever since *Helios* had been surprised by the Cardassian patrol five days earlier, the damage had been spreading, and there had been no chance to make more than temporary repairs. All the good he'd been able to do with the equipment stripped from *Gift of Flight* had been completely destroyed. It had been devastatingly bad luck that Gul Dukat's squadron had spotted them, just at the moment that it looked as though they might have escaped their pursuers. . . .

He glanced over his shoulder, toward the plotting table, and saw the captain looking back at him, a slight, gambler's smile tilting the corners of his mouth. Jarriel smiled back, unwillingly, and the captain beckoned to him. Jarriel gave his work a last assessing glance, and moved to obey.

The surface of the table was filled with a model of the system, the most probable positions of the Cardassian ships indicated by delicately shaded holographic models. Jarriel looked once at it, assessing both the tactical position and his own handiwork, then looked back at his captain. Demaree Kolovzon was tall for his people, topping Jarriel, himself not a small man, by half a head, and the lights of the table glinted in his slit-pupilled eyes. They were Kolovzon's least human feature—the Trehanna were remarkably humanoid in their outward appearance—and Jarriel met their gaze firmly. He knew better than to be fooled by the apparent congruences, but it helped to remind himself of the obvious differences.

"So," Kolovzon said. His voice was softly deep, with a timbre like the purr of a very large cat. "The Shield is holding?"

Jarriel nodded. "If it wasn't—"

Kolovzon grinned, showing teeth. "—we wouldn't be standing here. I take your point."

Jarriel nodded again.

"How long can we expect it to hold?" Kolovzon went on.

Jarriel sighed. This was the question he'd been dreading, the one to which he had no answer. "I don't know for certain, sir. The ship we took it from—you remember, the Ferengi trader two months ago? They had gotten the technology at second hand, had never tested it." He hesitated, judging the captain's mood, and added, "I suspect it was meant to be a last-ditch weapon against us."

To his relief, Kolovzon's smile widened for an instant. "It didn't work. But you're my engineer. What's your guess?"

"In theory," Jarriel began, carefully, "indefinitely. We're balanced very precisely, right above the point where the corona becomes dense enough to override the Shield. That assumes, however, that the Ferengi calculations were accurate."

"Isn't that a rather large assumption?" Kolovzon murmured. "Your Federation doesn't think much of them."

"Not entirely," Jarriel retorted, stung by the reminder of his past—it had been five years since he'd worked a Federation ship, and he'd served Kolovzon for four of them. "The Shield works, there's no question about that. And while the Ferengi may not be to your taste, they're not stupid. Or technologically backward."

Something ugly flickered briefly across Kolovzon's face, and Jarriel braced himself. He had scars already, from the captain's erratic temper. But then Kolovzon relaxed slowly. "I still want to know how long I can trust this thing."

I wish I knew, Jarriel thought. He said, "I would say, at least another ten hours. I'm showing strain building in the warp drive—I haven't had a chance to overhaul it since we met this damn squadron, I've been putting bandages on missing limbs down there, not making repairs—" He caught himself abruptly, made himself take two deep breaths, before continuing more calmly. "But, as I said, there shouldn't be a serious problem for at least ten hours."

Kolovzon nodded, and turned back to the plotting table. He rested his hands on the controls, staring pensively at the images, but made no changes, tilting his head to one side as he studied the display.

"Captain," Jarriel said. "The repair situation is getting serious. The Xawe ship wasn't nearly enough. I need—"

Kolovzon swung away from the table, and Jarriel braced himself again for a blow that didn't fall. "I know we need repairs," Kolovzon snarled. "You've told me we need repairs, shown me the damage, I haven't forgotten." He controlled his temper with a visible effort. "But there's nothing I or you can do about it until we get ourselves free of these damned Cardassians."

"Gul Dukat is very determined," Jarriel said, in his most neutral voice.

"I've pulled his ears once too often," Kolovzon said, "as you're the first to remind me." He looked back at the table. "Which is why I don't intend to hide here in this sun until he goes away. I want to deal with him, Jarriel, deal with him permanently."

Jarriel grimaced. "Captain—"

"Dukat thinks we're damaged, that we've gone to ground to wait him out," Kolovzon went on. "But if he continues on his current course, look here."

He touched keys, and the Cardassian ships in the tabletop display shifted position slightly. Squinting, Jarriel recognized Gul Dukat's flagship, just passing out of the shadow of the third planet, and the heavy cruiser that had inflicted most of the damage.

"They're trying a pincers movement," Kolovzon went on, his voice rich with contempt, "which is good of its kind, I suppose. But if we take the initiative, so—" He touched a final key, and the insubstantial model that was *Helios* emerged from the sun on a parabolic course that swept them past the Cardassian flagship. Miniature phaser bolts shot from the hologram, striking the Cardassian craft in a dozen places, and then the model *Helios* swept on, picking up speed as it swung around the gas giant, and accelerated out of the system at a speed not even the fast scout could match. "We can hit them first. If Dukat's ship is forced out of the hunt, the others won't pursue."

Or at least not as fiercely, Jarriel thought. He sighed, studying the images in the table's display. "This all depends on the Cardassians trying a pincer attack," he said slowly.

"What other tactic would they use?"

Jarriel nodded slowly. Cardassian tactics tended to be formalized; they hadn't been a major power long enough to train an innovative officer corps. It was a tribute to their grim determination that they'd gotten as far as they had.

Kolovzon was watching him with unblinking eyes. "Can the ship take it?"

Jarriel turned to study the strain gauges, a cluster of sickly yellow lights attached to nearly every console. "We have ninety-eight-percent normal shields," he said, "and we can shunt the power currently going to the Metaphasic Shield to main impulse—that'll come close to doubling our output, at least for the first twenty minutes."

"And the phasers?"

"Still at seventy percent of normal," Jarriel answered. "I can't guarantee you'll strike a killing blow."

Kolovzon grunted, dismissing the objection. "Have you got the cloaking device back on line?"

"Yes."

"Then we'll do it." Kolovzon touched another series of keys, produced an illusory screen, floating in the air in front of the main display. "The Cardassians should be right where I want them in twenty-eight minutes. Make sure everything's ready, Jarriel. I'll want to move instantly."

"Yes, Captain." Jarriel watched as the larger man turned

away, but made no move to follow. He was as ready as he would be; his technicians had made all the repairs they could under battle conditions. And they were a good crew, as good as any he'd served with before. Not for the first time, he wondered briefly where Kolovzon had found them—in the first year after he'd lost his Federation papers, he'd served on three ships, none of which had been able to match *Helios*'s crews for sheer competence. Kolovzon's people were good at their jobs; they were also as dangerous a crew as any he'd ever sailed with, to each other as much as to the enemy. Only Kolovzon's iron rule—an iron will enforced with an iron hand—kept them from turning on each other, and kept the ship from falling into deadly anarchy. And if anything ever happened to Kolovzon . . . He put the thought firmly aside. He'd made his plans for that eventuality—there were too many people on board who had no reason to love an ex-Federation citizen—and the lifepod was ready, stocked with oxygen and food and enough power to bring him into safe space again, and the false papers he would need to start over. Briefly, his hand touched the tiny sphere that hung on a fine chain around his neck. It contained the lock codes to his lifepod, his airlock, and would only be used when Kolovzon was dead. It was a numbing thought, and he shoved it away, refused to let it take root in his imagination. There was still work he could do to make sure *Helios* would survive this encounter; more, would emerge the victor.

"Gul Dukat wants this pirate very badly," Glinn Merid said.

Dijmas nodded, studying the latest tactical display. So far, their sensors had picked up nothing, no trace of the *Helios* anywhere in the system, no trace of anything except their own ships. But *Helios* had been seen to enter the system, and had not left it. . . . "Is blue watch back on station?" he asked, idly, his mind still on the problem in his screen.

"Yes, sir," Merid answered. "Gold watch is eating now, at yellow stations."

"Good." Dijmas frowned at the screen, facial ridges contracting. There was something there, something he should have realized—a tactical solution, hovering just below the level of consciousness, like the solution to a chess problem. "And the boarding party?"

"Armed and ready," Merid answered. There was a note of distaste in his voice, and Dijmas allowed himself a quick grin. Gul Dukat had had a running feud with this pirate; he would be grateful to the man who brought him in alive, or, failing that, brought an intact body for the Gul's revenge.

"Tell the men that there will be a commendation for the man who takes Kolovzon alive. And a bar of gold-pressed latinum from my prize share."

Merid nodded. "If we can board, sir. I don't think the pirate will let himself be taken."

Neither do I, Dijmas thought. *Kolovzon is just that little bit mad.* He said, "Still, it would please Gul Dukat—" He broke off abruptly, a new train of thought filling his mind. *Kolovzon is a little mad; there are no hiding places for sane men in this system. But what is there for a madman? Only the sun itself . . .* "Merid, what do you know about something called a Metaphasic Shield?"

"Metaphasic—?" Merid bit off the rest of his words, eyes wild. "The Federation! They have it, and the Ferengi—"

"And maybe *Helios.*" Dijmas swung around in his chair, so that he faced the main screen again. "Takel, raise the flagship. At once!"

"Sir." The technician's hands flashed across the control boards, and a face took shape in the screen. Not Dukat, Dijmas saw, and suppressed a curse.

"Onslaught here. What is it, *Heartless?"*

"Get Gul Dukat," Dijmas said. "At once. I know where *Helios* is hiding—"

Onslaught's officer started to respond, looking over his shoulder, but whatever he would have said was drowned in the sudden shrilling of alarms behind him. A second later, the same sound echoed on *Heartless's* bridge, and this time Dijmas did swear.

"Condition red," he said, and heard Merid repeating the command.

"Condition red, all hands combat stations. Condition red."

Check-lights flicked from red to green along Dijmas's status board, and a part of him registered that his crew had beaten their best drill time. And then all thought vanished as, in the viewscreen, the surface of the sun twisted, as though the liquid fire were rising to a boil. The surface split, fountained, and a ship exploded from the corona. It rose, trailing fire, and Dijmas could see the solar face painted on the projecting bridge, all too clear against the flames. *Helios* bore down on the flagship with increasing speed, a solar flare following it. Dijmas winced as he watched the readings shift, too slowly, *Onslaught* struggling to set its deflectors and bring its own phasers to bear. *Too late,* he thought, *too late. . . . Helios* fired then, a massive, full-power salvo that momentarily blanked *Heartless's* screens, and swept on without waiting to see the results of its attack.

"Sir, she's on an intercept course—" one of the technicians began, and Dijmas cut him off.

"Shields to maximum power. Stand by phasers."

Helios swelled in his screen, impossibly fast, boosted to near-warp speed by the slingshot effect of the gas giant. The grim face glared from its bridge, framed by the painted flames; for a crazed instant, Dijmas pictured that same image framed by the sun's corona.

"Helios is firing," Merid announced. "Ten seconds to impact."

Dijmas braced himself. "Fire when you have a target."

"Firing, sir," a technician said.

Heartless bucked as the phasers fired, momentarily draining power from the main engines. Then the viewscreen went white, and the entire ship seemed to stagger under the impact of a dozen phaser bolts. The lights in the command chamber flickered and went out, were replaced a heartbeat later by the dim glow of the emergency lights. Half the consoles were blank, their screens dead, but even as Dijmas registered that fact, the first flickered and produced a wavering emergency display.

"Damage control," he said, and smelled smoke drifting in the ventilators. Gul Dukat's voice was screaming in his ear, ordering his ships to pursue; Dijmas closed his mind to that, focusing on his own ship. "Damage control, report!"

"Emergency power on-line," Merid said, in a shaky voice. Dijmas looked at him, and saw blood welling from a cut along the line of a brow ridge. "Sickbay reports a fire on deck ten, under control. We've lost forward shields completely, rear shields at thirty percent. Engineering reports no permanent damage to the main power plant, but it will take twenty minutes to get the main power conduits flowing again. They say we've blown a dozen junction nodes; they're rerouting."

Dijmas nodded. "Casualties?"

"Five wounded in the boarding party—thrown against a bulkhead when the phasers hit."

"See to them," Dijmas said. "Tell Engineering to carry on, get us back to full power as soon as possible. And, Sensors, track that ship!"

"Tracking, sir," the sensorman answered, and Dijmas thanked the gods-who-are-not that he had a competent junior on that post. "They're heading for the edge of the system—they've gone to warp, sir."

"Damn." Dijmas slammed his fist against the arm of his chair in sheer frustration. "Did we hit her at all, Merid?"

His second-in-command spread his hands. "I can't be sure, sir. We may have, but it's impossible to tell."

Dijmas took a deep breath. "And *Onslaught?*"

"We've lost the transmission temporarily," Merid answered. "Our sensors show serious damage to the warp drive containers—"

As if in answer to his words, the viewscreen crackled, produced a static-banded image. Gul Dukat glared from its center, fixing his anger impartially on his own people and the departing pirate.

"Dijmas, report."

"We've suffered minor damage to our drive," Dijmas answered, "but we should be back to full power in twenty minutes."

"And the pirate?"

"Escaped, sir. We've no way of knowing if we damaged her." One of the technicians was signaling frantically from his station, and, out of the corner of his eye, Dijmas saw Merid move to look over his shoulder, then straighten, a sudden grin on his face. "Excuse me, sir, I think we have a fix on their wave emissions." Merid nodded, and Dijmas allowed himself an inaudible sigh of relief. "That's confirmed. We have a fix on their wave emissions, bearing—?"

"Two-four-zero mark seven-zero," Merid said.

"Two-four-zero mark seven-zero," Dijmas repeated. "Permission to pursue?"

"Granted," Dukat answered. "Relay that course to the rest of the squadron. Then get after him, or I will hold you personally responsible, Dijmas."

"Yes, sir," Dijmas said again. His mouth felt stiff, bloodless, as though he'd bitten into numbroot.

"Dukat out."

Dijmas touched the keys that shut down the communications channel, moving with excruciating care, unable quite to believe that Gul Dukat would blame him for any defeat, and furious that he could do nothing to stop him. *I knew,* he thought, *I knew where Helios was, I figured it out and warned you—but not quite in time. Damn you, Kolovzon. This is becoming personal.*

Sisko looked at his people, gathered around the operations table, and felt an unexpected sense of satisfaction. Dax sat at his right hand, a display box operating in front of her. Odo sat to his left, his face drawn as always into an unrevealing scowl. Kira sat beside him, fingers drumming nervously against the edge of the table, where she thought no one could see. Bashir sat opposite her, looking eager and wary by turns, as though he couldn't quite figure out if he was flattered to be there, and Sisko hid a smile. It had been some time since he had been able to pull his primary staff together for a conference; it was to their credit that there were no immediate emergencies demanding their attention. In spite of himself, his eyes strayed to O'Brien, who sat at the far end of the table where he could watch the secondary engineering consoles without turning his head. O'Brien had done well to make the balky, unfamiliar Cardassian technology work as well as it did; Sisko was no longer surprised when things functioned as intended. But they were a good crew, even the ones he had feared would be most difficult to work with: Kira, and the truly alien Odo. They were still difficult—Kira with her temper, and Odo with his peculiar and unswerving sense of law—but Sisko sensed a new ease with each of them, and hoped it was the beginning of a new phase for the station.

"Very well," he said, and felt all eyes turn to him. Ops was closed to the rest of the station's personnel for the duration of the meeting; only his senior staff were present. He could feel the tension that decision had caused, the unspoken fear that there had been some new attack by the pirate, and smiled, hoping to deflect that worry. "I've called you in to give you an update on the *Helios* incident, and to discuss Dax and O'Brien's analysis of the tapes *Ganges* secured." He nodded to Bashir. "Thus your presence, Doctor, though there may be medical issues to be discussed later."

"Sir," Bashir said.

"To business, then," Sisko said, and looked at Dax. "Lieutenant, I'd appreciate it if you'd give us a summary of Starfleet's latest information on this incident."

"Yes, sir." Dax favored the table with her impersonal, catlike smile. "Most of it's old news, actually. They confirmed that there have been forty-two attacks in the past five years that can be attributed to an otherwise unknown ship known as *Helios*. Their computers give us an eighty-three-percent probability that our pirate is the same ship, this *Helios*. The *Hammurabi* made a sweep along the Cardassian border where *Gift of Flight* was destroyed, but they didn't find anything you didn't spot, Major. And they did not see any sign of *Helios*—their commander reported that she thought *Helios* had run back across the border. They did report increased Cardassian traffic, mostly military, and Starfleet Intelligence has confirmed a military buildup there."

Kira made a small, strangled noise of disgust, but said nothing.

Dax went on placidly, "Intelligence suggests that this is a response to the attack on *Gift of Flight*, or to other attacks which the Cardassians have not made general knowledge, but nonetheless I think we should increase our own surveillance of the Bajor system."

Sisko nodded. "I agree. Odo, what about the merchant captains? Was there anything in their interviews that give us a hint of what *Helios* is up to?"

"No, sir." Even for Odo, he sounded out-of-temper. "I interviewed everyone who has arrived at the station from that sector, but none of them report anything out of the ordinary."

"Well, keep on it," Sisko said.

"Sir, I don't think there's anything to be gained from further questioning." Odo looked, if anything, faintly affronted by the suggestion.

Sisko looked at him. "Perhaps not, Constable. But there will be other ships coming to the station, and other crew members will talk, too. I want you to keep an ear out for anything else that might be useful."

"Ah." Odo leaned back slightly, visibly appeased. "Of course, Commander."

"Thank you." In spite of his best efforts, Sisko knew that he sounded sharp. But then, Odo could be fairly abrasive himself. There was no harm in occasionally giving him a taste of his own medicine. "Dax, I agree that the regular scanning routines should be beefed up—even without this pirate, if the Cardassians are more active than usual, I want to be sure we know everything that's happening out there."

"Sir," Kira said. "Have you informed Bajor of all this?"

Sisko stared at her, and admitted to himself that this was the one question he had hoped to avoid, primarily because he didn't yet have an answer. "I have informed all shipping, including Bajoran, of course, of the attack on *Gift of Flight*," he said, carefully, and was not surprised when Kira waved the words away.

"But you haven't informed the government on Bajor," she said. "Have you?"

Sisko took a deep breath. "No, Major, I have not. Frankly,

I wouldn't trouble the Bajoran government with something as vague as this."

"But—"

Sisko overrode her easily. "Major, all I could tell your government is that I have heard vague reports of some Cardassian military activity in their own sector of space—activity that is almost certainly directed toward internal problems. I see no reason to contact anyone until we have something definite to say."

Dax said, "Starfleet Intelligence is much more concerned about the pirate."

"Starfleet Intelligence," Kira muttered, but subsided.

Sisko could see from her expression that she was only momentarily silenced, and continued hastily, "I want the new scanning routines in place as soon as possible, Dax."

"Or course, Benjamin," the Trill answered, already busy with her controls.

"O'Brien," Sisko said.

"Commander." The curly-haired engineer looked up with a well-disguised start. His attention had clearly been miles away.

"Will you give us your analysis of the tapes from *Ganges,* please?" Sisko asked.

"Yes, sir." O'Brien leaned forward, cuing a display in his datapadd. "The information is all in the library computer in detail, but the high points are pretty simple. *Helios* is a hybrid of a lot of different technologies. It's a Klingon hull, but, oddly, a Romulan cloaking device; there are some Cardassian phaser mountings as well, plus some recognizable Federation stuff. As I said, the details are in my report. But the bottom line is, this ship is damn near as powerful as a Federation starship."

And a good deal more aggressive, Sisko thought. He said, "See if you can come up with a list of unique features. Things that will help Dax narrow her scan."

"Oh, it's all pretty damn unique," O'Brien muttered. He went on, more loudly, "Sorry, sir. I know what you mean. I'll see what I can come up with, but with the cloaking device to contend with, too . . ." He shook his head, visibly withdrawing, then shook himself again. "Oh, there is one other thing. About that cloaking device, I mean. I think—" He stressed the word. "—I can rig a program that will run as a subroutine within the main sensor program. It's sort of a virtual filter, homes in on the subspace frequencies where the wave emissions from a cloaking device are strongest, and amplifies them to where the computers can get a rough fix. The *T'Marisu* used it two years ago, against the Klingon renegades, and, even though Vulcan computers are a little different from what we have here, I think I can make it run."

"Excellent," Sisko said, and meant it. "Get that installed as soon as possible, Chief." He saw O'Brien open his mouth, possibly to protest, more probably to remind his commander of the list of things that needed overhaul, and lifted his hand to stop the words. "Make it your top priority."

O'Brien subsided, with a fleeting grin. "Aye, sir."

"Right." Sisko looked around the table. "Dr. Bashir. I want you to run a full check of the station's emergency medical capabilities."

"I've already done that, sir," Bashir said. "And, if I might make a suggestion?"

Sisko started to nod, but the young doctor was already hurtling on, and he contented himself with lifting an eyebrow.

"I've put together several supplementary medical kits— special equipment, some drugs that are in common use among the Sector Eighteen settlers, that sort of thing. And several kits that are specific to Bajoran physiology as well. I thought they might come in handy, if any more ships are attacked. They'd fit on the runabouts easily, they only mass about eleven kilograms—eleven point three three nine, to be precise. It shouldn't have an impact on engine performance."

Bashir still sounded like an eager puppy, but there was something more to this offer of his, Sisko thought, than his earlier overenthusiasm, an enthusiasm that bordered on the officious. And it wasn't a bad idea, always assuming that they found survivors the next time.

O'Brien scowled. "I don't see that it would do much good. Why should this pirate be any less efficient next time?"

Bashir's eyes dropped. "We might get—lucky," he said, with a flippancy that did not hide the sudden hurt.

"It's worth the effort," Sisko said. "See to it, Doctor, if you would."

"Yes, sir." Bashir flashed a smile, his usual good spirits apparently restored.

"I wish you would inform Bajor of the Cardassian activity, Commander," Kira said.

Sisko frowned. "We've been through that, Major. The answer is still no, not until we have something real to report. I don't want to be responsible for a panic on Bajor—or for giving some of the extremist groups an excuse to start another purge of so-called Cardassian sympathizers."

Kira's eyes dropped at that reminder of local politics, and this time Sisko knew he had her. "All right," she said, "sir. But I had to ask."

"Agreed, Major," Sisko said. *I understand perfectly—I understand your concern for your people, and your hatred of the Cardassians. But I—we, you and I both—have to walk a tightrope here.* There was too much at stake, for the Federation as well as for Bajor itself, for them to be anything but extremely cautious. *Too much at stake to make any mistakes at all,* a dry voice in his head corrected him. He shook that thought away, and looked around the operations table again. "Is there anything else?"

O'Brien shook his head, and Bashir said, "Not from me, sir."

"I think that covers everything, Benjamin," Dax said.

Kira shrugged, a faint, wry smile on her thin face. *Everything except telling Bajor,* the smile said.

"Ah. Commander," Odo said. "There is one thing I would like to discuss with you. It has nothing to do with this pirate, however."

Sisko nodded, puzzled, and looked at the others. "All right, then, that will be all. Odo, let's go into my office."

"Very well."

The constable followed Sisko into his office, remained standing while Sisko seated himself behind the desk. Sisko looked warily at him, and gestured toward the guest's chair. "Have a seat."

"Thank you, no," Odo answered. "I have been sitting, I would prefer to stand."

"Suit yourself," Sisko said. "What's on your mind?"

"Lady Diaadul. The Trehanna visitor."

"I remember." In spite of himself, Sisko smiled. He had caught a glimpse of her on the Promenade the day before, a slim figure wrapped in a blue veil the color of a summer sky, its edges thick with gold embroidery. The gold had glittered in the strong light, and the blue had been a striking spot of color against the harsh Cardassian architecture: a small bit of beauty in an otherwise unremarkable day. He had wondered what she looked like beneath the veil, and had decided that he didn't need, didn't want to know. The glimpse, the single image, had been enough, a reminder of the good things—a reminder even, in some pleasant, indirect fashion, of Jennifer. He had dreamed of her that night, and the pain had been reduced to a faint, melancholy knowledge, the awareness that she was indeed dead, and it was a dream.

Odo said, "I don't think she's what she seems."

"What?" Sisko frowned. "What do you mean?" Even as he spoke, he knew the words sounded angry, unreasonably so, and he was not surprised to see Odo pull back a little, his own habitual frown deepening in response.

"I mean that she's not behaving as I'd expect a Trehanna noble to behave," Odo said. "If you're questioning my competence, sir—"

"No." Sisko waved the words away. "Not at all."

Odo said nothing, still watching him, and Sisko waved his hand again.

"It's just—" He broke off then, unable to face explaining the surge of disappointment, of unreasonable disillusionment, that had filled him. He could barely explain it to himself, the glimpse of memory that seeing Diaadul had given him, and could not imagine beginning to tell Odo. "It's nothing," he said, more firmly, and put aside the memory of the blue-veiled figure. "How is her behavior unexpected?"

"I followed her to her meeting with Quark," Odo said. He smiled, thinly. "I was fortunate enough to be passing by when she went to see him. In any case, I followed her through the air ducts, and into Quark's office."

A spasm of something passed across his unfinished face. Chagrin? Sisko thought. Regret? It was gone then, too quick to be identified.

"At that point," Odo went on, "Quark suggested that she should go unveiled—"

"That must've gone over well," Sisko said. Even for Quark, that was less than subtle, bordered on stupidity.

"Quite. But not," Odo said, "as I'd expected." He put both hands on Sisko's desk, leaned forward slightly. "The Lady Diaadul picked Quark up by the collar of his jacket, set him down hard enough to rattle his pointed teeth, and told him to get on with business."

Sisko chuckled. "I bet that got his attention."

"They went into the inner office then." Odo gave the bad news without flinching. "I wasn't able to follow them."

"That's too bad," Sisko said. He could just picture the situation, the slim, veil-wrapped figure, picking up Quark and slamming him down again. It served the Ferengi right—and Quark in particular needed constantly to be reminded that females of other species were individuals in their own right. He became aware that Odo was still staring at him, and schooled himself to seriousness with an effort. "I'm not sure I see the point, Odo. That sounds like an aristocrat to me."

"Not to me," Odo said. "Or, more precisely, not like a Trehanna female. According to the library computers, they are trained to defer to males—all males, not just of their own species."

Sisko shook his head. "I don't know. Are noblewomen expected to defer to their social inferiors? That doesn't sound like the little I've heard about Trehanna society."

"I don't know how class and gender would balance out," Odo said. "I don't pretend to understand humanoids or their customs. But this I am certain of, Commander. Her behavior simply does not feel right."

Sisko looked at him for a long moment, impressed in spite of himself by the constable's obvious sincerity. And besides, he told himself, haven't you learned yet to trust Odo's hunches? "All right," he said slowly, "what do you recommend?"

"I'd like to continue to keep a watch on her," Odo said. "Personally, as well as more routine methods. And I'd like to be sure I have your support if I need to stop her leaving the station."

"That's an extreme measure," Sisko said, startled.

"I'm aware of it," Odo answered. "But if she isn't what she seems, then she has to be working for Quark—and I would like very much to put an end to his smuggling games once and for all."

"I doubt that's possible," Sisko said. "Short of killing him. Ferengi enjoy breaking the law."

Odo smiled. "And I enjoy stopping them."

Sisko sighed. The last thing he needed right now was to have to deal with another episode of Quark-and-Odo. Jake had said once, not thinking his father could hear, that the constable and the Ferengi was just like an old cartoon. *They keep bashing each other,* Jake had giggled, *keep laying traps and making trouble, and neither one of them ever even comes close to winning.* Sisko had stepped in then, given him a heavy-father lecture—for which he still felt slightly guilty—about respecting the law's agents as well as the law, but he had been unable to shake the too-apt image. He said, "I agree, you should continue surveillance, and I leave the arrangements to your discretion. But I'm not prepared to restrict her travel without a good reason. Bring me that reason, and I'm with you all the way."

Odo sat motionless for a fraction of a second, then nodded. "Agreed. Thank you, Commander."

"Oh, wait," Sisko said. "There's one other thing."

Odo turned back from the doorway. "Sir?"

"About your surveillance," Sisko said. "I'd suggest you recruit one of the women to help you—or, better yet, see if Major Kira would help out. I expect a Trehanna would be more likely to confide in someone of her own gender."

Odo nodded slowly, eyes widening. "A good point, Commander. I will ask Major Kira—with your authority, of course."

"Of course," Sisko said. He waited to smile until the door closed again behind the constable. That was, if he did say so himself, an elegant solution to a minor problem. With any luck, Kira would be busy enough with Odo's investigation to distract her from her need to warn Bajor. And he had meant exactly what he said: a woman who was expected to socialize only with other women would be more likely to talk to another woman than to Odo. Though, to be fair, Kira was not the most tactful person he'd ever met. . . . Perhaps it would have been better to suggest that Odo take on a woman's shape—or would that be worse, for Diaadul? Sisko tilted his head to one side, contemplating dizzying possibilities, and reached for the keyboard, calling up the library computer.

Half an hour later, he had a partial answer. If a Trehanna woman spoke to a man disguised as a woman, she was still culpable because she should have recognized him as a man, though extenuating circumstances were recognized. So, Sisko thought, a shape-shifter would probably fall under the same prohibition, except that she would be forgiven because there would be no plausible way to detect the deception. But she would still feel betrayed, if she found out—or would she? Did Odo actually have a gender? Could someone whose natural form was a shapeless liquid be said to have gender in any sense that was meaningful to Trehan's peculiar legal system? Or did his general choice of shape count, somehow? Sisko shook his head, glad he didn't have to deal with the minutiae of Trehanna law—worse than the worst of Starfleet protocol, worse than ambassadorial precedence— and closed the system down again. It was, he decided, a very good thing he'd decided to send Kira.

CHAPTER
5

DAX LEANED CLOSE to her console, watching as the indicators changed slowly from orange to yellow, and finally shaded slowly to green as the Vulcan filter's software mated itself to the main scanner program. When the last bar had turned to a deep and steady green, she ran her hands over the membrane boards, setting up a quick test sequence. The screen blanked for an instant, and then filled with numbers. Everything was well within operational limits—so far, she told herself. There was no knowing what would happen when she tried to run a purely Vulcan program—well, not purely Vulcan; O'Brien had made modifications already— on their hybrid system. The computers were mostly Cardassian with Federation boosters, but the scanners were Cardassian through and through, maximized for military effectiveness, and limited in the broader ranges that were of scientific interest. *We're nearly blind and deaf in some areas,* she thought, not for the first time, *and no one is willing to do anything about it.* Which wasn't entirely fair, either—both

Sisko and O'Brien had far more important things to worry about—but she was convinced that, sooner or later, the station was going to pay for its neglect of pure science.

"How's it going, Lieutenant?" O'Brien's voice said in her ear, and she jumped slightly.

"Fine, so far."

"Sorry. Didn't mean to startle you." O'Brien leaned over her shoulder, scanning the screen, and she slid her chair sideways to let him take a closer look. If it had been Bashir, now, she would have had a hard time resisting the impulse to tease him, to stay close, but O'Brien was a sober and sensible man—and far too much in love with his wife to notice anyone else.

"Ah, good." O'Brien leaned forward still further, tapped the screen. "You see there? I was hoping that would happen. You'll get thirty percent better resolution on the broad-beam scan with this system running." He leaned back again, grinning. "You see, Lieutenant, I do listen to you."

Dax smiled back. "I never thought you didn't, Chief. Thank you. That is helpful."

"I'll stick around if you'd like," O'Brien offered, "keep an eye on the hardware while you finish the fine-tuning."

Dax swung around in her chair to look directly up at him. "I thought you were off-watch now."

O'Brien shrugged. "I can stay a little longer. Just in case."

"And what will Keiko say?"

"She's Starfleet. She'll understand."

Despite the cheerful words, Dax saw the faint flicker of guilt that crossed the young man's face. Keiko O'Brien was Starfleet, all right, but she was also O'Brien's wife, and he was well aware of his obligations to her—obligations that all too often had to take a lower priority than O'Brien would have liked. Dax allowed herself a smile that barely wrinkled the skin at the corners of her eyes. "Miles," she said, and let her voice take on the faintly teasing note she used with

Bashir. "I appreciate the offer, but I don't anticipate any problems. And besides . . ." She smiled more openly this time. "I have been doing this for somewhat longer than you have."

O'Brien opened his mouth to protest, then blinked, and closed it again. "You have, haven't you," he said, blankly. "I forget sometimes."

"So," Dax went on, "I think you can safely leave me to it, Chief. And don't worry, I'll call you at the slightest hint of a problem."

"Frankly, Lieutenant," O'Brien said, "I hope I don't hear from you until tomorrow." He turned away, and a moment later, Dax heard the hiss of the turbolift descending out of Ops.

This was her favorite time of the station's day, between nineteen and twenty hours by the twenty-four-hour human clock. Ops was all but deserted, the day watch gone home, the night watch still in the transitional phases—the Bajoran tech who would take over O'Brien's station was on her nightly tour of the operational reactors, and Sisko's current deputy, Philips, was in conference, catching up on the events and decisions of Sisko's day. The only other person in Ops was the monitor technician, and Dax had never heard the Bajoran say an unnecessary word to anyone. He wasn't unfriendly; he had just withdrawn himself from everything except his work. Dax would have worried about him—had worried about him, until she encountered him once off-duty. The man had been standing on a table in the center of Quark's, the voice she had never heard raised above a murmur lifted in raucous, explicit—and very funny—song. He hadn't been drunk, she found out later; it was just his monthly night out. Looking at him now, hunched over his console, his coveralls drab even by Bajoran standards, she found herself wondering if she had hallucinated that earlier evening.

And that was none of her business. She turned back to her console, and let the quiet surround her. She could hear the hiss of the ventilators, the faint, distant hum of the power conduits, and the soft chirr and beep as the computer finished the last complex set of calculations and presented its results. She scanned the screen thoughtfully. The search pattern it displayed—the third revision of their standard scan—would now concentrate on the section of the Denorios Asteroid Belt that lay between the station and *Helios*'s last known position, and on the wedge of space beyond the asteroids. She studied it, made a final adjustment to the z-axis, and watched while the image re-formed. That was what she wanted, that precise area, there where the Belt ringed the Bajor system. There had been little study of the Belt, at least so far—the Bajorans had lacked the technical expertise, and the Cardassians had lacked interest —and she caught herself staring at the pale band with something remarkably like lust. At times like this, here when she was alone and she could expand into the silence, could feel most herself—*herselves*—she thought she wanted nothing more than to spend the rest of her life in search of pure knowledge.

And that was one of the greatest temptations of being Trill: to forget because of your own long life span that there were things that did demand immediate attention, instant action and reaction. She smiled to herself, acknowledging the new host's contribution, her youth and fire that made it so much easier to remember those things, and turned her attention to the new scanning routine. She touched a button, and watched the final dry calibration scroll across her screen. There was nothing left to do, then, but run the new system. She keyed in the sequence that pulled the entire system back on line, and set the scan for its maximum range. There was no point, she thought, in wasting even a single scan.

Her screen went white for a second as the system shifted into its new operating mode, and then began with numbers and symbols, all flowing past too fast for the eye to follow. The computer would sort it out within minutes, sift through the undifferentiated mass of data, and present it in order of interest and importance. She watched abstractedly, wondering if one day she would find something really interesting in the data discarded by the computers, and then the screen went dark again, displaying the same familiar starscape, the Denorios Belt barely a thicker haze against the starry darkness. A moment later, the computer beeped for her attention. Dax swung around to face it, and frowned slightly at the schematic presented on her screen. The computer was showing—something, a reading, possibly elevated thorium or related particles in a discrete area, possibly something else, but in any case something that stood out as an anomaly. Dax's frown deepened, and she touched keys to run the same scan again.

Two minutes later, the computer reported its verdict: whatever the sensors had picked up before was no longer present. The scan showed nothing unusual, just the random debris that filled the asteroid belt. Dax keyed the scan again, and turned back to the first results.

"Query," she said aloud. Sometimes it was easier to talk to the computer as though it were another Trill: her own thoughts flowed more freely, and it was easier to define what she needed from the computers. "Can you isolate the anomaly spotted in the first scan sequence?"

"The anomaly is isolated," the computer answered. "The scan showed a concentration of anterium ions, with a smaller thorium component, which has since vanished."

Thorium, Dax thought. Elevated thorium levels were not her favorite discovery right now—she was still wary of them, since the time their discovery had heralded the arrival of her own double, Bashir's fantasy-Jadzia, along with a few other oddities. She shook that memory aside—she had teased Bashir unmercifully, but it had been an awkward feeling nonetheless—and said, "List the possible causes."

"Listing possible causes in order of probability," the computer said. "First, imperfect calibration—there was nothing actually there."

"A reflex shadow," Dax said, half to herself. "Probability?"

"Forty-five percent."

Dax's eyebrows rose. "Continue with the list."

"Second, debris from an asteroid of unusual composition. Probability, twenty percent."

And I would call that estimate high, Dax thought. *I grant that the Denorios Belt hasn't been thoroughly explored, but I think we would have spotted anything that left an active trail—and besides, that doesn't explain why it vanished.*

"Third," the computer went on, "emissions from a cloaking device at point of closure. Probability, ten percent."

Cloaking device. Dax froze, staring at the innocuous image in her screen. In the secondary screen, the results of the third scan, and then the fourth, rolled past, monotonously blank. Only the first scan had spotted anything—but if it was *Helios* recloaking, she thought, only the first scan would. She ran her hand over the controls, setting the system to scan the Denorios Belt continuously, and then turned back to her working screen. The numbers were still there: a one-percent probability that her anomaly was a ship recloaking. One chance in a hundred that *Helios* was out there, waiting—for what? There was nothing to be gained from attacking DS9, but there was enough traffic through the wormhole already that a pirate might make a profit attacking. . . . She shook herself—tactics were Sisko's province, and his strength—and reached for the intercom button.

"Dax to Sisko."

It was a few minutes before Sisko answered, and when the screen lit, Dax could see Jake hovering, out of focus, in the background.

"Yes, Dax?"

"It's not an emergency, sir—" With Jake there, it was important to offer reassurance first, Dax thought. "—but something's come up that needs your attention."

Sisko was silent for a heartbeat, but when he spoke, his voice held no hint of any private regrets. "Problems with the station?"

"No, sir," Dax answered. "Something showed up briefly —very briefly!—on the scan."

"Damn." Sisko glared at the screen for an instant before he'd mastered himself. "I'll be right up."

The commander was as good as his word, appearing in Ops less than five minutes after Dax had shut down her working screen. "So," he said, and stepped out of the turbolift. "What's this about the scan?"

"I wouldn't call you if I didn't think it was important, Benjamin," Dax said, answering the anger she saw in his stance and movement.

"I know." Sisko sighed. "I'm sorry, Dax, it's just—well, you know I haven't had much time with Jake lately." He shook himself. "But that's beside the point. Show me what you spotted."

No, it isn't beside the point, Dax thought, and knew perfectly well she couldn't say it, any more than she could tell Sisko that his son might be happier with relatives or friends back on Mars or on some ship or station larger than DS9. She said, "When I started the new system, I got an anomalous reading on the first scan that hasn't been repeated." She smiled, aware of the sulfurous comment lurking just below the commander's polite smile. "Believe me, I wouldn't have called you for that, except for the analysis. Basically, the computer says it doesn't know what it saw, but it could be a reflex shadow, debris from an asteroid of unusual composition—or a ship caught at the instant of recloaking."

"Ah." Sisko stood very still for an instant. "You haven't picked it up again."

Dax shook her head. "No. And I've kept the scan running, centered on that general area of the Belt."

"What does the computer say the chances are?"

"A forty-five-percent chance it was a shadow, a twenty-percent chance it was asteroid debris, and ten percent that it was a ship."

"And what do you think?" Sisko smiled.

Dax smiled back, charmed once again by her old friend. "I think we can't ignore the possibility that it could be *Helios*."

"I agree." Sisko sighed. "All right, Dax, set up a general close-monitoring program—keep it focused on the Belt, if there is a ship out there, that's the only place for it to hide—but make sure we get some long-range scans as well. In the meantime—" He smiled again, the expression wry this time. "In the meantime, I need to inform the Bajoran government."

"Kira will be pleased," Dax murmured.

Sisko snorted. "I'm not doing it for her. And all I'm going to tell them is that we had a tentative sighting that might be related to the attack on *Gift of Flight*. It's their shipping that goes closest to the Denorios Belt, after all."

"You're not going to recommend that they avoid the Belt," Dax said, sharply. To do that would mean rerouting dozens of ships, disrupting hundreds of individuals' schedules.

Sisko looked mischievous, and, in that instant, years

younger. He sobered at once, but Dax could still see the amusement lurking in the corners of his eyes. "Not at all. It's not my place to tell Bajor what their ships should do. No, I'm just going to give them the information, tell them just how uncertain it is, and let them decide what to do with it." Even though he had been speaking softly, in a voice that would barely carry across Ops, he lowered his voice again. "At least that may keep them off my back for a while."

Dax nodded, not in the least surprised by the devious tactics. She said, "It should work."

"I hope so," Sisko answered. "So, get that scan into place, would you? I've got a feeling about this, Dax, and not a pleasant one."

Dax nodded, already running her hands over her controls. She heard him turn away, and said, softly enough that he could choose not to answer, "So do I, Benjamin. So do I."

O'Brien sat at the narrow table, watching Keiko manipulate the replicator, Molly at her heels alternately grabbing her mother's knees and babbling too quickly for either parent to follow. It seemed as though it had been months since he had been able to sit down to breakfast with his family, and the sheer unexpectedness of it filled him with a deep contentment. Keiko turned away from the replimat, her hands filled with hot dishes, and her frown dissolved at the sight of his smile.

"Miles," she said, "would you deal with Molly?"

Recalled to his duty, O'Brien held out his hands, saying, "Come to Daddy, Molly. You're underfoot."

"Am not," Molly said, but came trotting over.

O'Brien hoisted her into his lap. "And what's my big girl going to do today?"

"I don't know."

"You do, too," Keiko said, and set the plates on the

counter. "Tell Daddy where we're going. Do you remember where we're going?"

O'Brien looked down at the tiny, heart-shaped face. "Are you going somewhere, Molly?"

Molly frowned, put a finger in her mouth as though that would help her remember. "I'm going to school," she said, at last, and took her finger away to smile broadly. "I'm going to help!"

O'Brien suppressed a chuckle, and saw, over his daughter's head, Keiko give him a speaking glance. "I'm sure you're going to be a big help, sweetheart."

"I'm going to be a teacher," Molly insisted. "Just like Mommy."

"Mommy's a botanist, honey," O'Brien said. "She's just helping out with the school."

"I thought you wanted to be a science officer," Keiko said. She pulled a last plate out of the replicator, and set it on the table at Molly's place. "Like Dax."

Molly shook her head. "I want to be a teacher."

"And the day before yesterday, you wanted to be a starship captain," O'Brien said.

Molly nodded. "And a teacher."

"Your breakfast is ready, honey," Keiko said. "Come over here and let Daddy eat."

O'Brien set her down, and Keiko lifted the tiny girl into her special chair. The Cardassian furniture that they had inherited with their quarters had never been designed for children—*or if it had,* O'Brien thought, *I pity the poor brats.* O'Brien had spent fifteen hours of his precious spare time cutting down and rebuilding the original furniture until it was something Molly could comfortably, and safely, use. He and Keiko had tried to do the same thing with the rest of the quarters, but there had been little they could do to hide the harsh angles of the walls. He looked around again, remembering something one of his technicians had said about his quarters.

"D'you remember Jaan Ashe?" he said, and stood up to bring the rest of the plates to the table.

Keiko looked up from mixing Molly's egg-and-rice. "He's your second reactor technician, isn't he?"

O'Brien nodded, settled himself again in his place. "He said he bought some fabric when he was down on Bajor, used it to hang his walls. I think he may have painted it first, or else Chris did it, but he says it worked wonders. He sort of bunched it up around the corners, I think, softened up the angles a little."

Keiko gave the grey-and-brown walls a critical glance. "Do you think it would help?"

"It couldn't hurt," O'Brien answered, and Keiko smiled.

"That's true." She looked at Molly, visibly decided that the girl had her spoon under control, and turned to her own food. "It's better than what Torrie Aimatsu did."

"Oh?" O'Brien tried to put a face to the name, and failed.

"Torrie Aimatsu," Keiko said. "She's one of the science staff."

Thus prompted, O'Brien dredged up a vague impression of a raw-boned blonde—a cartographer, he thought, who usually worked on Bajor.

"She painted every wall in her quarters matte black," Keiko went on, "and the floor and the ceiling, too, and strung the whole thing with pinlights. She said if she had to live in inhospitable, alien space, it might as well be space she recognized. She got Dax to help her work out the constellations for her home planet. It's very effective, but I'm not sure I'd want to live there."

"I do," Molly said. "I want a room like Auntie Torrie."

"I don't think so, sweetheart," Keiko said.

Molly looked instinctively at her father, and O'Brien

shook his head. "You don't like sleeping without a night-light, darling. Do you really want a room that's dark all the time?"

"No," Molly said doubtfully, and O'Brien seized the moment to distract her.

"Don't you have to get ready for school?"

"Are you finished with your breakfast?" Keiko asked. "All right. Then go get your datapadd—the one with the *narvies* I bought you yesterday—and bring Mommy's jacket, too."

"OK, Mommy." Molly slid down out of her chair— O'Brien suppressed the urge to help, knowing he'd only get the familiar "I want to do it myself!" for an answer—and trotted off into the inner rooms.

Keiko said, "Miles, what's all this talk about a Cardassian pirate?"

O'Brien stared for a moment. He should know better than to be surprised by the station's grapevine, but that it had reached Keiko—and therefore the station's children—was still something of a surprise. He took a deep breath, not wanting to alarm, but knowing at the same time that Keiko needed to know the truth. "Well, it's not a Cardassian pirate," he began, and Keiko sighed.

"Yesterday, some of the older children were talking about it—Nog in particular, I think his uncle had another run-in with Odo—and I could see that some of the little ones were nervous. We have quite a few Bajoran kids in the classes now, and they can get really frightened about the Cardassians."

"Not without cause," O'Brien said. "But, as far as we know, it's not a Cardassian." He ran quickly through the destruction of *Gift of Flight,* not minimizing the brutality of the attack, but stressing that they had no reason to think that DS9 was in any danger. As he finished, Keiko held up her hand, and looked past him to the door.

"Molly, honey, would you bring Mommy her datapadd, too?"

"OK," Molly said, behind them, and O'Brien heard the door slide shut again behind her.

Keiko looked at him, her face very serious. "Should we—should I be worried, Miles?"

O'Brien sighed. "I don't know, Keiko. I think— Not yet, anyway."

"You'll let me know when I should worry?" Keiko asked, but she was smiling.

O'Brien smiled back, the expression a little crooked. "No fear, darling, if there's trouble, I want you worrying about it right along with me."

"It's nice to be needed," Keiko said, dryly.

O'Brien smiled again, and heard the door open behind him. Before he could say anything, either reassurance or a change of subject, the intercom sounded.

"Sisko to O'Brien."

Keiko's expression froze for a fleeting instant, and then, with an effort that made O'Brien's heart ache with sympathy, she smiled at her daughter. "All ready, Molly?"

O'Brien reached for the intercom switch, aware that Keiko—and Molly, too—was listening. "O'Brien here. What's up, Commander?"

"No emergency," Sisko said, and there was a dry note in his voice that suggested that, whatever it was, it might be worse than an emergency, "but there are some things we need to discuss. I'd like to see you in my office as soon as is practical, Chief."

"On my way," O'Brien answered. He looked at the table, at the last few bites of breakfast congealing on his plate, and picked it up one-handed. "O'Brien out," he said, and shoved the plate into the reclamation chute with unnecessary force.

"Let me know what's happening, Miles," Keiko said, and O'Brien swept her into a quick hug. He was not the most articulate of men, always, at least not with her, with the important things, and he hoped, as always, that the gesture would convey the words he couldn't find.

"As soon as I know anything," he said, "I'll tell you."

Keiko nodded, and held open the door. O'Brien touched her cheek, and went past her into the corridor.

Sisko was waiting in his office when O'Brien tapped on the door. He looked up at O'Brien's knock, and beckoned for the younger man to enter. O'Brien did as he was told, unsuccessfully trying to quell the sense of panic that fluttered in his stomach. The station's systems were in good order—or they had been the night before, and he would have been called earlier if something were seriously wrong —so it had to be *Helios. Or the Cardassians,* he added silently, *and I don't know which is worse.*

"Chief," Sisko said, and gestured at a chair. "Thanks for being so prompt."

"Not at all," O'Brien said, through a mouth gone suddenly a little dry, and seated himself opposite his commander. "What's up, sir?"

"Possibly nothing," Sisko said, "but there is a chance that *Helios,* or someone, is hiding in the Denorios Belt."

O'Brien whistled softly. *"Helios* hiding in the Belt," he repeated. "Sir, if the tapes we've cobbled together from *Gift of Flight* and *Ganges* are at all accurate—if they're half-accurate—this station could be in serious danger."

"I know." Sisko gave him a look, and the engineer realized suddenly that he might have overstepped himself this time.

"Sorry, sir. It's just—" O'Brien hesitated, then went on, "I was talking to Keiko this morning already. It seems the attack is becoming the talk of the station."

"I know that, too," Sisko said, but this time he smiled. It was a somewhat wry smile, but O'Brien allowed himself an almost imperceptible sigh of relief. "Which is part of what I wanted to talk to you about, Chief. I want you and your people to check out the station's weapons and our defensive systems. Make sure everything is in operating order, and make sure it can come on line at a moment's notice."

O'Brien nodded, already running a mental inventory. "Yes, sir. I can tell you already that our shields are in good shape, you can have them up, nothing to one hundred percent, in five seconds. Half capacity in one-point-seven-five seconds."

That was a little under the time needed to earn Starfleet's "excellent" rating, and O'Brien was a little hurt when Sisko merely nodded.

"That's good, Chief." The commander smiled suddenly. "In fact, I believe that's excellent. But what about our offensive capabilities?"

"Ah." O'Brien made a face. "Not as good, I'm afraid. I've never been able to get the phasers to more than eighty percent of the Cardassian normal rating, and I can't tell if that's because the Cardassians didn't give a damn if they blew up the station, or if there's something I haven't figured out in their sorry excuse for a manual. But I'll do what I can to get it up to the full rating."

"Thanks, Chief," Sisko said. "But there's one thing more."

"Sir?"

Sisko leaned forward slightly. "I need you to do it discreetly—without alarming the station personnel any more than they already are."

O'Brien lifted an eyebrow. What Sisko was asking was very nearly impossible, even on a starship, where everyone aboard knew the score. On DS9, where half the population wasn't even Starfleet, it was like asking Quark not to cheat a newcomer. "I can try," he said, and knew he sounded doubtful. "Uh, sir, are you expecting trouble?"

Sisko sighed. "Frankly, I don't know, Chief. When Dax spotted—whatever it was—the computers thought it was probably a reflex shadow, an artifact of the new program you and she put in place. But there's a ten-percent chance, no more than that, but no less, either, that it was a ship recloaking, and I don't dare take the chance. Not with the lives on this station. As for the rest—" He shrugged. "The military maneuvers that we've been hearing so much about seem to be staying well within the Cardassian borders now, and for a miracle, the political situation on Bajor seems momentarily stable, so . . . I don't know if I'm expecting trouble, Chief. But I intend to be prepared."

O'Brien nodded, recognizing a familiar attitude. "I'll do my best to keep things quiet. And if you'd like, I'll tell Keiko to do the same. Some of her kids have been worrying, sir, about the Cardassians and all."

"It couldn't hurt," Sisko said. "Tell her I'd be grateful."

"Aye, sir."

"And give me a report as soon as you know the weapons' status."

"I'll do that, Commander," O'Brien answered.

"Thanks, Chief," Sisko said, and looked down at his desktop again.

It was clear dismissal, but O'Brien lingered for an instant, wanting to say something, anything, that might help resolve the worry he saw in the commander's eyes. But there was nothing, and he knew it; he nodded again, in vague salute and acknowledgment, and left the commander's office, letting the door slide softly shut behind him.

The security office was as quiet as ever, with only the hiss of the ventilators and the faint, inevitable chirps and whirs from the banks of wall displays to break the silence. Kira sat opposite Odo in the constable's private office, and did her best to curb her rising anger.

"I'm not a baby-sitter," she said. "And I'm not a policeman—or a spy, for that matter. It's not my job to look after this person, this Trehanna—"

"Her name," Odo said, "is Diaadul. The Lady Diaadul." His expression didn't change—but then, Kira thought, resentfully, it almost never did. "And this wasn't my idea."

"Oh, I just bet I know whose it was," Kira muttered.

"Commander Sisko felt you would be very helpful on this job," Odo said. His thin mouth twitched, and Kira was suddenly certain that he was laughing. *At me?* she thought, and drew breath to protest, but the shapeshifter was already continuing. "Since the Lady Diaadul comes from a culture that does not encourage contact between members of the opposite sex, the commander felt that you might be more likely than I to gain her confidence if she were in trouble." This time, Odo did smile openly, the expression grim. "To speak frankly, Major, I doubt it—and I doubt there is a confidence to be gained. And that's the reason I want your help."

Kira's anger evaporated as quickly as it had formed. "What do you mean?"

"I mean," Odo said, "that I don't think she is everything she pretends to be. Or at least that her intentions are something other than what she's said." He explained how he had followed Diaadul to her meeting with Quark, and her unexpected reaction to the Ferengi's habitual leer. "Which, you must admit, is not the reaction one expects from a Trehanna noblewoman," he finished.

"No." Kira frowned, trying to match the scene Odo had just described with the veiled figure she had glimpsed on the Promenade. One of the other Bajorans had pointed Diaadul out to her: a mysterious, blue-veiled shape, very bright and almost frivolous-looking against the harsh Cardassian architecture. Gold had glittered from one wrist as she had lifted a hand to take something from a shopkeeper, and Kira had, in that moment, almost envied the deliberately fragile femininity. It was, in an odd way, almost a relief to hear Odo's suspicions. "Were you able to follow her to the inner office?"

"No." Odo's voice was a growl. "The inner space is on a separate ventilation system, I have to backtrack to reach it. And by the time I'd done that, they were gone."

"I see." Kira nodded. "All right, what do you want me to do?"

"I want you to do just what Commander Sisko asked," Odo answered. "Help me keep an eye on Diaadul. If she decides to confide in you, well and good—but the main thing I want is to be sure she's not able to cause us any trouble."

"All right," Kira said again. She had already learned, in the short time that she'd been on DS9, that Odo's suspicions were generally well founded. If Odo said someone needed watching, that person generally did—and all too often, needed restraint as well. Perhaps he'd developed that almost uncanny knack under the Cardassians; the gods knew, they would give anyone reason for suspicion. She had said as much to other Bajorans more than once—Odo was not an instantly lovable person, nor did he go out of his way to make himself agreeable—and had gotten only grudging agreement, more for her own rank, she suspected, than out of any respect for him. But they would learn, given time, as she had learned. "What kind of surveillance do you have on her now?"

"Protective only," Odo answered. "For the moment, that's all that can be justified."

And that, Kira thought, is Benjamin Sisko speaking, not you. The Federation was a great respecter of the letter of the law, even when it came to potential felons— Her thoughts broke off abruptly, stopped by the memory of a Bajoran mob hot in pursuit of a collaborator. There had been a young lieutenant, a woman, part of the original Federation team that had made the first agreement with the provisional government, and she and her people—all two of them— had stepped in front of the mob. They had held off the angry Bajorans until the rest of Kira's troops had come up, and order had been restored enough to let them take the suspected collaborators away. Kira had been impressed by the young lieutenant, had stopped to speak with her: a thin, tired-eyed woman, with dirt on her face and a rising bruise from a rock someone had thrown. *Do you want me to let you know what happens at the trial?* Kira had asked, and the lieutenant had shaken her head. *It doesn't matter,* she had answered. *You people will do what you like.* Kira had been shaken by the anger, and it had been weeks—and several trials—before she had fully understood the other woman's answer. She shook away that equivocal memory, and said, "So far. What do you know about her habits?"

"That they're innocuous," Odo answered. "She walks the Promenade, spends a few hours each evening at Quark's, and then retires to her quarters. She speaks to shopkeepers, and when spoken to, nothing more."

"It's not much to go on," Kira said, and wrinkled her nose at Odo's sudden scowl. "I know, her behavior with Quark was still suspicious. I said I'd help. I'll drop in to Quark's tonight. If she's there, I'll try to talk to her, see if I can find out anything."

Odo nodded. "Thank you, Major. I appreciate the help."

"You owe me," Kira said, cheerfully, and, after a moment, Odo nodded again. They had both learned the value of favors under Cardassian rule.

"I owe you."

"Great." Kira pushed herself to her feet, headed for the door. As she stepped outside, a thought struck her, something Odo had said before. She caught the door before it closed, leaned back into the little office. Odo looked up quizzically, one hand on the intercom button.

"Major?"

"What the hell did you mean, you doubted she'd confide in me?"

Odo smiled again, thinly, but with real amusement. "I didn't think you were quite her type."

Kira had a sudden vision of herself as the Trehanna would see her: brash, free-striding, more like a Trehanna male than a fellow woman. She grinned in spite of herself—sometimes Sisko could be a little obtuse—and let the door close behind her.

CHAPTER
6

JULIAN BASHIR MADE HIS WAY through the crowd that
thronged Quark's place, easing past Sardonian traders and
courtesans of indeterminate sex, as well as the occasional
Bajoran newcomer who looked as though he didn't know
whether to approve or to summon clerical authority to
cleanse the place. There were Ferengi as well, more than
usual, and Bashir, who was tall even for a human, found
himself having to divide his attention between his intended
destination and the floor around him to keep from walking
into the smaller people. He vaguely remembered that there
was a Ferengi ship in dock—the *Pickpocket,* or *Sticky-
Fingers,* or something like that—and wondered for an
instant if he shouldn't have stayed at home in his quarters.
But rumor also said that the mysterious Lady Diaadul spent
her evenings at Quark's, and Bashir had heard the other
stories that were sweeping the station. Not that she could
possibly be as attractive as Dax, he assured himself hastily,
but it was still incumbent on him, as a Starfleet officer, to be

available should the lady need assistance. And besides, rumor said that she was very beautiful indeed beneath her veils.

He fetched up against the bar at last, and stood leaning against it, catching his breath. All around him, the air was filled with the babble of voices, Bajorans dominating, though the sharp mutter of Ferengi formed a distinctive counterpoint. It was a weird and wonderful mixture, exactly the sort of thing he had joined Starfleet to experience, and he turned slowly, savoring the sights. A pair of humans stood outside one of the holosuites on the upper level, negotiating—arguing, more like, from the aggressive gestures—with one of Quark's henchmen; the rest of the balcony area and the main part of the bar were filled with species he had never seen before.

"And what can I get for you today, Doctor?"

That was Quark's voice, at once sharp and obsequious, and Bashir turned hurriedly back to face the bar.

"A terrevani tea, please," he answered, and Quark bowed, a little too deeply to be sincere.

"Is the doctor certain he wouldn't like something a little more, um, adventurous?" Quark gestured expansively to the gleaming bank of replicators that rose behind him. "We've just received an entirely new programming set, and our menu has expended accordingly. We have all sorts of stimulants. . . ."

"No, thank you," Bashir said firmly, and suspected he was blushing again. "Just the tea."

"Suit yourself," Quark answered. "Though I know for a fact that Lieutenant Dax always has ale."

"Tea," Bashir said again, wishing he didn't have to go through this every time Quark waited on him. "Just tea. Thank you."

Quark bowed again, his smile showing a ferocious range of teeth. "As you wish."

Bashir waited until he was out of earshot, and then allowed himself a long sigh of relief. Sometimes he thought the entire station had banded together to tease him for his novice status, and, while he knew such teasing was traditional, if not inevitable, it could be very tiresome sometimes. He glanced along the length of the bar, trying to guess the size of the crowd, and hoped that Quark would find someone else to wait on.

That wish went, unsurprisingly, unanswered: it would have taken an entire shipload of Kaldanni tourists to distract Quark from his amusements. He reappeared in record time—sometimes Bashir thought he was the only person on DS9 who got prompt and efficient service at Quark's—and set the foaming glass on the counter in front of Bashir.

"Someone's been asking about you, Doctor," he said.

"Oh, really?" In spite of himself, Bashir felt his heart leap. There were a number of young women on the station who intrigued him, as well as the apparently unattainable Dax herself. Maybe, just maybe, one of them had deigned to acknowledge his interest. . . .

"Oh, yes," Quark assured him, showing teeth again in the Ferengi parody of a human smile. "Quite a bit, in fact—you've made a hit, I'm sure."

"That's—nice," Bashir said, and reached for his credit chip to pay for his drink. He was pleased that both his hand and his voice were steady—if anything, he thought, he sounded not entirely enthusiastic at the prospect, and that, too, was good. It wouldn't do to seem too eager.

Quark waved away the stick. "No need, Doctor, your admirer's already taken care of it."

"Really?" Bashir heard his voice rise in spite of himself, heard, too, the undignified excitement in his answer. It couldn't be Dax, she was still too aloof—and, to be fair, she was a little old for him, or at least half of her was—but Kira had been less hostile toward him since they'd gone out after *Gift of Flight,* and the major was undeniably attractive, if more than a little intimidating. . . .

"Absolutely," Quark assured him, showing the full rank of pointed teeth, and leaned sideways slightly, gesturing toward the corner table. Bashir turned to look, schooling himself to a not too eager smile, and found himself looking directly at the ridged face of the only Cardassian left on DS9. Garak smiled back at him, the ridges curving alarmingly, and Bashir looked past the Cardassian's shoulders, hoping against hope to see Kira or Dax or anyone else waiting for him. The other tables in that corner were crowded with lizardlike Gemurra, and Garak lifted a long-fingered hand to beckon him over.

"Yes," Quark said, "Garak thinks quite well of you."

"How nice," Bashir said, through clenched teeth. "Quark—" But the Ferengi had already turned away, apparently oblivious to his calls, and Bashir knew from experience that Quark was perfectly capable of ignoring him for the rest of the night.

And there was really no reason to refuse the drink, in any case. Not only had Commander Sisko encouraged him, all of them, to be as courteous as possible to the Cardassians, but Garak could be, in his own odd fashion, a pleasant companion. Besides, spy or not, he did hear everything. Bashir threaded his way through the crowd to Garak's table. The Cardassian beamed up at him, and gestured to the empty chair.

"My dear Julian. Do join me. I've had so little chance lately to enjoy your company."

Bashir seated himself, setting the tea in front of him. He still wasn't entirely sure what game Garak was playing with him—the station grapevine swore that the Cardassian had only remained to spy on the station's new owners, though he suspected that there was more to Garak's friendliness than the sheer desire for information. "I've been rather busy," he said. Garak was watching him expectantly, still with that slight smile, and Bashir felt the blood rise to his face. "Thank you for the drink."

Garak's smile widened. "My pleasure, I assure you, Julian. It's a very small thing to do for one I consider a friend."

"What was it you wanted, Garak?" Bashir asked, and was instantly ashamed of his suspicions.

Garak spread his hands. They were incongruously beautiful, and the Cardassian used them to unexpected advantage. "Why, only to pursue our acquaintance. What else could I want? More would be—most inappropriate."

What more *could* he want? Bashir wondered, and a new and appalling series of possibilities seemed to open in front of him. He shook the thought away. "I'm sure."

Garak studied him for a moment longer, the lines at the corners of his eyes giving him an almost mischievous look, then leaned forward slightly. "And, in way of friendship, Julian . . . I think I should pass along to you something that I heard in my shop. I think it would interest you, and that you, of all people, would know what to do with it."

"Now you are making fun of me," Bashir said. The words slipped out involuntarily, and he felt himself blushing again. If Quark hadn't given him a hard time, and Dax before that, he would never have said such a thing, and especially not to Garak.

The Cardassian smiled openly this time, an expression so unlike his usual affectations that Bashir almost didn't recognize it, but said only, "Not—not in the information, Julian. I do think you will find it useful."

Bashir blinked, and the moment vanished. "I'll do what I can," he said, doubtfully, and Garak simpered at him.

"I'm sure you're more than capable, Julian. Much more." He leaned forward again, lowering his voice. "I had a customer in my shop today—one of the Aniona, such a difficult people to fit, especially with the asymmetric arms. It's one thing to have an odd number of arms, but the placement! A poor tailor's nightmare, I assure you! But that's not my point." The smile vanished as quickly as it had appeared, and Bashir tensed. "What my customer told me was that there's quite a lot of activity on the Cardassian side of the border—he usually brings his ship in through Cardassian space, it saves him time in the long run, always assuming the Guls don't confiscate his cargoes. He was quite worried, as you might imagine, didn't want to risk bringing in a cargo if he was just going to lose it in some attack. But what he was told, by a Gul with whom he's had some very profitable dealings, is that this activity, this massing of a fleet and all the troubles it's caused, hasn't a single thing to do with the Federation. Apparently there's a pirate loose on their side of the border, someone who's been something of a nuisance for quite a while now, and Gul Dukat has decided to put it down once and for all. However—"

He paused, and Bashir thought he saw a look of unholy satisfaction flit across the Cardassian's face.

"However," Garak continued smoothly, "Gul Dukat's efforts have been less than successful. My customer tells me that the day he cast off from the Sheraona Colony, everyone was talking about the pirate's escape. It seems that it hid in a sun's corona, and ambushed Gul Dukat's fleet. Several ships are said to have been badly damaged—Cardassian ships, I'm afraid—and the fleet has lost the pirate. But they're still looking, of course, and I understand that Gul Dukat is furious."

I just bet he is, Bashir thought. His mind was working furiously, untangling the implications of the story. If it was true—and it could be, it would fit all the other facts they'd gathered, and even the Cardassians would have no reason to love the pirate—then DS9 had less to worry about than they had thought. Of course, that could be exactly what Gul Dukat *wanted* them to think. He took a deep swallow of his tea, barely tasting it, and then nearly choked on unexpected carbonation. Quark had been adjusting the replicators again. . . .

Garak reached out solicitously, patted the younger man between the shoulder blades. "Are you all right, Julian? Yes, it is shocking news—but not, I think, precisely *bad* news."

Bashir took a deep breath and recovered himself, inwardly cursing Quark, Garak, the pirate, and all the other things that were making his life impossibly difficult just at the moment. "No," he said, "I suppose not. . . ."

"Though of course it does change everyone's calculations, doesn't it?" Garak went on, with bright, spurious sympathy. "Dear boy, what you're drinking! Do let me buy you something more to your taste."

Bashir shook his head. "No, thanks," he said, and took another hasty swallow of the tea.

"And someday," the Cardassian continued, with what sounded to Bashir like suddenly genuine concern, "you must come by my shop and let me dress you properly. It's a great shame that such a nicely built young man should be reduced to Starfleet uniform."

"That's regulations," Bashir said, relieved to have such an innocuous answer for once, and Garak sighed.

"Oh, I know. But you'd think they went out of their way to make humans look unattractive. Tell me, were the uniforms designed by a Vulcan?"

"By a committee, I think," Bashir answered. "A long time ago."

"That," Garak said darkly, "is fairly obvious."

Bashir drained what was left of his tea in a single gulp. "Thank you very much for the drink, Garak, but I really must be going now."

"Of course," Garak murmured. "And you're very welcome. I hope we can have another chat sometime when you're less—pressed."

"Definitely," Bashir agreed. "Thank you, Garak."

"Doctor," the Cardassian said.

Bashir turned back, lifting his thin eyebrows in unspoken question.

"The pirate ship is called *Helios*," Garak said. "And her captain is Demaree Kolovzon. Or so they say."

"Do they," Bashir echoed blankly, and wished he could think of something more intelligent to say. "Thank you, Garak, that's very interesting." He turned away, heading for the door, but not before he heard the Cardassian's murmur.

"Not at all. . . ."

Once back out on the Promenade, Bashir paused for a moment, collecting his thoughts. It was mercifully quiet, after the noise of Quark's, and he was glad of the chance to pull himself together before he called Sisko. Not that he had any choice—even someone as inexperienced as he was could see that this was the sort of information that, true or false, should be brought at once to the commanding officer —but he wasn't looking forward to disturbing Sisko at home.

Sisko was still in Ops when his communicator sounded. He frowned for just an instant—he was already behind schedule on half a dozen routine matters, and he knew from bitter experience that a comm call at this hour meant falling at least another day or so behind—but then mastered himself and touched his insignia. "Sisko here."

"It's Dr. Bashir, Commander."

As if I wouldn't recognize that voice, Sisko thought. He said, "Go ahead, Doctor."

"Sir, I've just— I wonder if I might have a word with you? In private?"

"Is it important?" The moment the words were out of his mouth, Sisko regretted them: he would not have questioned any other of his officers that way. Fortunately, Bashir didn't seem to notice.

"Yes, sir. I think it is."

Sisko sighed, assessing the firm voice. "I'm still in Ops, Doctor. Come on up."

He was never sure if he'd heard an answering sigh of relief. "On my way," Bashir answered, and cut the connection.

Bashir was as good as his word. He appeared in Sisko's doorway within minutes of signing off, tall and gangling, a look of almost comic perplexity on his improbably handsome face. Sisko eyed him without favor, but motioned him to the guest's chair.

"Well, Doctor?"

To his surprise, a faint, delicate color suffused Bashir's cheeks. "I've been approached—no, contacted, by Garak again," the doctor said, and Sisko looked down to hide his sudden grin. Garak enjoyed his little games, and his information was generally reliable enough to allow him to get away with it.

"What did Garak have to say?" he asked.

Bashir took a deep breath. "Even shorn of the irrelevant material, quite a lot, actually, sir. But I don't know how reliable it is." He outlined what Garak had told him, that Gul Dukat's pursuit of *Helios* was responsible for the rumors about a Cardassian military buildup, and that the Cardassian fleet had actually succeeded in cornering *Helios* briefly, before it broke away, leaving Gul Dukat with damaged ships and, though Bashir was careful to stress that this was his own guess, damaged pride. "The final thing Garak told me," he finished, "was the name of the pirate ship—and the captain's name. Demaree Kolovzon."

"Well done, Doctor," Sisko said. *And very well done, Garak, to get this to us so quickly—but is any of it true, I wonder? Or is it just what Gul Dukat wants us to think? He and Garak are old rivals, but when all's said and done, they're still both Cardassians. If it's a bluff, Garak's effectiveness would be permanently destroyed—we'd never trust him again—but that would be a very small price to pay for destroying DS9.* He sighed, shaking himself back to the present, and Bashir cleared his throat uncertainly.

"Commander, do you think this is true?"

Sisko looked at him. "I don't know," he said, after a moment. "At least, not yet. What I want you to do, Doctor, is to make me a complete record of the conversation— everything he said, everything you said, to the best of your memory. Do it now, while it's still fresh."

"Yes, sir," Bashir said, and Sisko could see the dull blush creep into his face again. "Um, sir, when you say everything . . ."

"I mean everything," Sisko said. He waited a beat, and then, seeing the look on the young doctor's face, added, "Everything that's of relevance to this story of his."

Bashir let out a heartfelt sigh. "Yes, sir. Thank you."

"Now, Bashir."

"Very good, sir," Bashir answered. Only then did a sudden look of dismay flicker across his face, and Sisko wondered what plans he'd inadvertently interrupted. But the look vanished as quickly as it had appeared, and Sisko acknowledged with grudging approval that at least the doctor seemed to have his priorities in order. Bashir pushed himself up from the guest's chair, long body unfolding to its full length, and let himself out of the office.

The door closed behind him, but Sisko didn't move, stared instead at the blank screen embedded in his desktop. There were tactical programs in the computer, programs that purported to be able to analyze intelligence data, but they needed facts to work with, not the rumor and innuendo that was all he actually had. If Garak's story was true, then they had little to worry about from the Cardassians—a mixed blessing, he added silently, since it meant that they should be worrying about *Helios* instead. And *Helios* was, to all reports, a formidable enemy.

All of which raised an interesting question, one that was diplomatically very tricky indeed. As far as *Helios* was concerned, Cardassian and Federation interests ran in tandem. Did the Federation want to offer formal, or informal, assistance in Gul Dukat's hunt? Fortunately, the decision wasn't his to make: it would be very hard to choose between working with the Cardassians and insuring the safety of the station. But this was a question that needed to be put before Starfleet as soon as possible. He ran his hand over a toggle menu, transforming the blank work screen to a subspace radio control board, and then began doggedly to enter the various codes that opened a secure line to Starfleet headquarters.

As he had more than half expected, neither of the admirals whom he attempted to contact were immediately available, and he resigned himself to several hours' wait in his office before one of them responded to the short version of Bashir's story that he had left with their aides. To his surprise, however, he had barely ordered a cup of coffee from one of the recently repaired replicators and was about to taste the suspiciously oily-looking liquid when the communications console signaled again. He set the cup aside with some relief, and touched the toggle that accepted the coded call and routed it into his larger desk-mounted screen. The screen went blue and silver, numbers and symbols flashing across its face as the code routines went into action, and then the screen split into two discrete images. The first was familiar, a thin, well-weathered man, his long face carved into deep lines, but the second, a fleshy, grey-blonde woman in civilian clothes, was at first glance unknown. Then the background behind her really registered, a night cityscape, all gold bars of light that were the windows of skyscrapers and the red of air-traffic steering lights and the occasional multicolored retro-neon display board that flashed its messages into the darkness, and he realized who she had to be. Vice-Admiral Estellan Angerich, retired from active service to head Six Branch of Starfleet Intelligence, was a shadowy but formidable presence in the Ansterra Sector. For her to sit in on this conference meant that someone, somewhere, was taking this threat very seriously indeed. Sisko felt a cold tingle of fear at the pit of his stomach, and was not reassured by her casual, social smile.

It was the other admiral, Joachim Ledesma, Sisko's ultimate commander, who spoke first, however. "Ben. I'm glad to have heard from you."

Sisko answered the implied reproach. "I've had nothing to report until now, sir. And I'm not sure myself how to interpret this—evidence."

He thought he saw the shadow of a grin cross Angerich's full lips, but she said nothing. Ledesma said, "And, frankly, neither are we. But Admiral Angerich will go into that in more detail later."

The blonde woman bowed her head.

"But if it is accurate," Ledesma went on, "Starfleet does have a policy."

Wonderful, Sisko thought. He waited.

"Frankly," Ledesma said, "we've been concerned about this pirate for some time now. Although it's been careful to avoid attacking Federation shipping, or crossing into Federation space—"

"Until now," Sisko said, unable to stop himself.

Ledesma paused, and nodded, acknowledging the point. "Until now. Which is a very mixed blessing, Ben. On the one hand, a good ship and its crew have been lost, which I can't, and don't, consider to be anything less than the disaster it is. But on the other . . ."

He paused again, and Angerich said, "It does give Starfleet a leverage we haven't had before." Her voice was deeply musical, with a faint, lilting accent that Sisko could not place. She smiled then, quick and wry. "Which is not to discount the destruction of *Gift of Flight,* but it's nice to have the chance possibly to do something about it."

Ledesma nodded. "Precisely. And that's where your information comes in, Ben."

"You have my preliminary report," Sisko said. "And Dr. Bashir is making out a full and detailed report, which I will pass to you as soon as it's completed."

"Dr. Julian Bashir," Angerich said. "He was the Cardassian agent's contact?"

"Yes," Sisko answered, and was suddenly certain, though her gaze did not shift by even a millimeter, that she had Bashir's file—and probably his own as well—open on a screen somewhere in front of her.

"Why did Garak choose Bashir?" Ledesma asked suddenly. "Surely he could have found someone more experienced —more politically aware, at least. That would tend to make me think this is a hoax, something to distract us from the military movements."

Sisko hesitated, wondering precisely how to answer, and saw another ghostly smile flicker across Angerich's face. "Garak has a peculiar sense of humor," he said at last, and Angerich nodded slightly.

"Contacting Bashir is consistent with Garak's usual habits," she said.

Ledesma nodded again, though he looked less than convinced. "In any case, we—Starfleet, that is—have no choice but to proceed for now as though the information is genuine. We want this pirate, this *Helios,* very badly, Ben. It's caused the deaths of too many good people, too many allies and too many ships, not to mention the value of the cargoes lost. We want it stopped, and this is our first best chance to do so. And if that means cooperating with the Cardassians, so be it."

"With—" Sisko broke off, aware of the logic of the admiral's words, but equally aware of their impracticality. "Sir, if this information is correct, Gul Dukat is in command of the pursuit squadron."

He was vaguely aware of Angerich looking at him with something like approval, but his attention was focused on Ledesma, who colored faintly. "I'm aware of that, Ben. And I'm aware of Gul Dukat's history and reputation. But he's not the man who destroyed *Gift of Flight,* either."

Sisko made a face. "I understand that, sir. And I can certainly see the advantages to cooperating with the Cardassians to take *Helios.* I'm just not sure the Cardassians will follow through."

"They've suffered more from *Helios* than we have," Ledesma said. "And they aren't stupid. They're as aware of their military deficiencies as we are, and we think—Intelligence's best guess—is that they would jump at the chance to get Starfleet to do their dirty work for them."

Sisko glanced in spite of himself at Angerich, who nodded once.

"And that's where the catch lies," Ledesma said. "I told you earlier, Ben, Starfleet wants *Helios* and her mysterious captain very badly. My orders are to do whatever I and mine can to capture *Helios,* prevent any more destruction—and at the same time, if at all possible, to return *Helios* and her people to the Federation for trial."

Sisko took a deep breath, fighting back anger as the implications of Ledesma's words tumbled through his mind. Starfleet wanted, in essence, exactly what the Cardassians wanted: help capturing the pirate, and then the opportunity to punish captain and crew without interference from the other side. The trouble was, there were more Cardassians in this area of space to enforce their desires. "With all due respect, sir," he began, with careful irony, "I don't see how that can be achieved without a substantial fleet to insist on it."

"I'm aware of that," Ledesma said. "Don't think I don't appreciate your position, Ben. But my orders are, if at all possible, to see that *Helios* and her people are tried in the Federation." Sisko drew breath to protest, and Ledesma held up his hand. "You'll be receiving my orders in the morning anyway, Ben, in the official communications packet, but I'll give you the gist of it now. If the opportunity arises, you're to use your discretion to bring *Helios* into our space for trial. Always with the understanding that DS9 and its safety is your first priority."

"I understand, sir," Sisko said. And he did understand, all too well. Ledesma had given him as much leeway as he could have hoped for, stressing discretion and the station's safety, but Starfleet wanted *Helios* very badly indeed. And he, Sisko, was expected to make every effort to get it for them.

"You may have unlikely allies," Angerich said, unexpectedly. "Given the chance, I expect *Helios's* people would rather be tried in the Federation."

That was probably true—the Cardassian piracy laws were as draconian as the rest of their system—but Sisko couldn't see that it was likely to help much.

Ledesma said, "In any case, Ben, I wanted to pass this on to you at once, so that you'd have as much time as possible to make your preparations."

"I appreciate that, sir," Sisko said, and meant it. If there was any chance at all that DS9 would have to face *Helios,* they would all need all the time they could muster. He stared into space for an instant, no longer seeing the faces in the communications screens. DS9's weapons systems were erratic; the shields had long been O'Brien's top priority, as there had seemed to be less reason to rush getting the phasers back up to their full capacity.

"As long as the situation is clear," Ledesma said. His eyes flickered for the first time, shifting toward a secondary screen that carried Angerich's image. "I do want to see your doctor's report as soon as you have it for me, but I think that's all for now, Ben. Unless Admiral Angerich has something more?"

"Just a few follow-up questions," the heavyset woman said. "Nothing terribly important."

Ledesma nodded. "Then I'll leave you to her, Ben. Keep me informed."

"I'll do that," Sisko answered, and Ledesma smiled.

"Ledesma out."

The image in the screen vanished, and a fraction of a second later Angerich's image expanded to fill the full screen. Her image remained the same size, centered against the brilliant cityscape, its details so clear that for an instant Sisko imagined he could make out a route sign on the nose of an elevated tram as it moved across the glittering buildings.

"Commander Sisko," Angerich said, thoughtfully, and Sisko marshaled his straying thoughts.

"Admiral."

"A lot of my questions will have to wait until I get Dr.

Bashir's report of this meeting," she began, "but for now, I'd like to get your impressions of all of this."

"Impressions?" Sisko frowned. An invitation like that could be either the making or the ruin of a commander, and the outcome depended less on the commander's answer than on the questioner's interpretation of the answer.

"Off the record, if you'd prefer," Angerich said, with a quick, wry smile that suggested she'd followed his thoughts.

Sisko shook his head. "No, Admiral, thank you, I'll stick my neck out in public if I have to. But I'd like to be sure what you're asking me to do."

"You're the commander on the spot," Angerich answered. "I'd like to get your thoughts—and your feelings, your hunches, I don't hold that intuition is an exclusively female talent—about what's going on. The things you wouldn't put in a report."

Sisko regarded her image warily. She looked, if anything, tired and overworked, the heavy face and body at odds with her reputation as one of Starfleet's more acute intelligence controllers—but if she was half as good as everyone said, Sisko reminded himself, she would be very good at that particular act. After all, how better to catch a Starfleet commander?

"You mentioned that your science officer spotted something, maybe just a sensor shadow, in your asteroid belt," Angerich prodded, still gently. "You admit the odds are against, but you still warned Bajor to take precautions with its shipping."

She let the obvious question hang unspoken, and Sisko sighed again. "You saw the report, Admiral. And the percentages the computer gave. I simply felt we couldn't afford to take any chances with so new a Federation ally. The Bajorans are better placed to decide what risks they feel like running than I am."

"And it keeps them off your back?" Angerich said. It was only just a question.

Sisko hesitated, then nodded. "It should be their decision, not mine—I don't have or seek that authority."

Angerich grinned, more broadly this time. "So, Commander, do you think it's *Helios* out there?"

Sisko blinked, startled by the direct question. "I think it could be, yes. And I think it's more than a ten-percent chance—more than that, though, I don't think we can afford not to assume it's *Helios.*" He paused again, gauging his chances, and said, "Do you think it's *Helios,* Admiral?"

Angerich's smile vanished, and she stared at him for a moment—almost, Sisko thought, as though she's really seeing me for the first time. "Well," she said, after a moment, "it's a fair question. Off the record, Sisko—this is my opinion, not Starfleet Intelligence's, I don't have enough hard fact to justify it, yet—off the record, yes, I think Garak's story is true. It feels right, it fits with other whispers and hints I've been getting. And if it's true, I think DS9, and you, should be very worried indeed."

Sisko nodded again, slowly. "Thank you, Admiral. I'll bear that in mind."

"Do that—and be sure you take it at its proper value." Angerich looked down at something on her desk, and looked up again, sighing. "I've another urgent call, Commander. Contact me if you have any further information."

"Very good, Admiral," Sisko said, and the screen went blank again. He stared at it for a long moment—for Angerich, of all people, to agree with his suspicions was at once encouraging and coldly frightening—and then touched keys to switch computer modes. "Computer. I want a full status report on our weapons systems, defensive and offensive capabilities, including any modifications or notes Mr. O'Brien has made on the subject."

"Confirmed," the computer answered, and a moment later Sisko's working screen filled with symbols. He sighed at the sheer volume of information—there were several dozen different files, most of which held subfiles and cross-referenced directories, and it would take hours just to begin to review the system—but settled himself to work. If it was *Helios* out there, DS9 would need every advantage he could find.

Miles O'Brien blinked in the harsh light of the reactor chamber, and felt another bead of sweat run down his face, tickling gently. He reached instinctively to wipe it off, and knocked his gloved hand against the faceplate of the antiradiation suit. He sighed—there were some reflexes you could never get rid of, no matter how many hours you spent in space suits or radiation gear—and blinked again, more rapidly, clearing the sweat from his eyes. It was always hot in the suits, however one adjusted the individual controls: maybe it was the radiation, or maybe just the thought of the radiation, that filled the chamber, produced by the sabotaged fusion reactor that ran riot behind the sealed doors and layers of poured lead. A few lights still blinked forlornly on the display panels—this had been the primary control room for this pair of reactors—but most of the screens were blank and dead. O'Brien glanced over his shoulder at the other technicians, Swannig and Carter, indistinguishable in their heavy protective suits except by the splash of red paint on Swannig's left elbow, and hoped that they would have time to finish their survey. *And you won't have time to finish if you stand here daydreaming,* he told himself sternly, and turned his attention to the console in front of him.

The access panel was placed badly, so that he had to go down on his knees, awkward in the heavy suit, and grope along the side of the console for the release button. He found it at last, tugged the panel forward when it refused to budge on its own, and winced at the mess of circuits and fused wire-and-strapping that it revealed. The Cardassians had sabotaged four of the six reactors before they turned over the station; two were hopelessly contaminated, but these two were at least potentially salvageable. *Though "potential" is a very big word,* O'Brien thought, and grunted as the first board came free at last, trailing a tangle of half-melted wires. *A very big word indeed.*

A chime sounded in his ear, in the speaker set into his helmet, and in the same moment a computer voice said sweetly, "Warning. You have reached safety limit one. You must leave the radiation area now. Warning. You have reached safety limit one."

O'Brien groaned, but there was no point in arguing with the medical computers. He left the board where it was—it certainly wasn't functional, and there was no way he could bring it with him, badly contaminated as it was—and crawled backward until he could push himself to his feet.

"Oh, hell," another voice said—Carter, the clear soprano unmistakable. "Chief, permission to extend my stay to safety limit two. I've almost finished tracing this conduit, and it's all functional so far."

O'Brien shook his head. "Sorry, Carter. This isn't an emergency. You can finish it tomorrow."

Carter's sigh was heavy in his ear. "Yes, Chief. But I'm so close!"

"Tomorrow," O'Brien said, and gestured for the two technicians to precede him through the heavy doors. He understood her eagerness, all right—if they could find enough still-functioning power conduits, they could maybe tap some of the reactor's power; it was still running, sort of, a power source all the more frustrating because they hadn't been able to bring it into service. More than that, these reactors had been designed to power the weapons systems: *If I can just get some power flowing from this one,* he thought, *just to juice up the main systems, I should be able to get the phasers working right, and maybe stiffen up the screens into the bargain.*

A portable decontamination station was locked to the hatchway. They stepped into the blued light of the first chamber, mercifully cool after the brilliance of the reactor control room, and Swannig resealed both hatches behind them.

"Green seal," he reported, after a moment, and O'Brien nodded.

"Run decontamination."

"Yes, sir," Carter said, and her gloved hands moved easily on the oversized controls. A thick mist, blued by the lights, hissed almost soundlessly from a hundred pores in the walls, rising until it filled the chamber completely. O'Brien turned in the fog as though it were a cleansing rain, lifting his arms and spreading his fingers to give the mist better access to every centimeter of the suit's surface. Through the fog, he could see the others doing the same, and heard Swannig whistling under his breath, a tune O'Brien didn't recognize. Carter apparently did: she chuckled, and hastily suppressed the sound.

"Radiation has dropped to acceptable levels," she announced, a moment later, and in the same moment the mist cut out, and the exhaust fans switched on. The mist vanished swiftly, dropping toward the floor where the exhaust vents were, and a minute later the light turned green over the second hatch. Swannig reached for the controls, hauled the door open, and they went through into the changing room. He closed the hatch behind them, whirling the handwheel.

"Green seal, Chief," he said. "All secure."

"Great," O'Brien said, and unlatched his helmet. He lifted it off, then freed himself from the heavy gloves and, finally, rubbed the sweat out of his eyes. The changing room was crowded, only a few meters between the rows of lockers that held the protective suits, and it took concentration to keep from bumping into each other. O'Brien wriggled out of the thick suit, retrieved the internal data cartridge from the recorder, then stowed the suit and the gloves, helmet, and boots in their locker. He tucked the cartridge into his belt, and then stood waiting while Swannig wrestled his equipment into place.

"Sorry, Chief," the shorter man said, and Carter muttered something half under her breath.

"Slow as molasses, Chris."

"All right," O'Brien said. "Let's get out of here."

Carter swung the hatch wheel, and they stepped out into the larger compartment. O'Brien stretched, glad to be out of the cumbersome suit, then slipped the cartridge into the nearest data reader. Out of the corner of his eye, he saw the two technicians exchange glances, and then come to look over his shoulder. They were much of a height—Carter was tall, Swannig on the short side—and both fair-skinned blonds, and O'Brien thought, not for the first time, that they looked more like brother and sister than any unrelated people had a right to do.

"So," Carter said, "what's this all about, anyway, Chief?"

O'Brien didn't answer for a moment, scrolling through the pages of raw data, then grunted with satisfaction as he found the section he wanted. "You said you nearly finished tracing this section?"

Carter leaned closer. "Yeah."

"How long will it take you, do you think?"

She shrugged. "Maybe twenty minutes—thirty if there's a problem."

"All right. We'll concentrate on that tomorrow, then." O'Brien looked at the rough diagram for another long moment, then turned to face his technicians. "What I'm looking for—and I want you to keep this under your hats for now, no spreading it around the station, or even to the other techs, Chris—is a way to tap some of that raw power. It looks to me as if we could tap this section of the old power conduit here without risking a radiation leak—put in an exchange node here at the old feeder."

Swannig leaned past him, frowning slightly. "We won't get much power out of it, not without risking overload. That system's not even close to stable."

"I know it," O'Brien said. "But I don't want much." He grinned in spite of himself, still unreasonably pleased by the possibilities. "Whatever we can tap, we feed it direct to the phasers—if everything goes right, according to my preliminary calculations we can double the phaser output for at least three minutes before we risk further damage to the reactors."

Swannig nodded slowly, still studying the diagram. "That assumes that the conduit's still sound out here, of course."

"It was good all the way in," Carter said. "There's less reason to expect damage there."

"And radiation levels are low enough there that we can do minor repairs," O'Brien said. "Then we install an exchange node here, and we're home free."

Both technicians nodded slowly, and Swannig said, "Elegant."

"It's that pirate, isn't it?" Carter asked. "That's what this is about."

O'Brien looked at her for a long moment, and nodded. "Commander Sisko wants us to take all possible precautions." He watched their faces, seeing the sudden sobering as the thought took form, and added, trying for a lighter note, "Besides, I've been wanting to get the phasers up to their proper ratings for a while now. But that's for tomorrow. Come on, I'll buy you a drink to celebrate."

The technicians grinned dutifully, but he could tell he hadn't entirely reassured them. *Well, it hasn't reassured me, either,* he thought, and followed them toward the nearest turbolift for the long ride up twenty-five levels to the Promenade. *It hasn't reassured me at all.*

CHAPTER
7

ODO STARED AT the list of ships currently in the docking ring, well aware that his face showed a very human expression of disgust. It was, he thought, something of a pity that there was no one here to observe the cultivated effect. But he had good reason to be disgusted: there, among the new arrivals, was a name that stood out like a beacon. He had been dealing with *Carabas* since his first days as constable, since the days of the Cardassian occupation, and he knew perfectly well what *Carabas* and her crew were really up to. Of course, under the Cardassians, *Carabas*'s two-man crew had run guns and software to the Bajoran resistance, but the Bajorans had never been their only customers. They had sold just about anything to just about anybody, and Odo had done his best to stop them, but he had never been able to get solid evidence against them. *I suppose I could have bought a conviction,* he thought—*the two smugglers certainly never scrupled to buy their way out of trouble, and the Cardassians running the station never hesitated to dispense their version of justice to the highest bidder—but it would not have been satisfying.* Nor would it have been right, and that, in the end, had been the deciding factor. And now *Carabas* was back on DS9.

For an instant, Odo considered contacting Sisko, recommending that the ship and its crew be expelled from the station, but even as he reached for his communicator he dismissed the thought. He had no evidence—had never been able to collect enough evidence to convince Gul Dukat, never mind Sisko. And Sisko would not consent to removing them without evidence. "Odo to Zhou."

There was a brief pause, and then the young ensign answered. "Zhou here. What can I do for you, sir?"

"This ship, the *Carabas,* that just landed. Is the crew still aboard?"

"No, sir, I don't think so—no, they left a few minutes ago. Is there a problem?"

"Not yet," Odo said. "I want a watch posted on that ship—at least two men, round-the-clock surveillance."

"Very well, Constable," Zhou said. "Should they be looking for anything in particular?"

"Anything at all," Odo said, grimly. "Do you have any idea where the crew went?"

"I don't," Zhou said, "but they were talking to Aimoto. Let me ask her."

There was a little silence, and Odo drummed his fingers almost soundlessly against the desktop. It was impossibly frustrating to know that *Carabas* and her crew were at best troublemakers, and at worst dangerous to the station, and to be able to do nothing about it . . .

"Sorry, Constable," Zhou said. "Aimoto says they said something about going to the Promenade, but that's all she knows."

"Thank you," Odo said, and cut the connection. That was actually quite enough: he knew the smugglers well enough to guess where they would be found. He pushed himself away from his desk, and headed out into the Promenade.

Most of the people crowding the shopfronts were Bajorans, but there were more than a few nonhumans, and a sprinkling of off-duty Starfleet personnel, made conspicuous by their uniforms. Odo made his way through the crowd, glancing quickly into Quark's—not particularly busy at this point in the station's day—and then rode the turbolift to level ten. There were fewer people there, as he had expected, a pair of Bajorans in drab work clothes busy at an open panel, and a Starfleet technician with her boyfriend. Beyond the technician, two men stood by one of the massive windows, peering intently toward the apparent emptiness that concealed the wormhole. Odo was frowning, trying to remember if a ship had been scheduled to go through the wormhole now, when blue-white light flared beyond the window. He blinked, and saw the familiar blue disk appear, swirling out from the now-visible wormhole. Its center swelled, almost too fast to follow, and opened, emitting a shaft of light. The wedge shape of a starship rose with it, dark against that brilliance. It hung open for an instant longer, vivid blue against the stars, and then spun back into itself, contracting to a pinpoint of light that flared and then went out. The two men stood motionless for a moment longer, and then the taller clapped the other on the shoulder and turned away.

"Looks like water going down the drain."

"A true romantic, you are." The second man stopped abruptly, smile vanishing as he saw Odo.

"Gentlemen," the constable said, and allowed himself a thin smile at their sudden wariness. "Mr. Möhrlein, Mr. Tama. I didn't expect to see you back on DS9."

"Constable Odo," Vilis Möhrlein said. He was the taller of the two, and very fair, with white-blond hair cut short around his face. He would, Odo thought, be considered quite handsome by most humans. "It's good to see you again."

"Nice to see you kept your job," Kerel Tama said, and showed teeth in a distinctly unfriendly grin. He was shorter than Möhrlein by a handsbreadth, and had darker, long brown hair straggling to his shoulders in an untidy mane. It was streaked with grey now, more than there had been the last time Odo had seen him, and the constable took some satisfaction in the change.

"I have some things to say to you, gentlemen," Odo went on, ignoring Tama's jibe.

"We're a little busy right now, Constable," Möhrlein said. "Got some people to see, some—business—to arrange. Can it wait?"

"We can talk here and now," Odo said, "or you can come down to my office. I'd be happy to send someone to escort you."

Tama's mouth twisted into a sour grimace. Möhrlein said, "I hardly think that's necessary. What's on your mind, Odo?"

"You." Odo smiled again, without friendliness. "I simply want you to know that I have my eyes on you. If you make the slightest untoward move, you will be thrown off this station so fast you'll think you're making warp speed. And you will be permanently banned from docking here. Too many things happen around you two."

"Now, wait a minute," Tama began, and Möhrlein cut in smoothly.

"This is Federation space now, Constable, you can't just ban us without good reason—without even a hearing."

"Do you really want a hearing, Möhrlein?" Odo asked, and was pleased to see the smuggler's gaze flicker. "Besides, this is a Bajoran station. There is a Federation presence here, but the station belongs to Bajor."

"And we've done good service to Bajor in our time," Tama said. "People will remember that."

"You did those services at a very high price," Odo answered. "I think your erstwhile customers will remember that, too."

Möhrlein said, "Constable, I know we've had our differences in the past, but that was under Cardassian rule." He spread his hands, displaying palms empty except for a long scar across the left, legacy of an argument with one of Gul Dukat's junior officers. Odo scowled, remembering that evening—he had been the one to pick up the pieces—and Möhrlein instantly closed his hand again. "We've gone legitimate since the war, gone back to honest trading. It's just too dangerous, now that the Federation's become a presence in this sector. It's not worth it."

"I find that hard to believe," Odo said. "The profits are still considerable."

Möhrlein shrugged. "We're getting old, Odo. I'm not up to that anymore, not that life." He looked at Odo, suddenly serious, the teasing note utterly vanished from his voice. "You can search *Carabas* from bow to stern—I'll even open up the old secret compartments for you. We're legit now, Odo. I can't afford not to be."

Odo considered them for a moment. His hand was weaker than they realized, or so he hoped—Sisko would never let him expel them without due process—but at least his bluff had gotten him this much of a concession. "I'll take you up on that offer, Möhrlein. Now."

Möhrlein opened his mouth as though to protest, closed it again. "All right," he said, "but at least let me call Quark, let him know I'll be delayed."

Quark, Odo thought. That doesn't give me a lot of confidence in your honesty. His lips thinned, but he gestured to the nearest intercom box. "Go ahead."

Möhrlein nodded, his expression still perfectly sober, and touched the intercom's miniature controls. "Quark?" A voice answered, barely audible from where Odo stood, and Möhrlein said, "Well, get him. Please."

There was another little pause, and Odo glanced at Tama, wondering just what had brought the two men back to DS9. He had always thought that they would use their ill-gotten gains to move closer in to the center of the Federation, where the profits and risks were both higher. . . . Tama saw him watching, and something, a flicker of irritation, or of regret, crossed his broad face. Or was there something more? Odo wondered. Something perhaps more like . . . fear? That seemed unlikely—Federation law was far less strict than Cardassian; all a smuggler risked was a fine or a possible jail term, not the loss of life or limb—but nonetheless the feeling persisted. Odo scowled again, wishing he understood human expressions more clearly, and dragged his attention back to Möhrlein.

"—going to be a little delay," the blond man was saying. "Customs problems." He paused, listening, and Odo could hear the angry cadence of Quark's words. Möhrlein grinned, slanting a glance at Tama, and said, "We'll be in as soon as it's settled, Quark. You shouldn't get so upset about these things—go find someone to rub your ears, that'd do you some good."

He took his finger off the button, cutting Quark off in mid-rant, and looked at Odo. "I—We're at your disposal, Constable."

"Then we'll go," Odo said, grimly. He touched his own communicator. "Inspection team, stand by, docking bay five."

It took the better part of two hours to go over *Carabas* with fine-grain scanners, and another hour to make a visual inspection of the cargo. Möhrlein was as good as his word, unsealing various hidden compartments, and Odo did his best to pretend he had known of all of them before. Some he had—he remembered, quite distinctly, the pleasure of prying open a section of floorboard that had proved to hide a shielded storage compartment; he remembered with equal clarity the bitterness of the disappointment when he realized it was empty—but he made a mental note of several others, promising himself that he would be sure to add those sections to the automatic search lists. The cargo was unexceptionable: spare machine parts for several different Bajoran groups, some agricultural hardware en route to the group trying to salvage the most damaged sections of Bajor's surface, and several starcrates of high-value, low-mass luxury items that Möhrlein claimed he had bought on speculation, hoping to sell them either to merchants on the station itself, or on Bajor. Odo went over those crates three times, but finally had to concede that they were exactly what they seemed.

"Very well," he said, at last, and gestured to the inspection team, dismissing them. "But things do seem to—happen around you, Möhrlein. I will be keeping an eye on you."

"I wouldn't expect otherwise," Möhrlein answered, and sounded almost resigned.

Odo nodded sharply, and stepped through the main hatch. He started down the ramp to the floor of the docking bay, and at the bottom glanced back, to see the two humans watching him, their faces completely without expression. Tama saw him turn, and forced a smile, lifting a hand in almost-mocking farewell. Odo's lips thinned, and he turned away. They were up to something, of that he felt certain; he was equally certain that he didn't have enough proof of it to convince Sisko to throw them off the station. But I will watch them, he promised himself. I, my people and I, will keep them under full surveillance, and the first wrong move they make—well, I will be ready for it.

It was busy in Ops, the bustle that always came at the end of the civilian day, and Dax found herself caught up as always in the whirl, dividing her attention between the station's sensor net, now at its maximum expansion, and the myriad demands of the changing crews. And then, at last, the flurry of activity died away again, the civilian crew gone off duty, only Starfleet personnel remaining for the night watch. Dax smiled to herself, acknowledging her enduring pleasure in the transformation, and turned her attention to the science console. The Vulcan filter seemed to be working as promised, but she was still less than happy with the Cardassian scanners. She ran her hands over the controls, calling up the diagnostics, and let the programs run, watching the readings flicker over her screens. Everything seemed to be in order—seemed to be better than in order, all systems functioning at top capacity. And still they had found nothing in the asteroid belt. She tilted her head to one side, studying the results of the most recent scan. Still nothing, not even a glimpse of an asteroid or any glitch in the system to explain that one anomalous reading, and that, she thought, made no sense at all. If it was *Helios,* cloaked or not, she would have expected to catch some hint of the ship's presence by now; if it wasn't, if it was either some natural phenomenon or an artifact of the scanners itself, it, whatever it was, should have happened again.

All right, she thought, let's apply some of the famous Trill science to the situation. It is unlikely to have been a reflex shadow; we haven't seen it again, in thirty-six hours of observation, and a miscalibration should have showed up by now. And it's unlikely to be an asteroid, for much the same reason. By orbital mechanics alone, an asteroid of that bizarre a composition couldn't've moved out of sensor range, unless it had its own impulse drive. And that leaves only a ship, a cloaked ship, and probably *Helios*. She stared at her working screen, called up the record of the first sighting for what seemed like the thousandth time. A light flashed red in her screen, bracketed an instant later by the gold lines of the tracking systems zeroing in on the sighting, and she frowned, startled. It looked somehow different this time, the numbers not as clear as she remembered—

"Dax to Sisko," she said, her hand flying to her communicator. "We have a second sighting."

Her hands danced across the membrane board, tuning the sensors tighter, locking everything she had onto that pinpoint light, but already the image was fading from her screen. She swore under her breath, words she had learned from Kira, pulled in a secondary system, then shook her head in disgust.

"You've lost it?" Sisko asked, coming up behind her, and Dax glanced up at him, acknowledging his presence, before she turned her attention back to her screen.

"I'm afraid so, Benjamin." She touched keys, setting the various analysis programs to work, and watched the strings of symbols march across her screens. "We had it for a half second longer this time, and I'm absolutely certain it's neither an asteroid or a sensor shadow. I had just checked the system myself, and asteroids don't just come and go like this."

"Even if it's in orbit, being eclipsed by something?" Sisko asked. There was something in his voice that told Dax he was grasping at straws.

"If that were the case, Benjamin, there would be some regularity to it all."

"I know." Sisko sighed, and looked past her toward the main viewer. Dax followed the line of his gaze almost by instinct, even though she knew there would be nothing there. The screen was blank, showing the distant starscape;

the Denorios Belt lay invisible in the foreground, a some-how menacing unseen presence.

And that, Dax thought, is utter foolishness. She looked back at her boards, focusing on the numbers that spilled across the screens. "It's a ship, Benjamin, cloaking and uncloaking. I'm sure of it."

"Do you have a fix on it?" Sisko asked.

"I had a fix," Dax said, and stressed the past tense. "I doubt anyone would remain stationary once they'd recloaked." She touched controls again, setting parameters. "Assuming they moved out at top impulse speed, they could be anywhere in this volume of space." The image filled her working screen, a faint blue sphere surrounding the deeper blue fleck of the sighted position. "I'm scanning that—" As she spoke, her hands moved, making it true. "—but so far, no, there's nothing. Not even with the Vulcan filter."

She heard Sisko sigh, and glanced up to see him frowning, brows drawn together as he looked from her screens to the main viewer and back again. "So why uncloak, if you've been hiding quite successfully? Why uncloak at all?"

Dax knew that the question was rhetorical, but answered anyway. "To drop a shuttle, to pick up a shuttle, to fire a weapon, to send or receive a subspace communication—" She broke off abruptly, eyes going wide, and Sisko nodded.

"That's the most likely answer, isn't it? Any signs of a transmission—?"

"Not so far," Dax answered. "We weren't scanning specifically for subspace transmissions, but if there was anything—" She broke off, calling up the station's general computer logs. "No incoming transmissions, we certainly would have picked that up, but let's just be sure that nothing is being sent to the pirate."

She heard Sisko grunt, but did not look up, concentrating instead on the screens that opened in front of her. The general log was too long to look at entry by entry, but the accounting subroutine flashed green, signaling that all transmissions were legitimately logged, and linked to a known and registered user. Dax ignored that—she had expected nothing less—and queried the backup system. There was a brief pause—it was an old and less efficient program, left over from the Cardassian occupation—and then the same message flashed on the screen. Everything was accounted for, except . . . Her eyes narrowed, and she touched keys, comparing the two results. Except that the checks did not match. She looked up at Sisko again, and was pleased to see that he was following the accounts as closely as she was.

"Bad news, Benjamin," she said. "The sums don't match up."

Sisko nodded. "Which means?"

Dax smiled ruefully. "Nothing yet, at least according to regulations. But I think—I'm certain someone's tapped into the subspace communications systems, and has erased their trail. That's the only thing that could lead to a discrepancy like this."

"Which means we have a spy on the station," Sisko said. "A spy for *Helios.*"

"I'm afraid so," Dax answered.

"Can the accounting logs give us any kind of lead on the person's identity?" Sisko asked.

Dax shook her head. "Not if the person's any good. All it will be able to tell us—unless we get stupendously lucky—is if and when the transmissions went out. Always assuming there has been more than one."

"There will have been," Sisko said, sourly, and Dax nodded in spite of herself. Sisko was right about that, and even the Trill had a proverb about troubles coming in multiple units.

"All right," Sisko went on, and Dax shook herself back to alertness. "From now on, I want the sensors maintained at yellow alert. I want to know if anything moves a centimeter in the Belt—and that includes scheduled Bajoran shipping. Second, I want you to beef up security in the station systems, see if we can trap this person if he tries to use subspace communications again. And I'll also see what Odo can do about real-world security."

"There are a fair number of ships in the docking ring," Dax agreed. "It would be easy enough to slip in unobserved."

"Odo's pretty careful about checking papers," Sisko said. "But he can double-check this bunch. The main thing, though, Dax, is to keep this person from contacting *Helios* again."

"I'll get right on it, Benjamin," Dax said.

"Good," Sisko said, and turned away.

Dax turned back to her console, calling up the schematics of the security fence surrounding the subspace communications system, studied its complex workings. There were places she could add trip wires, booby traps, places she could possibly improve the security—but all of that was moot if the spy had already completed his mission. For a moment, she felt a chill run down her spine at the thought— that *Helios* and her mad captain already had whatever information they wanted, were already on the offensive, ready to proceed with his plan—and then, firmly, put that aside. There was no point to it: all she could do was make the computer secure, and wait.

Kira stood in the doorway of the Bajoran temple, staring down the length of the Promenade. It was evening, the end of the civilian day, but only a few of the shops were closed. Instead, the crowd had changed, from the bustle of the serious businesspeople, moving quickly from dealer to dealer, buyer to seller and back again, to a slower crowd, mostly brightly dressed Bajorans, wandering from shop to shop, as intent on each other as on the goods displayed in the windows and open shopfronts. Kira sighed to herself, acknowledging a vague sense of inadequacy, and fixed her eyes on the veiled figure four shops down from the temple doors. Today Diaadul was dressed in green, a luminous, not-quite-emerald green embroidered with delicate gold shapes and a wide band of gold and silver flowers at the hem. Watching her, watching the delicate hand that emerged from the folds of the veil, the gold bangles looking almost too heavy for the fragile wrist, Kira felt a stab of—something. It was not jealousy, of that she felt certain, or, if it was, just a little bit, a sort of envy, it was not envy of the clothes or the old-fashioned and assumed fragility, but of the peace Trehan had had that allowed Diaadul to be so merely decorative. *And, let's be honest,* Kira thought, *I wouldn't want to live like her.* But she couldn't help wondering what it would be like to dress like that, to wear silk and useless jewelry and a veil heavy with precious metal. Then common sense reasserted itself, and she chortled in spite of herself at the incongruous image. If she put on a veil like Diaadul's, within five minutes it would be knotted around her neck or shoulders, flung out of the way to let her move freely again. *And that,* Kira admitted silently, *pretty much sums up why I haven't had a bit of success with this assignment. There's no way Diaadul would confide in me— there's no way that she could.*

The veiled figure was moving again, hands tucked again decorously into the folds of the veil, and Kira sighed, easing out from the shadow of the doors. She followed at a careful distance, grateful for the evening crowd that let her disguise her presence, and was not surprised when Diaadul turned again toward Quark's. This was the routine, the unvarying routine, and had been ever since the Trehanna arrived on the station. She spent her days in her quarters, and then, each evening exactly as the station went from day to night, she would emerge from her cabin and ride the turbolift to the Promenade. There, she would walk its length and back, apparently enjoying the crowds and the bright displays—though she had never bought anything, not in the eight days Kira had been following her—and then return to Quark's. At Quark's, she would buy a single flask of wine, studiously ignoring Quark's inevitable approaches, and sit for an hour, drinking. At the end of that hour, she would pay her bill, and return again to her quarters: *A steady, never-varying routine,* Kira thought, *and one that makes me very suspicious.* She had struck up a conversation with Diaadul one evening, and the woman had been polite but distant; when asked, she had said she was waiting for Quark to complete his part of their business. Quark had confirmed it—*which of course he would*—but Kira still had her doubts. It just didn't feel right that a Trehanna noble should spend so much time doing nothing. When she had broached it to Sisko, however, all the commander had done was agree to increase mechanical surveillance as well. *And I still say she's waiting for someone else,* Kira thought, and winced at the memory of her last interview with Sisko. She had said—*well, shouted*—the same thing at Sisko, and had been answered by one of his cold stares. *That may very well be true, Major,* he had said, *probably is true—but how the devil you expect to catch her contact if Odo puts her in the brig is beyond me.* Kira felt her face grow warm at the thought, but she couldn't rid herself of the nagging feeling that she was right. Diaadul was up to something, and her instinct, a sense of danger honed by the years of service with the Resistance, told her that the Trehanna had to be stopped first.

But there was no convincing Sisko of that, and Odo was already doing everything he could. Which left it her responsibility. Kira sighed, and paused just inside the entrance to Quark's. She glared at the first Ferengi who approached her, waving him away, and glanced quickly around the busy main floor. It was even more crowded than usual, the crews of a pair of Bajoran freighters filling all the tables along the far walls, and Kira hesitated only for an instant before taking the spiral stairs to the second level. Her favorite table, set in a corner close to the edge of the balcony, was empty, and she seated herself, turning her back to the wall as always. Leaning forward, she had a clear view of most of the lower level, from the bar itself, with its crowd of crewmen and station personnel, to the sea of tables and the gambling consoles. Diaadul had taken her usual place, tucked into a corner where she could watch the door, and even as Kira watched, a waiter—not Ferengi—brought her the usual beaker of wine. Diaadul thanked him with an abstracted nod, and tipped her head forward to bring the glass under the folds of the veiling.

And that, Kira thought, was absolutely as usual. She heard someone approaching her table, turned to see one of the younger Ferengi coming toward her, rubbing his hands together in a gesture almost a parody of Quark's.

"Major Kira, so nice to see you. And on the upper level, too." He tilted his head toward the doors that led to the holosuites. "I'm afraid we're all booked up for the first shift, but you're welcome to have a drink or two while you wait. Many people find that it—whets their imagination."

"You can get me a drink," Kira said, keeping a firm grip on her temper—there was nothing to be gained by letting any Ferengi know he'd angered her. "Kalmr claret. And that's all I want." She let him take three steps away before she spoke again. "And, Sorv?"

"Yes, Major?" The Ferengi turned back, his smirk imperfectly concealed.

"I'd be very careful if I were you what I offered to a Bajoran officer."

She saw him blink, the sudden blank expression that meant her words had hit home, and hid her own grin. "Just the claret, Sorv."

"Yes, Major." Sorv turned away again, sulking visibly, and this time Kira did allow herself to smile. Not that Sorv was such a difficult person to face down—he was the least obnoxious of the Ferengi who worked at Quark's—but it did have its satisfactions. Unlike the rest of the job, she added silently, and edged forward slightly, surveying the lower level again, picking out familiar faces in the crowd. Diaadul was still alone at her table, the vivid green of her veil bright even in the subdued lighting; Chief O'Brien was standing at the bar next to a pair of humans Kira didn't recognize—traders, by the cut of their clothes—and a man she recognized as one of Odo's deputies was standing at one of the gaming tables, feeding credit sticks methodically into the slot. Quark, behind the bar, seemed to be watching him, and Kira allowed herself another smile. Odo had been trying to prove that the gambling was less than honest for years. Her smile faded quickly. This was all exactly what she had come to expect, exactly the same thing that had happened the night before, and the night before that, and all the while—all the while, she thought, I know there's something very wrong.

O'Brien leaned against the bar, waiting to catch Quark's attention to place a second order. The place seemed busier than usual tonight, and he wondered for a moment if all the talk about a mysterious pirate was keeping ships in dock. He grinned to himself, leaned forward to check Quark's progress. If *Helios* really was out there, which he thought was less and less likely the more time passed from that possible sighting, but if it was . . . he had an answer for it, even as heavily armed as *Helios* seemed to be. He could feel himself grinning even more widely, and didn't bother to hide his pleasure. It was a neat trick he and his staff were pulling, an elegant modification that also meant they wouldn't have to try to bring one of the dangerously damaged fusion reactors back on line. All they would do, all they would have to do, was run a simple tap, patch an ordinary exchange node into the existing system, and divert some of the continued output from the damaged reactor into the phasers. His smile faded slightly at the thought. The station would be able to double the phasers' output, all right, but not for very long: ten minutes, his calculations showed, at the most. It wasn't much more than a bluff, but bluffs could be very effective against single ships, even against *Helios,* and Sisko had approved the idea. And if anyone could pull it off, he thought, Sisko was the man.

He leaned forward again, and bumped elbows with the man to his left. "Sorry," he began, and the stranger waved away the apology.

"No harm done. Busy tonight, isn't it?"

O'Brien nodded. The stranger was human, sounded as though he was from the Federation, something a little out of the ordinary here where most of the clients were Bajorans, and he found himself suddenly wanting to prolong the conversation. "Quark's tends to be popular. But this is a little worse than usual."

The stranger—he was tall and blond, with a crooked smile that went a long way toward mitigating the almost too-handsome features—grinned, and glanced down the bar. "And not getting any better. We put in our order ten minutes ago, and haven't seen the 'keep since. What's going on, is there a trade fair on Bajor?"

"I don't know," O'Brien said. "It might be that pirate everyone's talking about."

"The pirate," the blond man repeated, and exchanged a quick glance with the dark-haired man at his side. "Yeah, we've been hearing talk about that. You're Starfleet, do you think there's anything in it?"

O'Brien shrugged, suddenly uncertain of what he should say, and the blond smiled again. "I'm Vilis Möhrlein, by the way, and this is my partner Kerel Tama. We run the *Carabas,* out of Geroldin."

"Miles O'Brien," O'Brien said. "I don't think I know *Carabas,* except from 'Puss in Boots.'" The moment the words were out of his mouth, he wished them unsaid: it was highly unlikely that this pair of free-traders would have named their ship after a character out of a fairy tale. To his surprise, however, Tama grinned openly.

"You're the first one to get it."

"'My uncle the marquis of Carabas,'" Möhrlein quoted. "It works with the Cardassians, though—and you need all the authority you can get, dealing with the Guls. But how'd you know? I didn't think anybody read those stories any more."

"My daughter's fond of fairy tales," O'Brien said, and felt himself blushing. This was not the time to talk about Molly, or Keiko—and besides, he told himself, it was always worth hearing about another starship. "But, like I said, I don't think I've seen your ship."

"She's a Delta-class runner, Federation hull," Möhrlein said, accepting the change of subject with equanimity. "But we've modified the engines considerably—we can carry nearly three times our working mass in cargo."

O'Brien pursed his lips. "Impressive." In spite of himself, he knew he sounded skeptical, and he saw Tama grin.

"We brought in a Cardassian power plant," Möhrlein said. "Salvaged it during the war, from a junior frigate. It's clumsy, but there's power and to spare."

"You must've had fun modifying the reactor chambers," O'Brien said. If Möhrlein was telling the truth, or even part of it, he'd done a pretty piece of engineering, and O'Brien caught himself wondering if the other man would be willing to give him a tour of the ship. To get a Cardassian reactor to feed into a Federation hull's usual EPS system—you'd have to use transfer nodes, he thought, and probably a series transformer. "Did you put in their power conduit as well, or use a transformer?"

Möhrlein nodded. "Transformer, actually. I'm not fond of the conduit. I gather you're an engineer yourself, then?"

O'Brien nodded. "Chief of operations."

"Then you know about the reactors, all right," Möhrlein said. "You still run them here?"

"Oh, it's still a Cardassian station at heart," O'Brien said, more grimly than he'd intended. "You should see the living quarters."

"I'm not fond of Cardassian architecture," Möhrlein agreed. "But the power systems aren't bad."

"If you like raw power over safety, sure," O'Brien said, and Möhrlein grinned again.

"I've worked out a step-down system that keeps the ship happy," he began, and Tama touched his shoulder.

"Drinks are here, mate. Your turn to pay."

"Sorry," Möhrlein said, and reached into his pocket for a credit stick. Quark sneered at him, and made a production of checking the holographic seals to be sure it was genuine. "Bastard," Möhrlein said, without heat, and picked up two glasses. Tama held a third, O'Brien saw: *Meeting someone?* he wondered. *Or just greedy?*

"We should talk some more some time, Chief," Möhrlein said. "I'd be glad to show you over *Carabas,* if you're interested."

"Thanks," O'Brien said. "I might take you up on that."

"Vilis," Tama said, and nudged the taller man away from the bar. He looked back at O'Brien, smiling slightly in apology. "Sorry, Chief, but we've got a client to talk to."

"Don't let me keep you," O'Brien said, and turned back to the bar. Quark looked up at him, mouth open to show all his teeth.

"Do you plan to drink tonight, Chief, or are you going to go on polishing my bar?"

"Beer," O'Brien answered. "Just like last time."

"One beer coming right up," Quark said, in a tone that meant precisely the opposite, and turned away.

O'Brien sighed, and turned his back to the bar, leaning both elbows against it. It would be nice to see what the blond man—Möhrlein, the name was, an unusual one—had done to his *Carabas*. He craned his head to see where they had gone, and saw Möhrlein's blond head towering above a knot of Andreazna tourists. They, he and Tama, were heading for the table where Diaadul sat, alone, her glass almost emptied in front of her. *Good luck to you, boys,* O'Brien thought. *You'll need it to get anywhere with the mystery woman.* Möhrlein leaned close, and O'Brien felt his own mouth twist into a wry grin, anticipating the rejection. But then he saw Diaadul's hand move, gesturing to the empty chairs, and the two traders seated themselves opposite the Trehanna woman. O'Brien's eyebrows rose, and Quark's voice said behind him, "Your beer, Chief. But you might want to taste it first."

"What?" O'Brien turned back to the bar, took the foaming glass that Quark held out to him. The beer looked somehow odd, not quite the right deep gold, and he sniffed it warily. The aroma was definitely off, too yeasty, and he set the glass down with a sigh. "Replicators gone out again?"

"I'm afraid so," Quark answered, and this time, O'Brien thought, the smile looked all too genuine. "And since you're here, Chief, I thought you might take a look at it, and save yourself having to come back later."

"And save you the trouble of making an official request and going into an official queue," O'Brien muttered. Still, if he fixed it now, before the system had a chance to drift any further out of alignment, maybe he wouldn't have to come back. "Fine. But I don't expect to be charged for the beer. The real one."

Quark lifted the gate. O'Brien sighed, and ducked back

into the space behind the bar, already reaching for his tool kit.

Kira saw the strangers approach Diaadul's table, drinks in hand, and suppressed her own smile. They looked entirely too sure of themselves; she would enjoy seeing Diaadul turn them down, as she'd turned down every other approach since she came aboard the station. She saw the blond lean down—it was almost a half bow, far more respectful than she would have expected—and then Diaadul's hand came out from under her draperies, gesturing for them to be seated. The two men exchanged a quick glance, then set their drinks down, and took their places. They leaned close, clearly beginning a quiet conversation. Kira swore under her breath—*Why did I decide to come up here tonight of all nights?*—but put aside her regrets instantly, and touched her communicator.

"Kira to Odo."

There was no answer, and her lips tightened. "Kira to Odo. Come on, Odo, answer me."

There was still nothing, and she bit her lip, wondering if she should call Sisko instead. Then Odo answered, sounding slightly out of breath, and Kira allowed herself a sigh of relief.

"Odo here. What is it, Major?"

"Diaadul's met someone," Kira said. "Two men, human, I don't recognize them."

"Description?"

"One's tall, fair, very blond hair, the other's darker—" Kira broke off, seeing movement on the floor below. "Odo, they're moving. It looks like—they're going into the back rooms. Quark's private space." She started to slam her fist on the table, checked the gesture instantly. "I'm not placed to follow them."

"That's all right," Odo said. "Which room—which door?"

Kira leaned forward cautiously, not wanting to draw attention to herself. "The office section—I can't tell."

"All right," Odo said. "I'm taking over. Odo out."

Kira started to form a protest, but the connection was already broken. She sat back in her chair, hoping the constable knew what he was doing, and tried to look as though nothing had happened. *And, for all I really know, nothing has,* she thought. *Maybe Diaadul finally heard a proposition she liked.* The idea seemed unlikely, however, and she scanned the main level again, wondering if anyone else had noticed the Trehanna's odd behavior. Quark was busy behind the bar, dividing his attention between his customers and O'Brien, who was crouched over a replicator's access panel, tool kit in hand. The freighters' crews were busy at the gaming tables, and she saw a fistful of coins pass from one to another. *A typical night at Quark's,* she thought. *I just hope Odo can follow them.*

CHAPTER
8

ODO TOOK A DEEP BREATH, released the extruded arm and with it the communicator he had stashed at the head of the ventilator shaft, and allowed himself to flow back into the shape he had chosen. He could see his own reflection in the polished metal of the ventilator mouth, lit by the shaft of light that filtered in from the corridor: a *verrior,* one of his favorite shapes, a chameleon-like Bajoran lizard with which he had always felt a certain kinship. Its six feet, with their broad, sucker-tipped toes, and the low-slung body were perfectly adapted to the ventilators, especially in the main branches where the rush of air was strongest. And he would need all the grip he could manage, if his guess was right and Diaadul was heading for Quark's inner office. He took another deep breath, working his toes, and started down the narrow passage.

He bypassed his usual paths, heading straight for the main duct, and reached cautiously out into the rushing wind. Though every instinct screamed at him to hurry, that

Diaadul and the two smugglers—it couldn't be anyone else, not from Kira's description—were already in the private office, he made himself take his time placing his forefeet, twisting to be sure the suckers were firmly planted before he swung himself out into the wind. He blinked hard as the stream of air hit him head-on, eyes contracting to narrow slits, and for an instant he thought he was about to be carried away. And then a hind foot found its purchase, and then both middle feet, and he took his first cautious steps up the shaft.

He was big enough in this shape, heavy enough, that once his feet were in place he could move almost normally. It was absolutely dark, of course, and in this shape he had none of the special sense organs that would let him follow the splotches of paint he had used to mark the system, but he didn't really need it. The ventilation duct for Quark's private office ran directly from the main shaft; all Odo needed to do was point his face into the wind, and count the openings. The third shaft would be the one he wanted. He suppressed the need to hurry, knowing that that would increase the chances of a mistake, and made himself move methodically, aligning himself with the shaft's seam. He found the first opening quickly enough, and then the second, and turned down the third, blinking as he scrambled over the first set of baffles.

The wind diminished almost at once, its strength cut neatly in half, and he used his first and middle feet to lever himself over the secondary baffling. Ahead, the grille glowed yellow from the lights of the room beyond, and Odo finally let himself hurry, his six legs propelling him down the tunnel with surprising speed. He stopped just inside the grille, and rose on his rear and middle legs to peer through the grating, careful not to let his forefeet poke through the narrow openings. Sure enough, Diaadul was there, seated comfortably on the edge of Quark's desk-console; the smugglers were there, too, standing, Tama a little behind Möhrlein. They looked, Odo thought, as though they were waiting for orders.

"So," Diaadul said, and unwound her veil in a single lithe movement. Beneath it, she was older than Odo would have guessed from the habit of gesture and movement, and her dark hair was cut short around her thin, fine-boned face. Her eyes, blue and slit-pupilled, seemed even larger now that the rest of her face was revealed. "Not before time."

Möhrlein and Tama exchanged glances, and Möhrlein said, "We only docked today, Lady. It took us time to get the parts you wanted."

"And the papers that got us in here," Tama muttered.

Diaadul lifted an eyebrow. She had shed her fragility with the veil, so that the green tunic-and-trousers suit that she wore beneath it looked somehow incongruous on her. "As long as everything's there," she said. "That's all that matters to me—or to the captain."

"All present and accounted for," Möhrlein said. "Hardware and software both. As long as you have a decent engineer, which I know you do, the repairs should be a snap."

In the ventilator mouth, Odo ground his teeth in frustration. He had known, he had been absolutely certain, that Möhrlein and Tama had an illegal cargo somewhere, but where? He and his security crew had searched the ship thoroughly—*unless one of the apparently legal cargoes was in fact destined for Diaadul,* he thought suddenly. *And her mysterious captain—and I have a nasty feeling I know exactly who that "captain" is.*

"And the items for the cloaking device?" Diaadul asked.

"I told you, Lady, everything's there, everything on your list." Möhrlein looked at Tama, who nodded his confirmation. "Now there's just the small matter of payment."

"You don't really expect to be paid sight unseen," Diaadul said.

"I expect some compensation for the trouble I've gone to, yes," Möhrlein said. "We had a deal, Lady."

"Yes. Cash on delivery." Diaadul smiled.

"We've delivered."

Diaadul shook her head. "Not yet. The parts still have to get to *Helios*. The captain is waiting at the usual rendezvous. You'll be paid when we get there."

Tama made an odd, skeptical noise, the breath hissing through his teeth. "If we can get there. You lot have everything all stirred up, both sides of the border. This station's on practically full alert, and there's an entire Cardassian fleet just waiting for Kolovzon to show himself again."

"I thought you were the best," Diaadul said.

Möhrlein matched her previous smile. "Even we don't do miracles."

There was a little silence, and then Diaadul sighed. "How much does a miracle cost these days?"

"Half again over what we agreed on," Möhrlein said promptly. "Payable now."

Diaadul gave him a long stare, and even in the safety of the ventilator shaft Odo felt a chill run down his spine. Whatever else she was, Diaadul was clearly a person of authority aboard *Helios*. "All right," she said at last, and reached under the skirts of her tunic. She produced four bars of gold-pressed latinum, and held them out, saying, "The rest on delivery, as agreed."

Möhrlein nodded.

"Which will be when?" Diaadul asked.

"Another day or two," Möhrlein said. "Odo—the chief constable here—"

"I know Odo," Diaadul said.

"He's very good," Möhrlein went on. "I want to move

carefully—I'd like to be able to go on doing business here, Lady."

"That's too long," Diaadul said. She held up her hand to silence their protest, the bangles falling musically down her arm. "Fifteen hours. And I intend to go with you. I'm being watched."

Tama muttered something inaudible, and Möhrlein whistled softly. "You don't give us the easy ones, do you, Lady?"

"I understood the difficult jobs were your speciality," Diaadul murmured.

Möhrlein made a face, and looked at Tama.

The dark-haired man shrugged. "Seven hours to the rendezvous, on impulse engines. That gives us eight hours to make our arrangements. It can be done, but, my God, it's going to look thin."

"It'll have to," Möhrlein said, and sounded grim. "The trick will be getting you aboard, Lady."

Diaadul smiled. "Leave that to me."

Tama made a face—clearly, Odo thought, he was less comfortable than Möhrlein was with this job—but nodded reluctantly. "You'd better let us leave first, Lady. It was risk enough being seen with you."

"And vice versa," Diaadul said. "Go ahead. I'll be at your docking bay in three hours."

"It's bay five," Möhrlein began, and Diaadul smiled.

"I know."

Möhrlein turned away, and Odo didn't wait to see more. He released his grip on the inside of the ventilator grid, and dropped soundlessly to the floor. Not for the first time, he wished there were some easy way to carry his communicator with him in altered shape, but shook the thought angrily away. There was no time to waste worrying about things that couldn't be changed; the main thing now was to get back to his communicator, and warn Sisko.

The trip back through the ventilators was a little easier:

the airflow was at his back, and he was able to make better speed through the slick-floored tunnels. Even so, it seemed to take hours to reach the access panel where he had left his communicator. The panel gave onto a secluded corridor, and he made only a perfunctory check to be sure the space was empty before rearing onto his hind and middle feet to push the panel outward. He was already changing shape as he stepped out of the ventilator, so that the movement that had begun as a step turned for an instant into an almost liquid flow. In his humanoid shape again, he reached back into the opening for his communicator, and thumbed it once without pausing to reattach it to his chest.

"Odo to Sisko." He fit the panel back into place automatically, and stood, head cocked to one side as he waited for an answer. "Odo to Commander Sisko. Answer, please."

"Sisko here." The commander sounded preoccupied. "Unless it's urgent, Odo, I'm going to have to ask you to wait. We've sighted *Helios* again."

Odo glared at the communicator as though Sisko could see him. "I'm not surprised. I've been following Diaadul. She seems to be someone of considerable importance aboard the pirate ship."

"What—?" Sisko broke off as quickly as he'd spoken. "Go on, Constable."

Quickly, Odo outlined what he'd seen in Quark's office, emphasizing the planned rendezvous. When he'd finished, there was a little pause, and he imagined Sisko frowning at his own consoles.

"Good work, Odo," Sisko said at last. "So you think Diaadul will keep this rendezvous?"

"I'm certain of it, sir."

"All right. Keep up the surveillance on Diaadul and your smugglers—what were the names?"

"Möhrlein," Odo said, "and Tama. Of the *Carabas*. They're known to me."

"Right," Sisko went on. "Keep up the surveillance, but tell your people to stay well back. We don't want to tip them off beforehand. We—you will arrest them as soon as they try to go aboard *Carabas*."

Odo nodded, and then, remembering, said, "Yes, Commander. That will be a pleasure."

"I need answers, Odo, remember that," Sisko said.

Odo smiled, and was glad this time that the communicator was voice-only. "I guarantee you'll get them, sir."

Kira stood at the head of the crossover bridge that lay between the section of the habitat ring where Diaadul had been quartered and the docking ring, Odo's instructions ringing in her ears. *Pull back,* he had said, *let Diaadul think we've withdrawn our surveillance—wait for her at the head of the gamma bridge, that's the most direct route from her quarters to bay five.* Certainly that was true, Kira thought, and pretended a deep interest in a display panel as a group of Bajorans moved past, talking cheerfully about a lug-ball game as they went off duty. On the other hand, Diaadul must have had some idea she was being watched, and she surely wouldn't be stupid enough to take the most direct route to her rendezvous.

Kira sighed, and scanned the display panel again. She touched the screen to call up a listing of the ships in dock, this time actually making note of *Carabas*'s position. The runner was in docking bay five, adjacent to one of the larger cargo bays: very convenient, she thought, sourly, for getting secret cargoes on and off the station. And that wasn't being fair to Odo, or his crew. He had said from the beginning that Diaadul was up to something; it had taken good luck, and Odo's legendary persistence, to get onto it this quickly.

"Sisko to Kira."

The familiar voice broke into her thoughts, not loud, but

she glanced over her shoulder anyway before she answered. "Kira here, sir."

"We're at the docking port now. *Carabas* has requested takeoff clearance for oh one hundred hours tomorrow morning, and Odo's people report that Diaadul has left her quarters. They can't follow too closely, but she may be heading your way."

"I'll be on the lookout, sir," Kira said. "Kira out."

She eased back into the shadow of a mechanic's alcove even as she spoke, wedging herself between the cover of a Jeffries tube and a diagnostic console and its associated cables. It wasn't much cover, but she had discovered that, to most off-worlders, one Bajoran looked much like another. Oh, they recognized the gross differences of age and gender, but the subtler distinctions were hard to see. Of course—a small, genuinely amused smile quirked her lips, and vanished almost at once—of course, she herself had similar problems with several species.

She heard footsteps in the corridor, the soft sound barely audible above the gentle hiss of the ventilators, and turned instinctively so that she had her back to the corridor. A polished cover plate gave a distorted reflection of the scene behind her, and she fixed her eyes on its bronze surface, pretending to work at the console's limited touch pad. She heard the footsteps come closer still, and then, in the bronzed panel, saw the green-veiled shape that was unmistakably Diaadul move past, heading down the crossover bridge toward the docking ring. Kira held her breath, then made herself count slowly to a hundred, and then to a hundred again. That was the way she had always done it in the resistance, stayed in hiding, counting heartbeats, until it was clear to move again. . . . She shook that thought aside —this was not the time for those memories—and peered cautiously out of the alcove.

The corridor was empty except for another pair of technicians, both Starfleet, this time, heading back toward the main body of the station. Kira stepped out of the alcove, conscious of their curious looks, and started toward the docking bay. Once in the crossover bridge, there was no place Diaadul could go except into the docking ring, but even so, she moved carefully, glancing into any alcove or storage space that might afford Diaadul cover. They were all empty, and she paused at the airlock that led into the docking bay.

"Kira to Sisko."

"Sisko here."

The commander answered with reassuring promptness, and Kira allowed herself to think that this might work, after all. "Diaadul's entered the docking bay. She should be coming your way."

"Confirmed," Sisko answered. "You've done all that you can, Major. Join us here."

"Very good, sir. Kira out."

Kira released the communicator, studying the door suspiciously. Diaadul was beyond there, and the gods only knew what sort of weapon she had under that veiling—there was room enough to conceal a small arsenal. If she had calculated right, the Trehanna would be far ahead of her, heading directly for the docking port and *Carabas,* but Kira had been in the resistance long enough, had seen enough operations go desperately wrong, to be able entirely to trust to luck. She had her hand on her phaser as she opened the airlock's first door, was ready to draw as the system cycled and the inner door rolled back, opening onto the dimly lit corridors of the docking ring.

There was no one in sight, not even cargo handlers. Kira took a deep breath, no longer embarrassed by the practiced caution, and turned right, toward the cargo bay. It seemed that Sisko had cleared the corridors, or maybe it was just between the busy parts of the day and night shifts; at any rate, she met no one until she stepped through the hatch into the vast open space of the bay. She hesitated for a moment, and a cargo pod shimmered, the rounded shape twisting, stretching up and changing color until it had resolved itself into Odo's familiar shape.

"Major," he said. "This way."

Kira caught her breath—even knowing Odo, knowing he was on their side, it was hard to get used to the sight of his changes, of apparent flesh and bone flowing like the liquid he truly was—and made herself answer without emotion. "Diaadul's on her way."

"Over here," Odo said again, and Kira followed him through the maze of stacked crates and pallets to the hatch that gave directly onto the docking port. The great disk of the hatch was rolled back—standard procedure, when a ship was loading or off-loading a cargo—and Sisko and a pair of security men stood in its shadow, the youngest of the men peering carefully into the corridor.

Sisko nodded a greeting at their approach, but said nothing, his attention clearly on the space beyond the hatch.

"Anything yet?" Kira asked, and the younger security man ducked back into the doorway.

"I hear someone now, sir. I think it's Diaadul."

"Thank you, Liebowitz," Sisko said, softly, and gathered his command with a glance. "You all know what to do."

There was a murmur of agreement, and Kira found herself smiling fiercely. Oh, yes, she thought, I know exactly what to do. She drew her phaser, checking the power pack automatically, and saw Sisko's eyes on her.

"Stun only, Major," he said, and drew his own weapon.

"Sir," Kira said, not without regret, and adjusted the setting. She could hear something herself, now, footsteps, and, even more faintly, an odd, rustling sound. She frowned, cocking her head to one side to listen, and realized that it must be Diaadul's veil, the glossy folds of fabric skirring against each other.

"Wait for it," the older security man said, his voice a mere thread of sound, just above a whisper, and Kira saw Liebowitz relax slightly. She eased forward, keeping well in the shelter of the hatchway, flattened herself against the bulkhead at Liebowitz's side.

The footsteps were louder now, and then she heard a different step, louder and more heavily shod, and a man's voice said, "So there you are, Lady. We've been expecting you."

"Good," Diaadul said. She no longer sounded demure, Kira thought; this new voice was almost painfully incongruous with the heavy veil. She looked at Sisko, waiting for the signal, feeling her own shoulders painfully tense.

"Now," Sisko said, and stepped into the corridor.

Liebowitz was moving as he spoke, and Kira was right behind him, darting out into the corridor to get between the smuggler and his ship, phaser ready in her hands.

"Hands up," she said, "get your hands up now."

The smuggler—it was the blond, Möhrlein—turned, dangerously quickly, and Kira swung her phaser to cover him. "Freeze!"

He did as he was told, lifting both hands in instant surrender. "Major Kira, isn't it? What's wrong?"

He didn't sound as though his heart was in the protest, and Kira ignored him, kept the phaser leveled. At her side, Liebowitz did the same, his eyes wide, and the older security man circled cautiously to get behind Diaadul, cutting off their escape.

"Gentlemen," Sisko said. He was still in the hatchway, his own phaser already holstered again. "And lady. Or rather, it's only one gentleman, isn't it? Where's your partner, Möhrlein?"

Möhrlein hesitated only for a fraction of a second. "On board. Commander, I must protest—"

"Pointless," Odo cut in, with one of his edged smiles.

"Get Tama out here," Sisko said. He stepped out of the hatch, touched keys on the intercom that connected the ship to the docking port.

Möhrlein just looked at him, the handsome face gone suddenly hard and still. Kira had seen that look before, the cold calculation that would spend blood and lives, including his own, to get what he wanted, and lifted her phaser in answer.

"Don't even think it, Möhrlein."

He looked at her, and she saw the faint relaxation, shoulders slumping fractionally, that told her he'd believed her threat. "All right," he said, to Sisko, and stepped over to the intercom.

"Call him out here," Sisko said again, and stepped back from the panel, though he kept his hand on the controls.

Möhrlein nodded, and Sisko released the switch. "Kerel? We're busted."

"What—?" Tama's voice broke off, and Sisko slammed his hand on the controls again.

"Tama, this is Commander Sisko. We have your partner and Diaadul under arrest. Come out with your hands up—you've got no place to go."

There was a little silence, and then Möhrlein stirred. "Kerel. Do what he says."

There was another pause, and Kira found herself holding her breath. If Tama didn't do as he was told, they would have to force him out of his own starship—not an easy job at the best of times, and one they didn't have time for now. Or was Sisko tough enough to bluff them, threaten Möhrlein?

"All right," Tama said, and Kira released her breath in a long sigh. "I'm coming out."

"Hands on your head," Sisko said. "And slowly, please, Mr. Tama."

Automatically, Kira backed away from the short ramp that led up into *Carabas,* dividing her attention now between Möhrlein and the ship's main hatch. Liebowitz followed her, more slowly.

"I'm coming out," Tama's voice said again, this time from the hatch, and a moment later he appeared at the top of the ramp, his hands clasped firmly on top of his head. He made his way cautiously down the ramp, and stopped at Möhrlein's side.

"I really must protest," Möhrlein said again, but Sisko ignored him.

"Odo, make sure they're disarmed."

"With pleasure, Commander," the constable answered, and moved to search the smugglers. He ran a handheld scanner over first one, and then the other, and then, with an expression of distaste warring with a certain satisfaction, pulled a small phaser from under Möhrlein's loose vest.

"We travel in a lot of questionable places," Möhrlein said. "I have Federation permits for it."

"I'm sure you do," Sisko began, and in that instant, Diaadul moved. Ripping herself free of the confining veil, she flung herself for the hatch that led into the cargo bay, shoving the senior security man out of her way. Kira swore, caught flat-footed with the rest of them, and charged after her, Liebowitz at her side. She heard Sisko shouting for the smugglers to stay where they were, and then the commander's voice on the intercom, sounding a full security alert. Lights flashed behind her, the measured red strobing of the security alert, but Kira focused her attention on the dimly lit bay and the slim figure that had disappeared into the cover of the piled crates. She stopped, ducking automatically into the shadow of the nearest, most solid-looking container, and Liebowitz slammed into the metal beside her.

"Do you think she's armed, Major?"

"I don't think we should assume she isn't," Kira answered, and peered cautiously around the edge of the crate. Nothing was moving in the heavy shadows, and she took a deep breath. "What's her best way out?"

"There's only one other hatch," Liebowitz answered, and pointed with his phaser to a red light in the distance. "Over there—it gives onto the main corridor of the docking ring."

So that's where she's going, Kira thought. She touched her communicator. "Kira to Sisko."

"Sisko here. Are you all right, Major?"

"Yes, sir, but I need backup. We've got her cut off—" *I hope!* "—but we need a security team at the main corridor entrance to the cargo bay."

"On their way already, Major," Sisko answered. "Keep her pinned down if you can, but be careful."

"Right, sir," Kira answered, and took her hand off the communicator. It was going to take time to get a team in, especially since Sisko had cleared the area; it was up to her and Liebowitz to keep Diaadul occupied until their reinforcements arrived. She leaned cautiously around the crate again, straining her eyes in the dim light, and wished that the Cardassians had seen fit to install decent lighting. She grinned then, just for an instant—she had taken advantage of the Cardassians' fondness for dim lights more than once in her career—and looked back at Liebowitz. "She's got to be heading for that hatch. Cover me."

Liebowitz nodded, and edged forward so that he could just see around the piled crates. Kira saw his eyes move, scanning the enormous room, and then he nodded sharply. "Go, Major."

Kira darted forward, scuttling bent almost double toward the next set of crates. Her skin prickled, she expected every second to hear the snap of phaser fire, feel the searing heat of a beam across her sides or face, and then she was in the shadow of an enormous pile of metal-bound starcrates. She flattened herself against them, breathing hard, and counted to twenty before she peered around the edge of the crate. Phaser fire snapped at her, coming from the left side, where the crates offered no protection, and she threw herself down, rolling up to a shooting position in the shelter of another crate. She saw a shadow moving—Diaadul—and fired twice, the beams leaving green streaks across her eyesight.

"Liebowitz! Go right, flank her!"

The young security man responded instantly, and Kira popped up from behind her crate, firing at Diaadul's last position in the hope of providing cover. She saw Diaadul drop back, dodging between two piles of crates, and started after her, crouching low.

"Cover me!"

She heard Liebowitz fire again, steady as the best of her people during the war, heard Diaadul return fire, the bolt sizzling past too close for comfort, and ducked behind a single crate. They were getting closer and closer to the hatch, and there was still no sign of the backup team—

As if Diaadul had read her thoughts, the Trehanna rose suddenly from behind a crate, phaser in hand. She was already closer to the door than Kira had realized, and an awkward target; Kira swore once, already moving toward a better position, and saw Liebowitz rise out of the crates to her right, phaser leveled.

"Freeze, lady!"

Diaadul swung around and ducked in the same fluid motion, and Liebowitz's shot flashed harmlessly over her shoulder. She fired in the same instant, and the young man crumpled to the floor. Kira screamed a curse, and flung herself across the nearest crate, steadying herself against its bulk. She fired twice, three times, with barely time to aim, and then Diaadul was through the hatch, and the door rolled closed again behind her.

"Liebowitz," Kira said, though she was afraid she already knew the answer. She tucked her own phaser in her belt, and hurried toward him, dropped to her knees at his side, feeling for a pulse. There was no blood, but that didn't mean anything. . . . And then she felt the strong beat of his heart under her probing finger, and let out her breath in a gusty sigh of relief. For whatever reason—good sense, maybe, not wanting to risk a murder charge on top of everything else—Diaadul's phaser had been set on stun. She touched her communicator. "Kira to Sisko. Liebowitz is down, stunned. I'm leaving him for the doctor, and going after Diaadul."

She cut the channel without waiting for an answer, and turned to the hatch. She worked the controls, let the door's heavy disk roll back, and waited a few seconds before looking warily out into the corridor. There was no one in sight—not that she'd really expected Diaadul to hang around waiting for her, not with a security alert in effect and backup presumably on the way—but even so, she moved out carefully, phaser drawn and ready. *Where would I go, if I were Diaadul?* she thought. *She's lost her escape route, and there's no place to go on the station—if I were her, I'd be looking for another ship. Something I could fly myself, which means either lifepods or the runabouts. The runabouts are too well protected—the alert will have sealed their bays—so that means the lifepods or nothing.* She glanced instinctively at the directional plaques that decorated the walls throughout the station, pointing the way toward the nearest lifepod station or transporter bay, and ducked back as a phaser bolt struck the bulkhead above her head.

She caught a glimpse of Diaadul ducking back into a cross-corridor, and then she herself was scrambling into the protection of the nearest hatch. She fired twice toward the door, more to keep the other woman pinned down than out of any hope of actually hitting her, and then leaned back against the hatchway, wondering what to do next. If she remembered correctly—and that was always a big if—that corridor was a dead end, and it led into the interior, which meant no lifepods along its walls. And that meant that all she needed to do was keep Diaadul bottled up until Sisko's security team arrived. *Where the hell are they, anyway?* she wondered, and risked a glance around the edge of the hatch. A phaser bolt snapped past her head, badly aimed, but she saw no other sign of Diaadul. Kira fired back anyway, saw her own beam scorch the edge of the corridor mouth. It was still a stalemate, and she bit her lip, her phaser still ready, searching for some better shot.

The air further down the main corridor shivered, trembled with the familiar static of the transporter effect: Sisko had decided to beam the security team directly to the trouble spot, but they were materializing inside Diaadul's arc of fire. Kira charged, shouting wordlessly, hoping to distract Diaadul's attention for the crucial seconds the security team would need to materialize and regroup. She fired blindly, expecting every second to feel the freezing pain of a stun bolt—or the heat of a phaser set to kill—and saw her own shots fly wide, striking to either side of the corridor mouth. Then she heard a rumbling, felt it through the corridor floor, and saw the emergency hatch rolling shut, cutting them off from Diaadul. Kira dove for the narrowing opening, not stopping to think, heard one of the security team call her name, and then she was through, the hatch bruising her heels as it slammed home.

She rolled to her feet, too late aware of her vulnerability, and flattened her shoulders against the bulkhead in a vain attempt to make herself less of a target. Nothing was moving along the narrow tunnel, and she lifted her phaser, held her breath to listen. There were a couple of openings at the far end of the corridor, but those were dead-end rooms, one of them a maintenance bay, the other— She couldn't remember, but Diaadul had to be in one of them. Slowly, phaser at the ready, she took her first steps down the corridor, moving with all the stealth she had learned in her war.

And then, quite close, she heard a familiar sound, the metallic whine of a transporter. She froze, and then, too late, remembered just what was in the second room. It was one of the station's secondary transporter rooms, designed to move cargo around the docking ring, but fully capable, she thought grimly, of taking Diaadul anywhere on, or even off, the station. She headed for the transporter room at a dead run. It was empty, she could tell that at a glance; she shoved her phaser back into her belt, and bent over the controls.

"Kira to Sisko."

"Sisko. What's happening, Major?"

"She got away, sir." Kira gave the bad news baldly. "She triggered the emergency doors, and used the cargo transporter."

"Can you tell where she went?" Sisko asked.

"Just a minute," Kira answered, still staring at the controls. She touched the recall button, and the coordinates popped into view, along with the time of use: Diaadul's coordinates. "Yes, sir. She beamed herself back to the main part of the station, to the lower core—it looks as though she set it for level twenty-nine, near the engineering station." She took a deep breath, and set the controls to automatic. "I'm going after her."

"Hold it, Major," Sisko began.

"No, sir," Kira said, and stepped up onto the transporter platform. "Someone has to go, and I'm the closest."

There was a little silence. She braced herself for the dissolution of transporting, putting aside the consequences of disobedience for later. Sisko was a fair man, she would be able to convince him—or else it wouldn't really matter. The transporter whined, the sound building toward its climax, and in the fraction of a second before she vanished, she heard Sisko's voice.

"Very well. But be careful, Major."

CHAPTER
9

MILES O'BRIEN SWORE TO HIMSELF as he turned down the last corridor toward the temporary reactor control room, the words a rhythmic counterpoint to the sound of his feet on the heavy tiles. Stupid, stupid—he'd been careless earlier, left his tool kit and the datapadd containing his detailed plans in the workspace, and now he had to go back for them so he could finish fleshing out the last connecting nodes, unless he wanted to delay the installation of the new system by a good twelve hours. *Serves me right for being so bloody self-satisfied,* he thought. *I should've known the minute Quark asked me to fix the replimat that the evening was ruined.* And he was going to be later getting home than he'd planned—not that Keiko would say anything, she'd been Starfleet too long not to understand the demands of his job, and her own, but it galled him to miss reading Molly's bedtime story because of his own stupidity.

The new control room was dimly lit, just the blue of the standby lighting and the flicker of indicators on the single working console to show him his way. The space smelled of resin and the fainter, acrid tones of the Cardassian sealant they had been forced to use on the new lengths of conduit. O'Brien made a face at the scent—he had his doubts about the sealant—but touched the wall controls to turn on the main lighting. He stood for an instant, blinking in the sudden white flare of brilliance, until his eyes cleared and he saw the datapadd, tucked under a sheaf of insulating paper on the as yet uncompleted main console. He made a face, annoyed all over again at his carelessness—*It's no excuse, that there's too much to do, too many routine projects as well as this one, and this one with emergency priority*—and stepped across to collect it, triggering its screen automatically. He might as well, he thought, make sure all his basic data was correct, before he went ahead with the final plans.

He was well into the job, double-checking the last set of connections and the convoluted course of the diverted power conduit, when the security alarm sounded. He looked up sharply, and for a fraction of a second couldn't remember what that three-toned wail warned against. It wasn't a reactor breach, wasn't red alert, wasn't any of the engineering disasters that occasionally filled his nightmares. . . . And then he remembered, and touched his communicator.

"O'Brien to Ops."

"Dax here. Stand by, Chief."

O'Brien waited, glancing warily toward the still-open door of the compartment. Nothing was moving in the dimmed night lighting, nor had he expected there would be. This part of engineering was deserted, except during the day watches; the night shift's duty station was in the powerplant's monitoring station. *So what the hell's set this off? Full security alert, all security personnel report in—*

"Dax. Sorry, Chief, we have a situation on our hands."

"I'm down in the lower core," O'Brien said. "The temporary monitoring station. What's going on?"

"Odo identified Diaadul as an agent for the pirates," Dax answered, "but she broke free of arrest. Her two associates are in custody, but she's still free. Security has been alerted, has been dispatched to the docking ring, but the station will stay on alert until she's captured. All sections are to take appropriate precautions."

"Aye, Lieutenant," O'Brien answered automatically. If Diaadul—*and there's a surprise, after her delicate ways*— was still on the docking ring, the habitat should be safe enough. The main doors would be sealed, and Keiko would seal their quarters as well. Even so, he would be glad to get back to them, be absolutely certain that they were all right. He turned to leave, and then stopped, glancing around the secondary control room. The main monitoring station would already be sealed tight, security in full force to keep any intruders from tampering with the station's power supply, but this room . . . The new consoles gave some of the same access to the conduit system, and, because it wasn't fully on-line yet, was still being worked on, the anti-tampering systems weren't fully operational, either. The working console wasn't as good as the systems in the main station, of course, didn't access the truly crucial systems except indirectly—but a dedicated, or even half-educated, troublemaker could do enough damage through them to keep the station in an uproar for hours, maybe even days. He touched the wall controls again, resealing the main door. Then he glanced around the narrow compartment, already planning his next moves, and touched his communicator again.

"Dax, this is O'Brien."

"Dax here."

"I'm remaining in the new monitoring station to complete security shutdown of these systems."

There was a little pause, and then Dax said, sharply, "Are

you on your own down there, Chief? I can send a team to cover you."

"Yes," O'Brien said, and flicked a pair of switches on the main console, bringing its paired screens redly to life. "But I don't anticipate this taking me very long."

"I'm sending a team anyway," Dax said. "Dax out."

O'Brien grinned—Dax could be very maternal, for a creature who spent half its time male and the other half female—but said only, "Thanks, Dax. O'Brien out."

And I can't say I'm sorry she's sending backup, he added silently, touching the keys that brought up an internal menu. *This is a pretty deserted part of the station, and I am on my own right now, and unarmed.* The last wasn't a comforting thought, but it wasn't Starfleet policy for its personnel to go armed except on specific orders, and this was hardly a situation even Sisko—*or even Picard*—could have foreseen. He pushed the idea out of his mind, and focused his attention on the doubled screens.

He never, even later, knew how long he'd been working. The sound of the alarm had receded from his consciousness, too familiar to demand attention, and the second set of installation lights had faded from the left-hand screen, telling him that his standard password-and-palmprint access program was in place and ready to run, when he heard the sound of footsteps outside the compartment's door. He looked up, sharply, but the locking light still glowed red, and the footsteps sounded entirely too confident to belong to a fugitive. He relaxed slightly, and in the same instant a voice crackled over the intercom.

"Chief O'Brien? It's Macauslan, Security."

Definitely not the voice he had associated with Diaadul. O'Brien touched a final key, settling the program securely into local memory, and went to the door controls. He touched the switch that released the lock, and turned to face the opening door. Instead of one of Odo's deputies, or a Starfleet security officer, a slim, green-clad woman stood in the opening, a leveled phaser in her hand.

"Stand away from the controls."

O'Brien swore once, unable to believe he'd been this careless, but lifted his hands, and took a slow step back into the room.

"Move," Diaadul said, "or I will kill you."

Still reluctant, but knowing he had no other choice, O'Brien took two more steps backward. Diaadul, her eyes still fixed on him and her phaser leveled, sidled over to the door controls, and touched the keys that resealed the door. O'Brien bit back another curse as he saw the red light go on again.

"Now, Chief," Diaadul said, still in a voice he didn't recognize, a voice he belatedly realized was indeed her own, her true persona. "Your communicator. Take it off, and put it on the floor."

"What do you want with me?" O'Brien asked, and made no move to obey.

Diaadul extended her hand, the phaser leveled, and walked sideways again so that there was clear space between herself and the engineer. O'Brien turned with her, hating his helplessness. "I want your communicator," Diaadul said. "Take it off, now. Or I will shoot you down and take it."

And that, O'Brien thought, would do no one any good at all. Very slowly, he unhooked the badge from his tunic, held it palm out in his hand.

"On the floor," Diaadul said. "Slide it over to me."

O'Brien bent down, set the communicator carefully on the tiled floor. *If she picks it up,* he thought, *there'll be a moment when she's distracted—*

"Slide it to me," Diaadul said again.

O'Brien braced himself, and slid the bit of metal across the floor, ready to move the moment her attention wavered.

Diaadul never took her eyes off him, but reached out with one foot, and kicked the badge into the far corner, hopelessly out of reach. O'Brien bit his lip to hide his sudden fury. He could hear a voice speaking, faintly, from the communicator, and looked at Diaadul.

"They're calling me from Ops," he said, though he couldn't really distinguish the speaker. "If I don't answer, there'll be hell to pay."

"Eventually," Diaadul said. "But by then it will be too late." She gestured with her phaser, motioning him toward the empty bulkhead, away from the door controls and the dropped communicator. "Turn around and face the wall. Put your hands against it and lean forward."

O'Brien did as he was told, a cold chill running through him as he recognized a professional at work. There was almost nothing he could do in this position, not unless she got very careless, and there didn't seem to be much chance of that. He glanced carefully over his shoulder, and saw her reach into her tunic with her free hand, still without taking her eyes off him. She came out with a palm-sized communicator, and held it to her lips.

"Helios, this is Number One. *Helios,* this is Number One. Respond, *Helios."*

There was a slight pause, and O'Brien could hear static singing faintly from the system. Diaadul frowned slightly, and he allowed himself to hope, and then a voice sounded from the speaker.

"Helios."

"Abort plan one," Diaadul said. "I repeat, abort plan one. Commence plan two."

"Beginning plan two," the voice said promptly. "Confirm number of packages for pickup?"

"Two," Diaadul answered, and smiled openly now. "Two packages, *Helios.* We haven't lost yet, Demaree."

"Confirmed," *Helios* answered, and Diaadul took her

finger off the transmit button, tucked the communicator back into her tunic.

"Just what the hell do you think you're doing?" O'Brien demanded, and the Trehanna shook her head.

"Don't talk, Chief. Just keep very still."

The threat in her voice was unmistakable, and O'Brien resigned himself to wait. He had a bad feeling about this, a distinct sense that he already knew what Diaadul was up to, though he didn't yet know why. But if she had two "packages" for *Helios*, he had a nasty feeling that he was one of them. *Dax said she was sending Security*, he thought, *so where the hell are they?* There was no answer, and no point in wondering. He risked another quick glance over his shoulder, and saw Diaadul still watching, her great eyes fixed on him in unwinking, almost clinical assessment. She would have to make a major mistake before he'd have a chance to jump her—and so far, he thought bitterly, she was doing everything right.

Sisko's warning was still ringing in Kira's ears as she materialized on level twenty-nine. She crouched instinctively, scanning the night-lit corridor for any sign of Diaadul, and straightened cautiously when she realized the other woman was nowhere to be seen. She kept her own phaser in hand, however, and eased forward into the shelter of a sealed hatchway before she risked contacting the commander.

"Kira to Sisko." She had kept her voice low, barely more than a whisper—whispers carried; she had learned that long ago—but even so she winced, and glanced up and down the corridor again.

"Sisko here. What is it, Major?"

"I'm on level twenty-nine." Kira glanced at the plaque on the hatch above her head, translating its numbers and letters into location. "Sector eight, about halfway between the main turbolift shaft and the main monitoring station. No sign of Diaadul—and I don't know where she's heading." Probably toward the turbolifts, though, she added silently, except that a full security alert shuts them all down. Diaadul might not know that—but it would be standard procedure, and so far the Trehanna woman hadn't made that kind of mistake. That left engineering but, again, Kira couldn't see what the woman would gain from that.

"All right, Major," Sisko said, his voice sounding very loud in the silence of the deserted corridor. "Stay where you are. I'm sending a team to join you. We've sealed off the turbolifts, and every other occupied space in the lower core. She can't get far."

"Commander!" Dax's voice broke into the conversation, sounding more excited than Kira had ever heard her. "Commander, Chief O'Brien is in the new supplemental control room—alone, he was securing the station—and I can't raise him. He's not responding to my calls."

"Damn!" Sisko's curse crackled over the communicators, and then he had himself under control again. "All right. What's the location of the new control room?"

"Level thirty, sector nine," Dax answered.

"Sir—" Kira began, but Sisko was already speaking, overriding her response.

"Major Kira, get down there at once. See what's happened to O'Brien, and report. If he's a prisoner, stay out of sight, stay in contact, and keep security informed. I don't want you to take on Diaadul on your own."

"Yes, sir," Kira said. *And if the Chief's dead or injured,* she added silently, *I know enough to call Bashir. I just hope to hell it doesn't come to that.*

"The security team will follow you," Sisko went on. "You say your present location is secure?"

"As far as I can tell, sir," Kira answered. "I haven't seen any sign of Diaadul."

"Then I'm beaming them to your current location. Sisko out."

"Yes, sir," Kira said, and wondered if she was talking to empty space. It was a reasonable enough precaution, beaming the security team to her current location, but not entirely reassuring. They would have to move fast to catch up with her in time to do any good. She pushed herself out of the hatchway, glanced at a directional sign on the opposite wall, and started for the nearest Jeffries tube.

It wasn't a real Jeffries tube, of course, but the Cardassian equivalent, a wedge-shaped maintenance shaft lined with pull-out circuitry on two sides, and a ladder running down the third. The rungs were badly spaced for her height— Cardassian design again—and she had to alternately stretch and step short. She lowered herself cautiously down the narrow tunnel, bathed in the red glow of the emergency lighting, and paused about halfway down to touch her communicator.

"Kira to O'Brien. Kira to O'Brien. Please respond, Chief."

She listened for a long moment, but there was no answer. She hadn't really expected one, but even so, she felt a shiver run down her spine. Either O'Brien was Diaadul's prisoner, or he was lying somewhere, unconscious or dead. For an instant, she tried to persuade herself that the communicator might have malfunctioned, or that O'Brien might just have been careless, but the possibilities were vanishingly small. O'Brien took too much care of his equipment—was too professional, too much the Starfleet officer—to make such an error.

She reached the bottom of the tube, and turned her attention to the hatch. She needed both hands to work the cumbersome control wheel, and she made a face, reluctant to reholster her phaser, but there was no other choice. There was no way of telling if there was anyone in the corridor—

the tubes had been designed for maintenance, not sneaking around the station—and she braced herself for the worst as she heaved at the wheel. It resisted her efforts for a long moment, and then, just as she was beginning to think she might be stuck, it loosened abruptly, and she had to catch it to keep the hatch from rolling open too quickly. She took a deep breath, drawing her phaser, and eased the hatch out of its bed. She stopped when she had an opening maybe seven centimeters wide, and pressed her face against the narrow space. The alert lights pulsed at her, alternately red and orange, slightly out of synch with the still-sounding alarm, but she saw nothing moving in the flickering shadows. She rolled the hatch the rest of the way back into its bed, and clambered out into the corridor, letting the hatch fall shut again behind her.

Level thirty seemed quite deserted, no one moving along a corridor that contained only three doorways. There was nothing much down here, she remembered, except the engineering monitoring station; only the technical staff spent much time in the maze of corridors and maintenance spaces. A good place to hide, maybe too good: the solid-looking bulkheads concealed any number of crawl spaces and access tubes for the engineers' use. She shook herself then—if Diaadul had taken to the engineering spaces, there was nothing she, Kira, could do about it without significant backup—and checked her location again. The new control space was in sector nine: only a little farther, just around the corridor's gentle curve.

The control room's door was closed, the red light of a locked system gleaming above the outer panel. Kira stared at it for half a dozen heartbeats, suppressing her instinctive desire to charge ahead, and made herself stand quite still, looking up and down the corridor. The walls were mostly empty, except for another closed door perhaps fifteen meters ahead. It was the only possible cover, unless Diaadul had indeed gone to ground in the accessways. Kira eyed it warily, kept her phaser leveled on it as she eased toward the control room door. Nothing moved in the red-flashing shadows, but she flattened herself against the bulkhead anyway, twisting her body to provide a minimal target. The lock light still glowed steadily: *Either O'Brien has locked himself in,* she thought, *which would be the sensible thing to do, or Diaadul has locked herself in there with him. And if she has, I'll only make things worse by letting her know I'm out here.*

She looked at the control panel for a moment, then risked reholstering her phaser to study the boxy display system. Like so much of the station hardware, it was Cardassian, one of the pieces that hadn't yet been replaced with Starfleet's own equipment—but at least it was a system she knew. Very carefully, she touched a key sequence, hoping that O'Brien hadn't disabled the eavesdropping function, and allowed herself a sigh of relief when the familiar pattern appeared on the screen. The Cardassians liked to be able to keep their own people under surveillance; the Resistance had been quick to learn to use the inbuilt functions. She touched a second switch, easing up the volume, and heard O'Brien's familiar voice.

"—get away with it."

A woman's voice answered, not one that Kira recognized, but she knew it could be no one but Diaadul. "Be quiet, Chief. I won't tell you again."

There was no answer, but Kira had heard enough. She checked the eavesdrop function to be certain it was only a one-way transmission, and leaned back against the wall, reached for her communicator.

"Kira to Sisko."

The response was reassuringly prompt. "Sisko here."

"I'm at the new control room. Diaadul is in there with

Chief O'Brien, definitely holding him prisoner." Kira glanced back along the corridor in spite of herself. "Where's the security team?"

"On its way," Sisko answered. "Odo reports he's five minutes from your location. Wait for their arrival."

Kira made a face, but knew she couldn't handle this one on her own. "Very well," she began, and broke off as voices sounded again from inside the compartment. "Stand by, Commander."

"Two for pickup confirmed," Diaadul's voice said, from the speaker. "Commence beta phase now."

"Damn!" Kira bit off the rest of her words, knowing there was no time left, and reached for the command override box she had been issued when she joined Odo's security team. She slipped it over the control surfaces, and triggered the key sequence. "No time, Commander. I'm going in."

"Major—" Sisko's voice stopped abruptly, but Kira had no time to wonder why. The telltales on top of the override box went green at last, and she kicked the door release. The heavy hatch rolled back, groaning softly, and she ducked through the opening, phaser ready.

"Hold it right there!"

She caught a quick glimpse of Diaadul in the center of the room, already whirling like a dancer, and O'Brien leaning, arms outstretched and palms flat against the wall, and then Diaadul fired, and O'Brien crumpled to the ground. Kira cried out, wordlessly, unable to believe what she had seen, and in the same instant knew she'd made a fatal mistake. She flung herself down and sideways even as Diaadul fired, but the bolt creased her side, flinging her painfully against the bulkhead. She tried to breathe, her vision fading, realized that she was only stunned, and then even that ceased to matter and she collapsed bonelessly to the floor.

* * *

Diaadul waited, her phaser still leveled, until she was sure the Bajoran was truly unconscious, then crossed to the wall controls to close and relock the door. Kira had dropped her own weapon; the Trehanna kicked it carefully out of reach, then picked it up, setting it on the nearest console. Then she tucked her own phaser back beneath her tunic and reached for the package of sensor pickups that she carried in her pocket. She hadn't expected Kira to find her so quickly, but, on balance, it might not be a bad thing to have two hostages. O'Brien was needed for several reasons, could not be threatened too convincingly—Jarriel's repairs were proceeding all too slowly, and another engineer might well make a difference—but Kira was perfectly expendable. *At least to us,* Diaadul added, and smiled slightly. *She won't be expendable to Sisko, and that, at least, will buy us time.*

She set the first pickup on O'Brien's collar, working the tiny clips into the fabric to keep it secure, and then returned to Kira's slumped body. She ran her hands over the other woman's uniform, found and removed the communicator and Kira's spare phaser, a tiny holdout model, and attached the second pickup to the Bajoran's jacket. Then she stepped back, reaching for her communicator.

"Diaadul to *Helios.* There are three packages for pickup now."

There was no answer, but she hadn't expected one: once the plan had entered its beta phase, there would be no time to spare for a response. Everything now depended on *Helios,* on Kolovzon's legendary timing. . . . She glanced in spite of herself at the locked door, and hoped it would be enough. If Kira had found her, then the rest of the security team, the Starfleet security officers and the dough-faced, shape-changing constable, could not be far behind. And then an alarm whooped from the intercom's speakers, a sound that even she recognized as Starfleet's red alert. She grinned then, no longer bothering to hide her smile, and leaned back against the console, waiting for the final phase to begin.

In Ops, Sisko leaned forward as though he could drag an answer out of the communications console. "Major—" He broke off as indicators flicked out, informing him that Kira had broken contact. "Damn the woman! Doesn't she have the faintest idea of discipline?"

He saw the nearest Bajoran look away, eyes hooding, and mastered his temper with an effort. "Odo! Make all speed to support Major Kira, she's gone in alone."

"What?" The constable's displeasure was evident in his tone, but he made no other protest. "We're on our way, Commander."

Sisko grimaced, but there was nothing more he could do. They'd bungled this one, all of them, himself in particular— he should have listened to Odo, put Diaadul under arrest the moment anything had seemed odd about her—

A tone sounded, from the main navigation systems, and Dax said, "Commander, I'm picking up a disturbance, it might be a wave emission, moving toward us from the general direction of the Denorios Belt."

"Put it on the main screen," Sisko ordered, automatically, and Dax touched keys to obey. The image in the screen shifted, became a different patch of starscape, empty except for the faint, star-scatter haze of the Belt in the background.

"We're not picking up anything else," Dax said, doubtfully. "Just through the filter—"

And then the screen shimmered, wavering as though it were about to melt, to dissolve, and a ship appeared. Massive, slab-sided, it wheeled on its long axis until it faced the station, the image of a solar face blazoned across the protruding bridge.

"Sound red alert," Sisko said, and felt the calm of absolute disaster surround him. "Dax, stand by the shields, ready at full power."

"Red alert, sir," a Bajoran acknowledged, and in the same instant the familiar alarm sounded, whooping through the station. Sisko closed his mind to the image of the station's civilian population, running frantically toward their disaster stations, then looked back at the screen.

"Get me a good fix on that ship."

"Got it, sir," another of the Bajorans answered. "Sensors are locked on."

"Stand by phasers," Sisko said.

"Standing by," someone answered, and an engineering technician, Swannig, Sisko thought, lifted his head from his screen.

"Sir, we're not getting anything from the new conduit. All the controls are dead, and I'm not able to activate them from here."

"How much power do we have for the phasers?" Sisko demanded. In the screen, *Helios* grew larger, swinging again to reveal a flank scored and pitted as though by heavy fire. "Dax, put their course on the main viewer."

He didn't hear her acknowledgment, but a moment later, a secondary screen appeared, with *Deep Space Nine* at the center and *Helios*'s projected course laid out as a green parabola. If the pirate continued on her present heading, she would sweep around the station, and swing back out into the asteroid belt, using the station's disproportionately high artificial gravitational field to create a minor slingshot effect. It was a clever tactic, Sisko admitted sourly, and one that gave the ship a clear field of fire for as much as four interminable minutes. . . .

"Sir, phasers are at seventy-five percent of the Cardassian rating," Swannig reported.

"Commander," Dax said. "Preliminary readings suggest that won't be enough to penetrate *Helios*'s shield."

"Can we route power from deflectors to the phasers?" Sisko asked.

Swannig bent over his console. "Not without dropping shields below the recommended limits."

"Sir, *Helios* is approaching phaser range now," one of the Bajorans reported, his voice high and strained.

"Raise our shields, Dax," Sisko said, grimly, and braced himself against the nearest console.

"Raising shields—" Dax broke off abruptly, her eyes widening in horrified disbelief. "Sir, the shields don't answer. We have no deflectors."

"Get them up," Sisko said, through clenched teeth. "Come on, Dax." In the screen, *Helios* loomed ever larger, the wedge-shaped icon in the secondary screen already beginning its turn to circle the station. She was well within phaser range, but still holding fire, and Sisko's hands tightened on the edge of the console. Any minute now, he thought, any minute he'd see the flare of white light that meant *Helios* was firing, that meant DS9 would be destroyed— "Shields?" he snapped again, and saw Dax shake her head.

"The system's not responding, sir."

Out of the corner of his eye, Sisko saw Swannig and a Bajoran technician fling themselves to the floorplates, ripping frantically at the plates that gave access to the weapons console's inner workings. In the main viewer the stars swung crazily behind *Helios*, the green wedge accelerating perceptibly along its track. Sisko caught a glimpse of more damage, metal ripped like paper along one side of the pirate's hull, a weapon turret peeled back and hanging as if by a thread of metal, and then *Helios* was past, accelerating away from the station at near warp speed. The image shimmered again, like heat—like an illusion, Sisko thought, bitterly—and vanished.

"Tracking the wave emissions," Dax said, and almost at once shook her head. "I've lost her. I'm sorry, Benjamin."

Sisko sighed, shook his own head. "Keep scanning, you may pick up something." He stared for a moment at the empty screen, unable to understand what had happened. *Helios* had us dead to rights, he thought. Why the hell didn't she fire?

"Try the shields now, Lieutenant," Swannig said, and Dax bent over her console.

"Shields are responding normally," she reported, a moment later. "I don't know what went wrong."

"Well, find out," Sisko snapped. "We may not be so lucky next time."

He stood in the center of Ops, hands still resting on the edge of the operations table. The whole thing had been over in minutes, hardly time to respond—*but plenty of time to attack,* he thought, bitterly. *If we'd had power.* He stared at the main viewer, half expecting to see the pirate reappear, returning to finish what it had started, but the screen stayed blank, the same seemingly empty starfield filling its surface. He took a deep breath, and touched his communicator. "Dr. Bashir. Any casualties?"

There was a little pause before the young man answered, sounding out of breath. A baby was wailing in the background, sounding more outraged than hurt. "Nothing serious, Commander. Some bruises when the turbolifts shut down, and a sprained ankle from falling off a ladder. All under control."

Let's be grateful for small favors, Sisko thought. "Carry on, Doctor," he said, and broke the connection.

"Commander," Swannig said. "I've located the problem."

"Well?" Sisko turned to face him, saw the younger man

push himself up off the floorplates, and rub his clean hands reflexively down the front of his uniform.

"Something tripped the emergency cutouts," Swannig said. "It's there to prevent increased demand from over-loading the system—the Cardassians had troubles with time lag, you could ask for more than the conduits could carry if you weren't sensitive to it, and then you'd risk blowing the entire system. It's supposed to have an instant reset feature, but that seems to have been disabled, I don't know how. I've reset it manually, and disabled the cutout. It shouldn't happen again."

Sisko nodded, still chilled by the narrow escape. If *Helios* had fired, DS9 would have been completely defenseless, and even a single shot from that overweaponed monster would have been enough to do serious damage to the station. *So why didn't they attack?* "All right, Ensign," he said aloud. "Dax, stand down from red alert, but keep us on yellow alert for now." A thought struck him, frighteningly plausible, and he made an effort to keep his face expressionless. "And raise Odo for me."

"Yes, Commander," Dax said, and a moment later Odo's voice crackled through the nearest speaker.

"What's going on, Commander?"

Sisko grinned in spite of himself at the constable's famil-iar attitude, and heard a choking sound as someone sup-pressed a giggle. "The station was in imminent danger of attack, Constable. I'm sorry if that disrupted your plans."

There was a little silence, and when Odo spoke again, his voice lacked some of its usual asperity. "I take it that the emergency is over?"

"For now," Sisko answered. "Where are you, Odo, and what's your status?"

"I'm in the secondary control room," Odo answered. "Neither Chief O'Brien nor Major Kira—nor, for that matter, Lady Diaadul—are anywhere to be found." There was a little pause, and then the constable added, thoughtfully, "We did find their communicators, however."

"O'Brien's and Kira's?" Sisko asked, though he thought he knew the answer.

"Yes."

Missing people, abandoned communicators, and an abortive attack on the station: it was a suggestive, and unpleasant, combination. Sisko sighed, and said, without much hope, "Take your people and keep searching the area. Report the minute you find anything."

He distinctly heard Odo's sigh, but the constable said only, "Very well, Commander. Odo out."

"Dax," Sisko said, and the Trill looked up expectantly. "Pull the recordings of the attack, and put them through to my office. Then I want to talk to you and—" He stopped abruptly. He had almost said Major Kira, and that was a painful reminder of how much he'd already come to depend on the Bajoran. "I want to go over them in my office," he finished, and turned away before anyone could read the concern on his face.

Dax was as efficient as ever. The first reports were already flashing onto his screen as he took his place behind the desk. Dax herself appeared in the doorway a moment later, her lovely face set into a grim mask.

"Bad news, Benjamin," she said, and took her place opposite him. "I've run the sensor records of *Helios*'s approach through the broad-band system, and . . ."

Her voice trailed off, and Sisko said it for her. "You spotted a transporter beam."

"I think you should see for yourself," Dax said, and nodded.

Sisko leaned forward as the new images filled his screen. *Helios* hung at the center of the image, frozen against the stars, the marks of battle starkly visible on her sides.

"I'm beginning the tape two minutes into the attack run," Dax said. "She's just starting her turn around the station."

Sisko nodded, staring at the ship as it jerked into motion, shifting frame by frame across a starfield that was beginning to streak as the station's cameras could no longer cope with the relative motion. He saw the ship tilt slowly, exposing more damage, the torn turret he had noticed before, and dark lines of carbon scoring across the unpainted surface of the hull.

"And this is the enhanced view," Dax said.

In the screen, angles sharpened, as though a light had been turned up. A haze of color, like a faint, rainbowed halo, appeared around the ship's stern, highlighting emissions from the hidden engines; more halos appeared, surrounding the weapon turrets and picking out the sealed mouths of photon-torpedo launchers. The ship lurched forward again, and a haze appeared beneath its belly, a glowing golden light almost invisible against the bright hull. In the next frame, the light had already become a beam, stabbing halfway to the station; in the next and the one following, the beam reached past the edge of the screen, clearly extending toward the station. There was more, but Sisko leaned back, looking instead at Dax.

"Preliminary analysis suggests that that—" She gestured to the beam, now pulling back into the ship. "—is consistent with a transporter in operation."

"Which means we can assume that Kira and O'Brien are prisoners on board that monster," Sisko said. "And presumably the shields didn't work because someone on *Helios* lowered them."

"Or someone on the station," Dax said. "I don't think we can eliminate that possibility."

It was, in fact, the more likely option, and Sisko grimaced at the thought. "No one on board this station has any reason to support *Helios*—they're all equally at risk. Except those smugglers, and Diaadul herself."

Dax was already busy with a datapadd. "The smugglers were under restraint before the attack began, and remain so."

"Which leaves Diaadul," Sisko said. "Could she have lowered the shields from O'Brien's new monitoring station?"

Dax tilted her head to one side. "I don't know, Benjamin. I don't think so, but I don't know what her technical skills are like."

Sisko stared for a moment at the screen, no longer seeing the pirate ship's jerky progress. Instead, a new and frightening possibility opened up in front of him, one in which someone on board the station was a spy for *Helios*—worse than that, a saboteur—and he was left without either the chief engineer he needed to repair the damage, or the full security complement he needed to prevent it. He heard a tap at the door and looked up sharply, to see Swannig standing in the doorway.

"I'm sorry to interrupt, sir, but we've found the problem."

"Yes?" Sisko said, and beckoned the technician in.

"With the shields, sir. We were virused."

Dax gave a little exclamation of impatience. "I should've guessed—should've considered the possibility. Especially with someone playing around with our accounting systems."

Swannig glanced at her. "It was the same kind of program, Lieutenant, the same hand, I'd say. That's how we found it so quickly, ran a scan from the program you'd found."

Dax shook her head, her lips compressed in self-disgust, and Sisko said, "Go on."

"It wasn't really a virus, sir," Swannig said, "more of a Trojan horse. It masquerades as a standard subrepair routine—somebody's gotten a good copy of Starfleet programming—until it gets the trigger signal, which is the general shutdown of nonessential systems that goes out automatically with red alert. At that point, it disables the reset and substitutes its own data for the data usually sent by the override sensors, with the result that, the minute you call for shields, the whole system shuts down."

"Clever," Sisko said, sourly.

Swannig nodded. "It's a pretty neat little program. I'd recommend that we keep and dissect it for possible later use."

Sisko eyed him with ill-concealed distaste, and saw Dax hide a sudden and fugitive smile. *Technicians,* he thought, and said, "Have you cleaned it out of the systems, Swannig?"

"Oh, yes, sir," Swannig answered. "We reinstalled everything, and I have the copies on an isolated machine."

"All right," Sisko said. "Carry on."

"Very good, sir," Swannig said, and turned away.

Sisko let the office door close behind him before he spoke again. "So. Diaadul installed it, do you think?"

Dax nodded thoughtfully. "That would make sense, Commander. I'm nearly positive she was the one to install the accounting ghosts, and this would be consistent with that."

That was a relief, and Sisko allowed himself a long sigh. The thought of screening DS9's population for possible agents had not been a pleasant one. "So they made that attack to kidnap Kira and O'Brien?" He shook his head. "That doesn't make sense."

"Or to pick up Diaadul," Dax said. "Odo said she was clearly important."

"But why, if they were expecting to get those parts from

the smugglers, did they then go to the effort of kidnapping two of my officers?" Sisko said. "They must expect retaliation."

Dax looked up suddenly, her eyes gleaming. "Unless—"

"Unless this was a backup plan," Sisko said.

Dax nodded in agreement, her eyes fixed on the screen. "There were machine parts in the ship, things that could be converted to starship use—"

"—and *Helios* was pretty obviously damaged," Sisko finished for her. "So. Did Diaadul intend from the first to kidnap O'Brien, or was it just a lucky accident?"

"I don't think *Helios* and her captain leave much to chance," Dax said, suddenly sober.

Sisko nodded slowly, his own momentary elation vanishing. Whether it was serendipity or a well-made plan hardly mattered: O'Brien, and Kira, were still missing.

As if to confirm his thoughts, a light flashed on his desktop, and Odo's voice spoke from the speaker. "Odo to Sisko."

"Sisko here. Any luck?"

"None," Odo answered, and Sisko thought he heard more than the usual impatience in the constable's voice. *But then,* he thought, *in his own way, Odo is almost fond of Kira. . . .* "We've searched sector nine thoroughly, and are extending our efforts to sectors eight and ten. But I don't expect to find them on board, sir."

"Probably not," Sisko agreed. "We have indications that someone transported to *Helios* from the station during the attack run. It's likely that Kira and O'Brien were taken."

He heard a faint sound from the communicator, almost as though Odo had growled. He paused, but heard nothing more, and went on, "I want you to detail enough men to search the station completely, top to bottom. We'll remain at yellow alert until you're finished. I want to be absolutely certain that our people aren't lying somewhere hurt—and I want to be sure we don't have any unwanted visitors."

Odo didn't answer at once, and Sisko imagined him staring into space, preparing a protest at his commander's stupidity. But Odo's answer, when it came, was perfectly mild. "I'll organize that at once, Commander. And inform you when it's finished."

"Good. Sisko out." Sisko looked at Dax. "In the meantime, let's see if we can track down that damned pirate."

Though they worked hard for the next two hours, even the most careful scanning showed no sign of the *Helios*'s wave emissions. Sisko accepted the twentieth negative report without a change of expression, and said to the Bajoran technician who brought the report, "Keep looking."

"Commander, the constable reports that the search parties have reached the Promenade, and there's still no sign of either our people or Diaadul," another Bajoran said.

Sisko said, "Tell the constable thank you, and carry on." He saw Dax turn away from her console, frowning slightly, and his own brows contracted in a scowl. "And, yes, Lieutenant, we will stay at yellow alert until it's done."

"Yes, sir," Dax said, with an abstracted air. "Sir, we're receiving a subspace transmission. Its point of origin is just beyond our borders."

Sisko swore under his breath. He had been more than half expecting the Cardassians to show up, to make his life complete; he supposed he should be grateful it was only via subspace radio. "Put it on the main viewer, Lieutenant."

"Aye, sir," Dax answered. "Putting it through to the main viewer."

The screen lit, glowed briefly reddish brown before a familiar head and shoulders appeared in its center. Gul Dukat stared out from the screen, his lips curved into a smile that moved the heavy facial ridges, but did not reach his eyes. "Commander Sisko," he said. "How relieved I am to see you're still with us."

I'm sure, Sisko thought. He said, "Gul Dukat. I'm— touched—by your concern." He paused, and when the Cardassian showed no sign of continuing, said heavily, "To what do we owe the honor of this call?"

"As you know, our fleet has been tracking a dangerous pirate, one we've been chasing for some time. We've spotted that ship off your station, Commander—you were fortunate to come to no harm." Dukat's smile widened briefly, baring teeth. "We are in pursuit of that ship, and in earnest of our continued peaceful intentions toward the Federation, I am informing you personally of our intention to continue to pursue it into Federation space as necessary."

Sisko opened his mouth to answer, and Dukat held up his hand.

"Please, Commander, this is a purely internal affair. Our only concern is *Helios;* we want to prevent her captain from taking her through the wormhole, and, of course, to capture her and her crew if possible."

"And if not?" Sisko asked, before the Cardassian could go on.

"My orders are to destroy her," Dukat answered. "My orders also instruct me to consider any interference from *Deep Space Nine,* or from any of Starfleet, as if it were aid given to *Helios*—that is, as an act of war."

"Two of my people have been taken prisoner, and are currently being held on *Helios,* " Sisko said. "We're taking all measures to secure their release. I hereby request that you hold off until they're freed."

"Your—carelessness—can hardly be considered my concern," Dukat said. "We have our orders."

"Your situation can hardly be considered hot pursuit," Sisko objected. "Besides, there's no reason to assume that *Helios* hasn't already returned to Cardassian space."

"You're stalling, Commander," Dukat said, with another toothed smile that went oddly with his gentle voice. "I intend to pursue *Helios* and capture or destroy it. And I repeat, the Cardassian Empire will consider any interference with my mission as an act of war." He lifted his hand, obviously signaling to an offscreen subordinate, and the image vanished.

"Transmission ends, sir," a technician said.

Sisko nodded, still staring at the blank screen. The worst thing was, Dukat was right: he had been stalling, and not doing it very well. *I have two people prisoner on the pirate,* he thought, *and another four hundred on the station, all of whom are my responsibility, but my orders . . .* He smiled suddenly, unaware of the sudden curious looks of the crew in Ops. *My orders are to take* Helios *myself.* His smile faded as quickly as it had appeared. *My orders . . . To obey is to risk O'Brien and Kira's lives, which is their job and mine. That's well and good, and I could do—something—to hold the Cardassians back. But that would mean putting DS9 in the center of a major battle, a battle it and I can't win. And that is something I cannot, will not risk. No matter what my orders.*

CHAPTER
10

O'BRIEN STRUGGLED BACK to consciousness, his head aching, body tingling with the aftereffects of a stun blast. Something was very wrong; he was aware of that in the first instant, and killed his instinctive desire to sit up and look around. He lay still instead, eyes shut, and listened. The hiss of air in the ventilators sounded different, more like a starship than the station's system—*and not like a Federation ship, either,* he added, silently. There was something in the faint sounds of the ship's systems, a stuttering rumble almost at the edge of hearing, that confirmed his suspicions: whatever the ship was—and there was really only one likely possibility—it was neither Federation-built, nor in perfect repair.

He let his head fall to one side, still feigning unconsciousness, and opened one eye a crack. Bright light jabbed at him, and it took all his strength to keep from wincing. And then his sight cleared, and he could see the red-brown stuff of the mattress cover—he was lying on a bunk, he realized—and then, beyond that, the purple-glowing lattice of a forcefield that ran across the mouth of what could only be a cell. There were three figures beyond the forcefield: Diaadul, now dressed in work clothes and looking for the first time like the dangerous person she truly was, and two strangers. One of them was human, thin and brown-haired; the other was tall and broad-shouldered, not human, but not a species O'Brien recognized at a glance.

He closed his eye again, slowly, not wanting to draw their attention until he felt a little stronger, and tried to work out exactly how he'd gotten here. Where "here" was was no problem: "here" had to be *Helios,* and at least one of the men had to be her captain, Kolovzon, but how he'd been brought aboard he didn't know. He remembered Diaadul signaling *Helios,* announcing her two packages for pickup, but then his memories grew more chaotic. Kira had burst through the door, and then—

He twitched in spite of himself, remembering the shock of the phaser bolt, and knew he'd betrayed himself. He shifted his weight, rolling his head away from the barricaded door, and opened his eyes again, this time to the pale dull gold of a lightly padded wall. What had happened to Kira—?

"Chief O'Brien."

That was Diaadul's voice, and O'Brien held himself motionless for an instant, wondering how he should respond. He let his head roll back to face the forcefield. All three of the strangers were still there, though the nonhuman male had taken a step forward, so that he was a little in advance of the others.

"Good to see you're with us, Chief," the nonhuman male said. "Welcome to the *Helios.*"

So tell me something I don't know, O'Brien thought. He didn't respond at once, but levered himself cautiously into a sitting position. The headache was receding quickly, though the pins-and-needles stinging his hands was still frighteningly present—*but once that goes,* he thought, *I've got a chance. In the meantime, let's play sick. I need all the advantages I can pry out of the situation.* He mumbled something, pleased with the tremulous sound of his own voice, and put both hands to his face, looking out through the barrier of his fingers. "What the hell—?"

"You're on board the *Helios,*" Diaadul said. "Our prisoner."

"And Kira?" O'Brien demanded. He took his hands away from his eyes, fixed the woman with an angry stare.

The nonhuman grinned, showing teeth, but Diaadul said, flatly, "In the next cell. Stunned, but unhurt."

"I want to see her," O'Brien said.

The nonhuman's grin widened. "That can be arranged, Chief. On conditions, of course."

O'Brien pushed himself to his feet, his original plan forgotten, overridden by his concern for Kira, and came forward until he stood only centimeters from the opening and the softly spitting forcefield. This close, he could hear the faint hum of its generators, and the hairs on his arms stirred, lifted by the electricity. It was obviously a powerful field, and he was careful to keep his hands well away from its purplish glow. "What conditions, Kolovzon?"

"You know me," the nonhuman said.

Up close, O'Brien could see the slit-pupilled eyes, like Diaadul's, and the same oddly delicate length to his fingers: another Trehanna, then. He nodded. "I've heard your name."

"That may simplify things," Kolovzon said. "Your Commander Sisko has very seriously inconvenienced me, Mr. O'Brien. I have no interest whatsoever in your station, but he's seen fit to interfere with a shipment of parts and software that I need to repair my ship."

"That's what Diaadul came for," O'Brien said, when it became clear that some answer was expected of him. There was a look in Kolovzon's eyes, a fey lightness, that made him very nervous.

"That's right," Kolovzon answered, and for a second, O'Brien thought the Trehanna sounded almost approving. "Since your commander has blocked that shipment, however, I have no choice but to get my repairs done by other means. Such as yourself, Chief O'Brien."

"You can go to hell," O'Brien said. "I'm not helping you—"

Kolovzon lifted a hand. "I think you will want to reconsider your position," he said, and O'Brien shook his head.

"You can't force me to work for you. Not without doing me enough damage that I won't be able to do the work."

"How fortunate," Kolovzon said, "that we won't have to rely on direct intimidation. Diaadul, you did well, bringing the Bajoran."

"Thank you, Captain," Diaadul murmured, her face expressionless.

The human male stirred at Kolovzon's side. "Captain—"

"Your protest is noted, Jarriel." Kolovzon looked back at O'Brien, the slitted pupils suddenly fixed unblinkingly on the prisoner. "You're quite correct, it would be very difficult to judge the application of physical force correctly—as you say, one runs the risk of doing more hurt than one intends, and the prisoner has too much chance of incapacitating himself. However, I'm under no such restraints where Major Kira is concerned. You have a simple choice, Mr. O'Brien. You can either help repair *Helios*, or you can watch the Bajoran die, as slowly and as painfully as I can manage."

O'Brien stared back at him, momentarily silenced by the appalling clarity of his threat, and heard someone moving beyond the wall to his left.

"Chief, don't do it," Kira called. She sounded shaky, but otherwise none the worse for being stunned.

Kolovzon ignored her, still watching O'Brien. "Well, Chief?"

O'Brien swallowed hard, tasting bile. He had absolutely no doubt that the Trehanna meant exactly what he said, and there was no way he could stand by and watch Kolovzon torture Kira. "All right," he said, and heard himself sullen and reluctant. "All right."

Kolovzon nodded slowly. "You understand, of course, that any attempt to escape—any attempt to make any sort of trouble for my people—will be punished the same way."

O'Brien glared at him, but managed the expected response. "Yes."

"All right." Kolovzon gestured to Diaadul, who retreated smoothly from the doorway, easing a phaser out from under her shirt. "There's no time like the present to begin, is there? I will cut the forcefield, and you will come out without causing us any trouble."

"I've agreed to what you want," O'Brien said. "Isn't that enough?"

"I expect you to make it so," Kolovzon answered. He touched a control box mounted on the far wall—well out of reach from the cells, O'Brien noted, but maybe not completely out of the range of something heavy thrown through the gap in the forcefield's lattice—and the lines of purple light flickered once and disappeared.

O'Brien took a cautious step forward, and Kolovzon seized him by the shoulder, shoved him bodily toward the human male. O'Brien swung around, fists clenching automatically, and the human said, "I wouldn't."

O'Brien glanced at him, good sense reasserting itself, and Kolovzon said, "My chief engineer, Cytryn Jarriel."

O'Brien nodded, his eyes flicking over the stranger. He was thin, brown hair going grey at the sides, and there were heavy fatigue shadows under his eyes.

"Diaadul," Kolovzon said, and the woman nodded.

"The escort's laid on."

O'Brien sighed, almost imperceptibly—he had hoped that with only Jarriel to deal with, he might find some way to escape—and Jarriel said, "Come on."

O'Brien sighed again, and followed the other engineer out into the main corridor. As Diaadul had said, there were two men, one human or close, the other massive and unfamiliar, with thick blue skin mottled with indigo lumps like warts, each with a phase rifle clasped to his chest, waiting outside the heavy door. They fell into step behind O'Brien, who looked back once, and resigned himself to wait. There was nothing to do but follow Jarriel, try to memorize *Helios*'s layout, and hope for a change of luck.

He was reasonably familiar with the Klingon hull that *Helios* had been built from, but the modifications had been extensive, and it was hard to work out their route's relationship to the ships with which he was most familiar. He had been fairly certain that the detention cells were near the ship's outer surfaces—no one wasted the most protected spaces, at the core of the ship, on prisoners—and he guessed after a few minutes that they had turned into one of the major core-to-hull arteries. The bulkheads were marked with a dark yellow stripe, and when the corridor ended at a bank of turbolifts, O'Brien knew he had guessed correctly: the yellow stripe did mark the ventral corridor that ran from bridge to stern on most Klingon hulls. Knowing that, he could find his way to lifepods or transporters—if, of course, he could get away from his guards. And even if he could, there was still Kira to think about. His brief pleasure vanished, and he let himself be herded into the first turbolift.

"Engineering," Jarriel said, and the carrier lurched into motion.

O'Brien braced himself against the jerky movement, and looked at the other engineer with narrowed eyes. "You've taken a lot of damage."

The blue-skinned guard growled something, and Jarriel said, "Oh, shut up, Tess, anyone can tell that."

The guard subsided, rattling his weapon against his chest. Jarriel looked at O'Brien. "Yeah, we took some damage, O'Brien. And you better hope you can figure out how to repair it, or else the captain's going to leave DS9 short an engineer."

"Can't you handle it?" O'Brien asked, and achieved a sneer.

Jarriel smiled, lopsidedly. "Wait until you see it, *kurin,* then you tell me."

That did not sound promising. O'Brien looked away, watching the floor indicators flash past overhead. The little exchange had told him two things: first, the damage to *Helios* was more serious than even Dax had guessed, and, second, Jarriel was confident enough of his skills that he couldn't be drawn into doing something stupid. *At least, not by insulting his work,* O'Brien thought.

The turbolift slowed, then jerked abruptly to a stop. O'Brien stumbled sideways, unprepared for the sudden deceleration, and Jarriel caught him by the shoulder. The human guard sneered, but Jarriel said nothing, merely twisted the old-fashioned control to open the turbolift's door. They stepped out onto a catwalk perhaps halfway up the side of the massive engine space, and into a scene that made O'Brien catch his breath in shock. *Helios* had taken damage, all right, more damage than he'd seen on a starship since he'd left the *Enterprise.* Cables, bright-orange emergency couplings, glossy black temporary bindings, red and green builders' cables, and twists of multicolored wires that looked like nothing he'd ever seen wove through the open volume, bypassing damaged consoles and linking the surviving systems to each other. To the left, one entire monitoring panel was dark; beside it, another flashed wildly, readings just below the critical points. To the right, two other panels were mostly dark, a few warning lights flickering wanly along their screens. O'Brien swore under his breath, unable quite to believe what he was seeing. At least one of the reaction chambers was completely dead, two more had fallen below the restart minimums, and the fourth . . . O'Brien's eyes fixed on the flashing lights, the vertical indicators glowing red-orange and bobbing just below the warning line. The fourth was so close to critical that it would take only the slightest misjudgment from the technicians who hovered at that console to push it over the edge.

Even as he thought that, one of the technicians in that group—a woman, he realized abruptly, though she was so bundled in heavy coveralls that her sex was not immediately apparent—looked up and lifted a hand in greeting.

"Still holding, Chief, but I don't know how long. And the cloaking device is looking wonky again."

"Damn. Well, keep juggling, *kurin*, we've maybe got some help," Jarriel said, and smiled again at O'Brien. "We took a direct hit on the engine space, you see."

O'Brien nodded slowly, drawn in spite of himself to the problem in front of him. And Jarriel must be good, he thought, if he's kept the ship running this long, with this much damage. "You've lost, what, three reactor chambers?" he asked. "And you're losing control of the reaction on that one. Dump it, Jarriel, that's my advice."

Jarriel shook his head. "Sorry, that's not possible. Got another solution?"

"Not possible?" O'Brien stared at him. "You know as well as I do—if you're any kind of engineer, you know you can't keep that reactor running. It will overload, and then you'll not only lose the chamber, you'll destroy the entire ship."

And anything else in the near vicinity, he added silently. The thought was chilling—*How close are we to DS9, to Keiko?*—and he shook it away, made himself scowl at Jarriel. "I doubt your captain thinks it's worth the risk, Jarriel."

"You'd be surprised," Jarriel murmured. He said, more loudly, "I'll shut it down the minute someone shows me how I can get more power. If I had the parts *Carabas* was bringing us—bridging bars, replacement circuits—" He broke off, shaking his head. "Suffice it to say, this is what we've got. And I need all the power the system's putting out right now."

O'Brien looked around the devastated chamber, torn between fear and anger and a strange, furtive admiration for anyone who could keep this collection of junk and disasters running at all. "All right," he said, and knew he sounded less than certain. "Let's take a look at it, see what I can do."

It took him less than an hour to realize that Jarriel had done everything that he himself would have done—*except shut down that bloody reactor*—but he spun out his tour by another hour in the vague hope that it might somehow buy Sisko the time he needed to get him and Kira out of this situation. Jarriel followed him, silent except when O'Brien asked a technical question; the half-dozen technicians, all looking as worn as Jarriel himself, barely seemed to notice their presence. Finally, however, O'Brien had made his way from one end of the chamber to the other, and had checked the damaged reactors twice. He turned toward the console that monitored the dead reactor, and Jarriel said, "Well, O'Brien?"

O'Brien sighed, and looked back at him. "What the hell is a Starfleet engineer doing on this ship?"

Jarriel blinked once, startled and then gave one of his twisted smiles. "I was never Starfleet."

"That's Starfleet training, all of it." O'Brien gestured to the strung cables, and then to the monitoring stations opposite. "And it's Starfleet procedure to handle shutdown like that, not Klingon or Cardassian, and definitely not Federation merchant shipping. So, what made you join up with a bunch of pirates?"

"I never made it into Starfleet," Jarriel said. "For—various reasons. I learned the technique from an old drunk who used to be Starfleet: you might say the method was better than the source." He paused, shook his head. "And there's no point in stalling, O'Brien. What's your verdict?"

O'Brien hesitated. What would happen when he told the truth, or was he better off pretending there was something he could do, in hopes of immobilizing the ship until Sisko could make his move? It was an article of faith that Sisko would do something to rescue them. Then, slowly, he shook his head. Jarriel was good, too good to fool like that. "You're lucky this much of it still works, and I'm none too happy about that number-two reactor. There's nothing I can do that you haven't done. This lot won't be fixed short of dry dock—you could do patchwork, maybe, if you had the parts, but that's all."

"If," Jarriel echoed, and grinned. "Well, you don't see miracles every day." He nodded to the nearest guard, and turned to the intercom, touched a key code. "Captain, Jarriel here."

There was only a little wait before Kolovzon's voice crackled from the speaker. O'Brien could just make out the words, and strained to hear.

"So, Jarriel. What's the answer?"

"Pretty much what I told you," Jarriel answered, and O'Brien had to admire the offhand note in the engineer's voice. Kolovzon was not a man to whom he would care to tell bad news. "There's damn all we can do without the parts Möhrlein was bringing, and probably dry dock after that. And the number-two reactor is still barely subcritical."

"But it is within limits," Kolovzon said.

"Just barely," Jarriel answered. "And I'm not making promises."

O'Brien couldn't tell if the next noise was a hiss of annoyance or just static in the system. Kolovzon said, "All right, bring him to the bridge. And send Tesshan for the Bajoran. I want them both here at once."

"On our way," Jarriel answered. He nodded to the blue-skinned guard. "You heard the captain, Tess. Bring Major Kira to the bridge."

Tesshan nodded, and turned away. The ladders creaked audibly as he climbed back to the turbolift platform. Jarriel beckoned to the remaining guard. "Let's go."

By the time they'd reached *Helios*'s bridge, O'Brien was certain he understood the ship's basic layout. Which meant there was some hope of finding a transporter room or, better still, a lifeboat station—if only he could get away for long enough to look. And if he could bring Kira with him: he couldn't leave her behind, at Kolovzon's mercy, any more than she would leave him. But something was bound to happen. Someone, sometime, would get careless, and they'd have their chance; in the meantime, he would bide his time, and wait for an opening.

The bridge was surprisingly spacious, a crew of seven gathered in the forward section under Diaadul's watchful supervision, while Kolovzon stood in solitary splendor beside the plotting table that filled most of the aftercabin. The blue-skinned guard was there ahead of them, waiting deferentially at the edge of that space. Kira stood behind him, scowling, but her frown vanished for an instant when she saw O'Brien.

"Chief—" she began, and Tesshan nudged her with the barrel of his phaser rifle.

"Shut up, you."

Kolovzon turned his head as though he had only just

noticed their presence. "So, Jarriel. You're sure of this verdict, then?"

"Yes." Jarriel motioned for O'Brien to join Kira, and himself took his place beside the plotting table. "I told you I didn't think this would help."

"Ah." Kolovzon smiled, showing teeth, and O'Brien felt a chill run up his spine. He glanced at Kira, and saw his own wariness mirrored in her eyes.

"There you're wrong," Kolovzon went on, still smiling. "Our Number One did well to bring them aboard—to bring both of them, in fact." He stepped away from the table, and turned to face his prisoners. "You two are the currency that will buy back my missing parts. It's a very simple exchange."

"Sisko will never do it," Kira said, fiercely. "He's not going to bargain with you—"

Tesshan poked her sharply with the rifle barrel, and she broke off, glaring at the blue-skinned guard. Kolovzon said, "I do hope you're wrong, Major. But then, I have every reason to think he values your lives."

"He'll never do it," Kira said again, but she sounded less sure. Kolovzon ignored her, and stalked past them into the forward section.

O'Brien said nothing. There was nothing to say: Sisko couldn't agree to an exchange like that; even if it weren't against Starfleet policy, it would be impossible to agree to it without leaving DS9 perpetually vulnerable to the same tactics. Kira was staring after the Trehanna, an expression almost of pain on her mobile face, and O'Brien stared at her, willing her to hang on. Sisko wouldn't just leave them here, not without making some effort to rescue them, even if he couldn't agree to Kolovzon's bargain. All they had to do—all they could do—was wait, and be ready.

* * *

Sisko sat with Dax at the operations table, staring at the results of the latest in-depth sensor scan. Like the last one—like the last five—it showed no signs of the cloaked ship, not even the faintest tickle of a wave emission. It was as if the ship had vanished completely, and, in his worst fantasies, Sisko wondered if *Helios* had already fled the system, or, worse still, if it had somehow imploded, destroyed everyone and everything aboard. Both were unlikely, but the double vision had haunted him in his sleep, and he had been glad to return to Ops to face the real crisis.

"So there's nothing new," he said aloud, and Dax shook her head.

"I'm sorry, Benjamin. We're working on it, but we don't really have any options until we can locate *Helios* again."

"And not very many when we do," Sisko said, sourly. DS9 was in no position to fight—not only were both the station and the two runabouts outgunned by *Helios,* but Gul Dukat had contacted the station again to inform them that his government would construe any Federation attack on the pirate as unwarranted interference in Cardassian goals. For a moment, Sisko considered trying to get the Bajoran government to take temporary command of one of the runabouts—the Cardassians had said nothing about a Bajoran attack—but the runabouts were still outgunned, no matter whose markings they carried. "All right," he said aloud. "Our first priority has to be to get the hostages back. Is there any way we can transport them off again?"

Dax tipped her head to one side. "It's impossible at the moment, Benjamin. *Helios* is cloaked, and presumably will be shielded the minute she uncloaks—and in any case, Odo found both O'Brien's and Kira's communicators in the secondary monitoring station. Even if we were lucky enough to catch *Helios* with deflectors down and in transporter range, it would take us time, maybe as much as five or six minutes, to scan the ship and find our people, and even then I couldn't absolutely guarantee the accuracy of the scan."

Sisko nodded—it was no more than he'd expected—and looked down at the empty screen in front of him. "Can we do anything with the runabouts?" He was talking to himself as much as to Dax, and was not surprised when he didn't get an immediate answer. In any case, any attempt to rescue them from the runabouts would face the same problems: they would still have to find *Helios,* somehow get on board, and then escape.

"Sir!" a technician called, and in the same instant a proximity alarm sounded. "Sir, *Helios* is uncloaking!"

"Go to red alert," Sisko said, pushing himself away from the table. "Shields on full." He heard the instant acknowledgment, and the hoot of the alarm, but his eyes were on the main viewer, where *Helios* hung against the stars like a battered mountain. "Dax, scan them, see if you can find our people."

"Yes, sir," Dax said, but shook her head almost at once. "They're heavily shielded. Our scanners can't penetrate."

Sisko nodded. "Position?"

"They're just sitting there," Dax answered.

"Let me know the minute they start to move," Sisko said. "Maintain red alert." Was it possible that they were too badly damaged to attack? he wondered.

"Sir," the technician said again. "The pirate's hailing us."

"Ah." Sisko hadn't realized he'd spoken aloud. "Put it on the main viewer."

The screen clouded briefly, and cleared to reveal a broad-faced, broad-shouldered man—no, Sisko corrected himself, not a man, a Trehanna. The eyes, luminous blue, were slit-pupiled and slightly down-tilted; the mouth was wide, and curled into a faint, unpleasant smile. "Commander Sisko? I'm Demaree Kolovzon, master of *Helios.*"

Sisko nodded, wary. "I'm Sisko."

"You have some things that belong to me," Kolovzon went on. "But I'm prepared to make a deal."

"You are holding two of my officers," Sisko said. "Release them, and then we can discuss any deals that can be made."

Kolovzon shook his head, smile widening. "I'm afraid not, Commander. That is my trade, very simply. Return the parts I bought and paid for—you are interfering with commerce, Commander—and I will return your officers, unharmed. Refuse, and I will return them piece by bloody piece."

"If you harm them," Sisko began, and Kolovzon held up his hand,

"Attack, and I will kill them. I want that understood as well."

Sisko's lips tightened. He had no doubt that the Trehanna was more than capable of carrying out his threats—he had *Gift of Flight*'s destruction to prove it, if nothing else—but the thought of giving Kolovzon what he wanted, the parts that would let him continue his attacks on shipping, was equally impossible. "You should know, Kolovzon, that the Federation isn't the only factor involved here. There is a Cardassian battle fleet in the area, and it's very interested in your whereabouts. I would suggest that you return my people as quickly as possible, before the Cardassians arrive to make your life more difficult."

Kolovzon blinked, the luminous blue briefly hidden, and for a moment Sisko thought he had startled the pirate. Then Kolovzon's expression hardened again, and he shook his head. "I do hope it won't come to that, Sisko. This is Bajoran space, and I'm sure your Bajoran friends wouldn't want to see a Cardassian fleet trespassing." For an instant his voice was rich with mimicry, but steadied at once to his normal tone. "If they approach too closely, I will use your station as a screen."

"That—" Sisko broke off, but Kolovzon finished his protest for him.

"Yes, that would put your station at the center of any battle. And I assure you my first shots will be directed at your central core."

Sisko glared at the screen, mastered his rage with an effort. Unless he agreed to Kolovzon's terms, he would condemn O'Brien and Kira to a painful death—and, more than that, put the entire station and its largely Bajoran population at risk of complete destruction. His eyes slid for an instant to the weapons station, but there was no help to be found there. Even with the help of O'Brien's modifications, DS9 had no hope of standing up to the firepower on board *Helios*. "Very well," he said slowly. "I am prepared to beam the smugglers' cargo across to you, provided you transport one of my people first as an earnest of your good faith." He hadn't expected Kolovzon to agree, had hoped more to get the pirate to lower his shields so that Dax could find and rescue the hostages, and was not surprised when Kolovzon shook his head.

"I think not. Send *Carabas* out to meet us; I will transport the parts from her, and return your people the same way."

"Very well." Sisko took a deep breath, hating the concession, knowing that there was no chance at all of Kolovzon's keeping his end of the bargain. Still, a rendezvous might offer some opportunity of rescuing the hostages, and at least it kept *Helios* away from the station.

"Good," Kolovzon said. "I'm transmitting coordinates now; I'll expect to see *Carabas* at that point in exactly four hours. Kolovzon out."

The screen winked out. Sisko took another deep breath, biting back anger, and one of the technicians said, "Coordinates received, sir."

"All right," Sisko said. "Put them through to my office. Dax, get Odo, Bashir, and—who's handling O'Brien's job?"

"I am, Commander," a woman said, from the weapons console.

"And Carter," Sisko finished. "I want you all in my office immediately."

It didn't take long to assemble what was left of his staff. Looking around the little office, Sisko was all too aware of the missing faces, of the empty space where Kira usually sat, of Carter's thin face replacing O'Brien's. He put the thought aside, and turned his attention to the reports already filling his screen. "All right," he said, "let's begin at the beginning. Any luck tracking *Helios?*"

"*Helios* has not recloaked," Dax said, "which is good and bad news. We have a good fix on her, and a good sensor readout. The ship is shielded but we're picking up definite power fluctuations even through the shielding. That suggests that the damage is more extensive than we thought, which may explain why Kolovzon's willing to go to all this trouble to get his parts."

"And the bad news?" Sisko asked.

"The Cardassians have picked up *Helios*'s presence," Dax said, "if not the actual transmission. We're tracking their fleet, and at their present speed, they're only six hours from DS9. If they push things, Benjamin, they could be here in five."

Sisko nodded. He didn't need—none of them needed—to have the implications spelled out for them: if he wasn't able to rescue O'Brien and Kira and somehow deal with *Helios* in five hours, six at the outside, *Deep Space Nine* would find itself in the center of a space battle it could not win. "Carter, what's the status of O'Brien's modifications?"

The technician shrugged. "Everything is installed, Commander, and it will run, but the new system was never meant to do more than provide a temporary boost to the phasers."

Which wouldn't be enough, if DS9 was faced with a real battle rather than a hit-and-run encounter. Sisko sighed. And without O'Brien—Carter was better than competent, but she lacked the chief of operations' years of experience with balky machinery. Which left—what? They couldn't fight, and they couldn't give in to Kolovzon's demands. At least *Helios* was no longer cloaked; it was just a shame her shields were still intact. . . . Sisko frowned then, a plan slowly taking shape in his mind. "Dax—Carter. Have you managed to analyze that Trojan horse you found, the one that shut down our shields?"

Carter blinked, obviously taken aback. "I've got a clean copy in isolated storage—"

"I've run a preliminary study," Dax said, "but there hasn't been time to do anything more with it."

"Would it work on *Helios*'s systems?" Sisko asked.

Dax's eyes widened, and she reached for a datapadd. "As far as I can tell from our sensor readings, the way our systems interact with and interpret the systems on *Helios*, they're at least compatible."

"Pretty much anyone who can get them uses Federation computers," Carter said. "Or clones."

Odo said, grim-voiced, "The pirate will have had his pick of the looted ships."

"I agree," Sisko said. "Dax, Carter, I want you to pull that program, see if you can modify it so that we can use it against *Helios*. Odo—" He smiled in spite of himself, enjoying the irony. "—bring the smugglers to my office. I think I may have some work for them."

"Sir," the constable said, and turned to go.

"Commander," Bashir said.

Sisko looked at him in some surprise. He had almost forgotten that the younger man was there. "Yes, Doctor?"

"I'd like to go with you."

Sisko blinked. "Go with me—?"

"Yes, sir." Bashir fixed him with a firm stare. "Or whoever takes *Carabas* to the rendezvous."

Sisko swallowed his incredulous laughter, knowing it was born more of the tension of the moment than a legitimate response to the request. "You're needed here, Doctor, on the station. If this doesn't work—and I don't even have a definite plan yet—DS9 will be under attack, and it'll take every member of the medical staff just to perform first aid."

"If *Helios* attacks DS9," Bashir said, "there won't be enough survivors to need first aid. Sir." Sisko took a deep breath, readying a blistering reprimand, and the younger man plunged on. "On the other hand, one doctor on *Carabas* might make a great deal of difference, not just to individuals, but to the station's ultimate survival."

Sisko swallowed his retort, and admitted silently that Bashir was right about one thing. If *Helios* did attack the station, there probably wouldn't be many survivors, and those few would be too busy getting to the lifeboats to worry about medical treatment. "I suppose I follow your argument, Doctor, but that doesn't mean I agree with it." Bashir started to say something, and Sisko held up his hand. "I'll bear it in mind, Bashir. But no promises."

Bashir swallowed whatever else he would have said, protest or plea. "Thank you, Commander," he said, and left the office.

Odo returned to Ops in record time, the smugglers following docilely at his heels. He had taken no chances of their escaping, Sisko saw: a pair of security men had come with them, and despite Odo's misgivings about weapons, both men were visibly armed. "Bring them into my office," Sisko said, and returned to his desk while the group filed in. The two smugglers looked tired, but none the worse for their time in Odo's cells—*which is probably more than I can say about my people on* Helios, Sisko thought, and did his best to suppress his anger.

"Gentlemen," he said aloud. "You're in a position to do me a significant service."

The two exchanged wary glances, and Möhrlein said, in a voice that was far less confident than his words, "I'm glad to hear it. . . ."

Sisko ignored him. "Kolovzon wants your cargo very badly, to the point that he's kidnapped two of my officers in an attempt to get it. I'm impounding your ship, and its contents, to be used as I see fit to get my people back."

Again, the two smugglers exchanged a look, and Möhrlein said, "Commander, that ship is our livelihood."

"You're professional smugglers," Odo pointed out. "And you still have charges to face once this is over."

"We haven't been convicted," Tama said.

"Yet," Odo said.

"Gentlemen," Sisko said again. "Your guilt or innocence is for the courts to decide once this is over; right now, I'm more concerned about protecting this station."

Möhrlein said, "Am I right in thinking Kolovzon's set a rendezvous, for *Helios* and *Carabas?*"

Sisko nodded, wary again.

Möhrlein looked at Tama, who made a face, and nodded. Möhrlein looked back to Sisko, his handsome face setting into a determined mask. "If you're going to take *Carabas* out there, you're going to need our help. We've made a lot of modifications over the years; no one who isn't intimately familiar with them is going to be able to do more than keep the ship on course. And if you're going to get away after you've rescued your people—however you plan to do it, but you've got to be planning something—you're going to need to do some fancy flying."

Sisko looked at Odo. "You know these people, and their ship. Is this true?"

Odo nodded, mouth pursed as though he'd bitten into something sour. *"Carabas* is heavily modified. The Cardassians used to complain about it."

Sisko looked back at Möhrlein. "Even granting your point, why should I trust you, Mr. Möhrlein? Particularly when you were working with Kolovzon from the beginning."

"I didn't have a lot of choice," Möhrlein said. "I owed Kolovzon the ship, my ship—he had us dead to rights, with nowhere to run but back into Cardassian space, and the Cardassians aren't exactly fond of us. Demaree never forgets a favor owed him, and I want to be out from under the obligation. Besides, he'll kill us anyway: from his point of view, we lost him his cargo." He slanted another glance at Tama, seemed to receive some unspoken signal. "And we'd also hope that our cooperation now would be taken into consideration at our trial."

That made a great deal of sense, Sisko thought, at least if you looked at it from a professional's point of view. Cooperate now, and hope to bargain for a reduced or suspended sentence—and if half of what Odo said about their work for the Resistance was true, they might well get off with a minor sentence. He wasn't sure how he felt about the possibility. *But it hardly matters,* he thought. *Not if they can help us get O'Brien and Kira back safely.* It might not be fully justice, but at least it might save both his officers and his station. "You said you knew Kolovzon," he said. "What do you know about his ship?"

"We've been aboard it," Möhrlein said, cautiously. "Done some work on its systems, brought in parts and all."

Sisko bit back an exclamation of triumph. "Do you know where Kolovzon would hold prisoners?"

Tama gave a snort of laughter, and Möhrlein said, "Intimately."

"Could you indicate it on a plan?" Odo asked.

Möhrlein nodded. "The ship's a standard Klingon beta-class hull. The outer hull fittings have been extensively modified, but the interior has stayed pretty much as built—all the pressure bulkheads are in their original positions."

Sisko touched keys to access the library computer, called up the plans for the beta-class hull, and projected them onto a secondary screen. "Show me."

Möhrlein reached for a stylus, and, leaning forward, began to draw lines. Tama bent close, occasionally murmuring a correction, and finally took the stylus out of the taller man's hand and sketched a final series of curves along the main corridor. "That's pretty much it," he said, and set the stylus down. "Like Vilis said, they left the pressure bulkheads where they were."

Sisko nodded, studying the screen. If the smugglers were right—and there was little reason for them to lie, not facing either a good chance of death with the rest of the station, or at best trial on Bajor—then the cells lay along the starboard side, close against the hull. Which should mean, he thought, that we should be able to lock onto Kira and O'Brien without too much difficulty, with only a few levels of the hull to block our sensors. He touched the intercom. "Dax, would you come in here, please?"

The Trill appeared in the doorway almost at once, her beautiful face grave. "I'm afraid we haven't gotten any further on the Trojan horse, Benjamin. It's intact, and will function, but everything depends on whether or not it will run in *Helios*'s computers."

"We'll get to that in a minute," Sisko said. "For now, look at this." He pointed to the plan on his upfolded screen, and Dax leaned close to look at it. For a fleeting instant, Sisko was very aware of the faint, pleasant scent she wore—not at all like Curzon Dax, who had smelled more of a musky tea he had liked, and, at the end, of old age—and then she had leaned back again.

237

"This is *Helios?*" It was hardly a question, and she didn't wait for an answer. "If those are the cells—and if they're being held there—we could pick them out of there. Assuming, of course, we can persuade *Helios*'s computers to lower their shields."

"Nice to have it confirmed," Sisko murmured. "All right, Mr. Möhrlein, what can you tell me about *Helios*'s computer systems?"

Möhrlein opened his mouth to reply, then closed it, looked at Tama. "You tell them, Kerel."

Tama shrugged. "I've written software for them, and patched programs they took off of other ships. The basic hardware is Ferengi, but it runs Federation software—it's an older version of your operating system, maybe a couple versions back, I'm not sure."

"Would this Trojan horse, the program Diaadul used to disable our shields, would it function in *Helios*'s computers?" Dax asked.

There was an odd expression on Möhrlein's face, and again it was Tama who answered. "You'd have to rewrite it, but, yeah, with modifications, sure."

"Could you rewrite it?" Sisko asked.

Tama looked at Möhrlein, who shrugged. "Might as well tell him, mate."

"I wrote it," Tama said. "I can rewrite it."

Dax said, "I don't know, Commander. It would be quicker to let him do it, certainly, but I couldn't guarantee that the program would do what he promised. And I'm not sure that risk is worth taking."

Tama said, "Look, we're in no better shape than you are, stuck on this station waiting for Demaree Kolovzon—or the Cardassians—to blast us out of space—"

"And you're hoping to accumulate points for good behavior," Odo murmured.

"I don't deny it," Tama said. "But I wrote that program, I

know it inside and out—and you know it works, better than anything you could brew up in the same amount of time. I can rework it so that it'll run in *Helios*'s systems, I guarantee it. After that, it's up to you to figure out how to get it into the loop."

There was a note in the smuggler's voice, a sort of professional pride, that made Sisko nod. He looked at Dax, and saw the same agreement in her face.

"If he can do it," she said, "I know how to trick *Helios*'s computers into taking it in."

"Right, then," Sisko said. This was the best, maybe the only chance he was going to get to save both his officers and the station, and he intended to seize it with both hands. "How much time will it take to reach the rendezvous coordinates?"

"Fifty-six minutes at medium impulse power," Dax answered.

"Which leaves us little less than three hours," Sisko said. "Tama, you'll work with Lieutenant Dax. I want that program rewritten as quickly as possible. If we can insert that into the pirate's computers, there's a good chance that, even if Kolovzon doesn't keep his word, either you, Dax, or one of us on *Carabas* will be able to locate and rescue Kira and O'Brien."

"One of *us,* Commander?" Dax asked.

"That's right," Sisko said, and glared at her, daring her to say anything more. The Trill tilted her head to one side.

"Are you sure that's advisable, sir? One of us—"

"I want you to stay on DS9," Sisko said. "You're my science officer, you have the most experience with the sensor system here, and I will need your help to find our people." He smiled, and knew it went slightly awry. "Besides, who else could I send? Bashir?"

Dax smiled back in spite of herself. "All right, Benjamin, I—" She looked over her shoulder at the smugglers. "—we will get to work. But this is not going to be easy." She pushed herself to her feet, and beckoned to Tama. The smugglers, and Odo and the security men, followed her reluctantly out of the little office.

Sisko watched them go, the wry smile still twisting his face. It was a gamble, all right, and one of the biggest of his career, with the most at stake. If everything went right, he would save both his people and his station; if everything went wrong— He tried to shake the thought away, and failed. If everything went wrong, then the station would almost certainly be destroyed, and with it, his son, his fellow officers and friends, and hundreds of civilians whom he didn't even know. *So we can't fail,* he told himself sternly. *Or if we fail, it has to be* Carabas *that pays the price.*

CHAPTER
11

O'BRIEN LEANED AGAINST the wall that separated him from the cell that held Kira, and leaned forward so that he could feel the forcefield buzzing a centimeter from his skin, peering toward the entrance to the cell block. The blue-skinned guard was just visible through the armor-glass door, but there were no other guards in the block. *Of course,* O'Brien thought sourly, *that doesn't mean there isn't surveillance.* He looked around, scanning the junction of bulkheads and ceiling, and picked out at least two odd protrusions that probably contained cameras and recording equipment, but there were bound to be other devices hidden elsewhere. Not, he added silently, that there was much he could do about it if he found them.

Underfoot, the floorplates trembled, and a sound just at the edge of hearing rumbled through the compartment, a low groan like metal shifting against metal. O'Brien held his breath, listening for alarms, and in the next cell, Kira said, "What the hell was that?"

"I don't know," O'Brien said. "This ship's under a lot of strain, it could've been interior plates shifting." Or a structural member bending out of true, or— There was no point in imagining the worst, and he refused to think about the overworked reactor.

"It didn't sound good," Kira muttered.

O'Brien grunted his agreement, still listening to the faint sound of aftershocks crackling through the ship. Probably a structural member, he decided, after a moment. And as long as it doesn't bend more than a couple of degrees, *Helios* could still stand warp drive without coming apart at the seams.

"The repairs are probably starting to break down," he said aloud, as much for the comfort of hearing his own voice as to tell the Bajoran anything she didn't know. "Their engineer's good, but the ship's a mess."

"Does that mean Sisko might be able to take them?" Kira asked. "Damn, how long have we been here?"

O'Brien shrugged. Without his communicator, he had no access to the ship's chronometer, and there was no time display in the cell block. "Maybe three hours, maybe a little more."

"Which means the deadline is coming up," Kira said. "Damn it, Chief, we have to do something."

"Such as?" O'Brien asked. "I'm with you all the way, Major, but I don't see any way of getting out of these cells."

He heard footsteps, Kira moving restlessly around the perimeter of her prison, and then the dull thud as she kicked the shared wall. "All right," Kira said. "But we can't just sit here and wait to be rescued."

"I think we'd better do just that," O'Brien said. "Look, Major, I know this type of ship. The cell block is just inside the hull, there's only a thin skin between us and space."

"How reassuring," Kira said.

"The point is," O'Brien said, "there's only a meter or so

242

for the sensors to penetrate at this point. If they can figure out some way to get through the cloaking device—and the shape this ship is in, it wouldn't take much to overload the systems—they shouldn't have any trouble finding us to transport."

"We didn't have any luck breaking through the cloaking device before," Kira said.

She had put her finger with depressing accuracy on the weakest point of his plan, and O'Brien sighed. "I know. But I'm damned if I see any way to break through these forcefields." He turned as he spoke, running his eyes over the seamless bulkheads. The Klingons had built their cells to hold fellow Klingons, whose average body mass and strength was significantly greater than the average human being's. The walls were made of spun-and-fused carbon fiber; there was no sign of a check port, or anything that might give him even limited access to the control systems that must lie behind the dull grey surface.

"Do you think Sisko will agree to the trade?" Kira asked, after a moment.

"I don't see how he can," O'Brien answered. "He'll do something, I'm sure of that, but give up those parts in a straight exchange—I don't see how he can."

There was a little silence then, and then the sound of Kira's footsteps moving moodily around the edges of her cell. O'Brien leaned against the shared bulkhead, staring into the purple lattice of the forcefield until it left a green network across his vision. No, there was no way Sisko could agree to the trade. All he and Kira could do was wait, have faith, and be ready for anything.

Sisko stood at the head of the lock that led into docking port five, Dax at his side. Behind him, in the short tunnel that was the extended lock, the two smugglers completed their preflight preparations under the watchful eye of Odo and a pair of his deputies. Sisko made a final note on the padd, then scrawled his name across the gleaming screen.

"I'm leaving you in command, Dax," he said, though they both knew that was the only possibility. "Your highest priority is the protection of the station—and if that means abandoning, or even sacrificing, *Carabas,* I expect you to do just that."

"If it comes to that, Benjamin," Dax said, her beautiful face absolutely serious, "you know I will. But I trust it won't."

"I hope not, too," Sisko said, with a sudden grin. "In fact, I'm betting on it."

"Commander!" That was Odo's voice, and Sisko turned, to see the constable standing in the open hatch. "Möhrlein reports that everything's ready for launch."

"All right," Sisko said and turned back to Dax. "This is it, then, old friend. Take care of the station for me."

"You know I will, Benjamin," Dax said softly.

Sisko nodded, and held out the datapadd. Dax took it, glanced at the words that filled the screen, and held out her hand.

"I have command, sir." Her voice was suddenly formal.

"Carry on, then, Lieutenant," Sisko answered, his own voice equally formal—there was nothing he could say, nothing that would be equal to the moment; it was better to take refuge in the familiar Starfleet formulae—and turned toward *Carabas.*

"Commander."

The new voice stopped him in his tracks, and he turned back to see Bashir standing in the lock, medical kit in his hands.

"Commander, I wondered if you had a ruling on my earlier request."

Sisko hesitated for a moment, weighing the odds. To take

PROUD HELIOS

Bashir was to deprive the station of its chief medical officer, but it was also to add another Starfleet officer to his team, when he was already desperately short of people. And Bashir had Starfleet computer training, something else he could use, if they had to install Tama's virus. And if either Kira or O'Brien was injured . . . There were other doctors on DS9. He nodded, slowly. "All right, Doctor, come aboard."

"Thank you, sir." Bashir stepped past Dax, visibly struggling to control his smile, and Sisko gestured for him to precede him into the ship.

Carabas was small even by merchant small-ships standards, the main fore-and-aft corridor barely wide enough for two people to walk abreast. The control room was cramped, the twin control stations tucked forward under a main screen that followed the curve of the ship's nose. Möhrlein was already settled in front of the port-side console, his hands busy with the old-fashioned controls. Tama was seated at a secondary station directly behind Möhrlein—ship's computer and sensors, Sisko thought, from the arrangement of the screens and the patterns drifting across their dull surfaces—and there was a bank of four passenger couches in the center of the room, arranged around a tabletop control-and-display console. Odo and Bashir were already seated there, Bashir with his medical kit open between his feet, head down over its contents. A tiny transporter station filled the remaining space, crammed into the corner opposite Tama's position, its console and control boxes spilling over into the passenger space. The security men were nowhere in sight. Sisko frowned, looked at Odo, and the constable said, "I sent my deputies to check out the rest of the ship, to make sure there aren't any unpleasant surprises."

Sisko nodded, and took his place at the starboard console.

Möhrlein said, without looking up from his controls, "It'd be better if you left them on the station, Commander. We're going to be pushing my life-support systems as it is."

"With only seven people aboard?" Sisko asked.

Möhrlein shrugged. "We don't usually carry passengers."

It made sense, and Sisko nodded. "When your people report in, Odo, send them ashore."

"Sir," Odo said, and an instant later, a voice sounded softly from his communicator. "All right," he said. "Take Arvan and go back to the station." He waited for an acknowledgment, and looked at Sisko. "My deputies report that everything's in order."

"Good," Sisko said. "Möhrlein, how long before we can launch?"

"As soon as your people are off my ship," the smuggler said, and as if in response, a light flared red and then green on his screen.

"Hatch is sealed," Tama announced. "And the lock's resealed, too. All systems show the launch area is clear."

Möhrlein looked at Sisko. "We're ready when you are, Commander."

Sisko looked at the chronometer display already flashing on his screen: in exactly one hour, Carabas had to be at the rendezvous point. "Launch," he said, and Möhrlein echoed him instantly.

"Launching now."

Carabas lifted smoothly from the docking port, internal gravity taking over without the lurch Sisko had come to expect from small ships' systems. It swung low over the station's docking ring, and pivoted onto the heading that would take them out to the rendezvous point in the required time. Sisko watched the silver-grey skin of the station slide past in the viewscreen, and a screen unfolded from the console in front of him.

"Incoming communications," Tama said, from his station, and the screen lit and windowed, displaying Dax's face.

"DS9 to *Carabas.*"

Sisko reached for the communications tablet, found the response button after only a moment's search. "Sisko here. Go ahead, Dax."

"*Helios* has spotted your launch," Dax said. "She's moving toward the rendezvous point at minimum impulse. She should be there when you arrive."

"And the Cardassians?"

"They'll be in phaser range in three hours," Dax answered.

"Thanks, Dax," Sisko said. "Keep us informed of any changes. Sisko out."

The communications screen went blank, and folded itself back into the console. Sisko watched it go without really seeing it, his attention focused on Möhrlein at *Carabas*'s main controls. The ship did handle oddly, Möhrlein's hands and fingers in nearly constant motion across the double-banked consoles, and the impulse engines hummed like a musical instrument, their singing note varying in pitch and intensity as the output shifted fractionally with each change of setting. The pilot's display was overlaid with a series of gravity marks, and a set of fluctuating grids that seemed to indicate relative time-and-distance; the latter, like the other controls, seemed to vary constantly within fairly wide limits, but, after a while, Sisko began to understand how the systems interacted. *I could do it if I had to,* he thought, *but it wouldn't be easy. It's just as well Möhrlein agreed to come along.*

"How do you manage in warp drive?" he asked. "You must have some kind of autopilot."

Möhrlein shook his head. "We switch to a different control set in warp. It's much more stable—it was just under impulse that we needed this precise a control."

That made sense, at least for a smuggler, Sisko acknowledged. They would need to be able to slip into a system, into orbit, even down onto a planet, without being detected by local sensors, or at least without being spotted until they wanted to be.

"Vilis," Tama said, from his station at the rear of the compartment. *"Helios* is coming into view."

"Put it on the screen," Sisko said.

There was a pause, no more than a fraction of a second, and Tama obeyed. The pirate ship hung at the center of the screen, tiny in the distance, its hull white against the stars. "We'll be in transporter range in ten minutes," Tama said. "At the rendezvous in fifteen."

Sisko nodded, watching as the tiny shape grew steadily larger, took on angles and harsh shadows. The hull showed more carbon scoring than he had noticed in its attack on the station, and in places the plates of the outer hull had been peeled back like the skin of an orange. He saw again the damaged weapons turret, attached only by a single metal strut; saw beyond that a long line of dull grey where the hull surface had been burned away. That streak—almost certainly from a phaser bolt that had penetrated *Helios*'s shields—ended in a blasted crater that might once have held a sensor pod. Now its edges were curled outward like the petals of a flower, blown into that shape by an internal explosion, and Sisko could see winking lights deep in the hole, where a temporary shield was in place to hold the broken hull plates. *Helios* had suffered appalling damage— it was astonishing that she was still spaceworthy, much less still underway and apparently ready to fight, and Sisko was conscious of a sneaking admiration for anyone who could get that ship this far into Federation space. He killed the thought—this was the ship that had destroyed the *Gift of Flight*—and looked at Möhrlein.

"Are you ready to transport your cargo?"

"As ready as we'll ever be," Möhrlein answered. "There's no transporter in the hold, we'll have to move it up here to send it across. Don't worry, we've got antigravs and sleds, but I'll need help moving it."

Sisko nodded. "That we can provide."

"We're at the rendezvous coordinates," Tama announced.

"Right," Sisko said, as much to himself as to the others, and then, more loudly, "Open a channel to the pirate."

"Hailing now," Tama answered. The impulse engines powered down, and there was a little silence, so profound that Sisko could hear the others' breathing mixed with the faint hiss of the ventilators.

"Helios is answering," Tama said at last, and the communications screen unfolded itself from Sisko's console. Kolovzon's image looked out of it, the broad face set still into a faint smile.

"So, *Carabas.* And Commander Sisko. You're very timely."

"We're prepared to transport your cargo," Sisko said, flatly. "Once you return my people."

"I think not, Commander," Kolovzon said. "Transport the cargo first."

Sisko shook his head. "No. I've no proof that they're still alive."

Kolovzon's smile widened briefly. "True enough. Transport half the cargo, I'll send you your Major Kira. Then you send me the rest of my cargo, and I'll return your engineer. I think that's a fair bargain."

Hardly, Sisko thought, *but I think it's the best I'm likely to get. And with the Cardassians on the way, I don't have time to push you.* He said, "It'll take us some time to get the cargo to our transporter—"

"About ten minutes," Möhrlein said, softly.

"—about ten minutes before you'll receive your first load," Sisko finished.

"Agreed," Kolovzon said. "Inform me when you're ready to transport. In the meantime—" He showed teeth suddenly, in a smile that lacked all humor or goodwill. "In the meantime, I'll bring your people to the transporter room. My officers have orders to kill them first, if anything— untoward—comes aboard. *Helios* out."

The communications screen folded itself neatly back into the console, and Sisko swung around to face his crew. "All right. Odo, Bashir, Tama, start getting the cargo up here so that we can begin transporting it across."

"Yes, sir," Bashir said, and levered himself up out of his couch.

Odo copied him more slowly, and said, "Commander, I doubt we can trust Kolovzon. I'd like to transport across— disguised as part of the cargo, of course. I may be able to help free our people."

"Not on, mate," Möhrlein said, before Sisko could answer. "They scan everything as it comes aboard. You'd be picked up as organic—or at least not what you're supposed to be—the minute you showed up on the platform."

"It's not worth the risk," Sisko said. "Get the cargo up here. We'll get Major Kira back, and then see what we can do."

O'Brien heard the first sound of footsteps outside the cell-block door, and looked up sharply. In the next cell, Kira swore to herself, a Bajoran obscenity that the engineer didn't recognize, and then he heard her feet move closer to the front of her cell.

"It must be time," she said, and her voice was absolutely steady.

"Must be," O'Brien agreed, and moved to join her. He had to admire her even as he envied her calm—and even as he knew that she would be just as tense as he beneath the outward display. *You'd have to be subnormal not to be afraid; the brave ones are the ones who don't let it affect their actions.* He took a deep breath as the outer door slid open, bracing himself for instant action, for anything, and held himself ready as Diaadul walked into the corridor that ran beside the cells.

"You're lucky today," the Trehanna said, bluntly. "Your commander values you."

O'Brien snorted in spite of himself, and heard Kira mutter something under her breath. Whatever else was going on, it wasn't like Sisko to give in without a fight. Oh, the commander might try something devious, but he wouldn't just give in. Diaadul smiled thinly, as if she'd read the thought.

"Commander Sisko has agreed to exchange the first half of our cargo for you, Major, and the second for the engineer." She lifted a hand—she still wore the bangles she had worn on the station, and they fell with a musical clashing down from her wrist—to beckon the guards who waited in the doorway. "I'm under orders to bring you to the transporter room for the exchange. However, I'm under no orders to transport you conscious, so any trouble, and I'll have you stunned and carried down. Do you understand?"

She is, O'Brien thought, *extremely efficient—something I'd respect, in other circumstances.* "I understand," he said, and heard Kira echo him.

Diaadul's efficiency did not slip as she brought them under guard to the main transporter room. The compartment was crowded, three crew members in work clothes and carrying grav-haulers standing by the platform, while a group of four stood by with drawn phasers. Jarriel, looking more tired than ever, stood at the controls. Diaadul motioned O'Brien and Kira into the most distant corner, their guards still following, and nodded to Jarriel.

"Everything set, Cytryn?"

"I'm ready, anyway," Jarriel answered.

"That should be enough," Diaadul said, and stepped to the intercom. "Bridge, this is Number One. We're ready to transport."

"Shields are down," a voice answered. "Ready to receive, *Carabas*."

"Receiving," Jarriel said.

His voice was almost drowned in the familiar whine of the transporter. The beam filled the chamber, and then the first of the cargo crates coalesced in its field. A fraction of a second later, three more appeared: that would be the limit of *Carabas*'s transporter system, O'Brien thought, and wondered if there was any way he, or Sisko, could take advantage of that.

"That's the start," Jarriel said, as the beam faded again. "Come on, *kurini*, clear the pad for the next load."

His technicians leaped to obey, grav-handlers ready, and tugged the crates off the pad. Two of them, straining even with the help of the handling devices, edged the crates toward the waiting sled; the third turned back toward the platform.

"Ready to receive," Jarriel said again, and the transporter whined.

Four more crates appeared, and his technicians leaped to shift them. O'Brien eyed the crates as they piled up on the sled, and wondered if they could possibly contain enough material to do more than provide a temporary repair. At his side, Kira said, "He can't do this—Sisko, I mean. He can't give in to them."

Another batch of four crates appeared as she spoke, and the sweating technicians leaped to pull them away, clearing the pad for the next shipment. O'Brien said, into the burst of activity, "You might try trusting him, Major." He didn't dare say more, even with the noise to cover him, but Kira gave him a sudden sharp glance.

"All right," Diaadul said. "You, Kira. Onto the platform."

"What about O'Brien?" Kira asked. She didn't move, and Diaadul made a face of disgust.

"He'll be sent across as soon as we receive the last of the cargo. So the soonest you move, the soonest you'll both be back on your station." Her face hardened. "Move, Kira."

Reluctantly, the Bajoran did as she was told. She took her place on the pad, eyes darting once from side to side as though she was looking for a way out, but the guards still had phaser rifles fixed on her and on O'Brien. She subsided, slowly, her face a mask.

"Coordinates locked in," Jarriel said. "Energizing." His hand moved on the archaic slide controls, and the transporter whined again. Kira seemed to dissolve into a glittering shadow, and then into nothing, and O'Brien let out the breath he had been holding. He was alone on *Helios*.

"The rest of the cargo's on its way," a voice said from the intercom, and Jarriel bent to adjust his settings. O'Brien shook himself as the cargo exchange resumed. If the pirates kept their word—*a big if*, he admitted, wryly, *but not completely impossible*—he would be on *Carabas* and back on DS9 within a few hours. If they didn't—well, without Kira to worry about, he had more options. Kolovzon could no longer use her against him, and it was easier for a single individual to seize a chance, to parlay a moment's inattention into an opening for an escape . . .

"*Carabas* says that's the last of it," the voice on the intercom said.

O'Brien took a deep breath, and a single step forward, bracing himself for the worst.

"Sorry," Diaadul said. She looked at Jarriel. "Captain's

orders, Cytryn. The engineer's to stay on board until we get the repairs done—and the more he helps, the faster it'll be over."

"That's crazy, Diaa," Jarriel said. "We've got enough trouble with Starfleet, we don't need more."

The Trehanna shrugged, her bracelets clashing as she reholstered her phaser. "Take it up with the captain if you've got a problem, Cytryn. It's his direct order—his idea, not mine."

Jarriel swore under his breath, but returned his attention to the transporter console. O'Brien watched him go through the familiar motions, powering down the system, concentrating on that until he had his own anger under control. He should've known better than to expect anything but a doublecross from *Helios* and her crew—and if he had known it, so would have Sisko. He would wait, and see what happened. And if nothing presented itself, he promised silently, he would make his own opportunity.

"No response from the sender," Möhrlein said.

"I'm not picking up any trace of Chief O'Brien," Bashir began, from his place at the transporter controls, and then Tama leaned back in his chair, swearing.

"Deflectors are up again," he announced. "I can't get through."

"Damn!" Kira pounded her fists on the side of the transporter console, narrowly missing Bashir's fingers. "I told you you should've sent me back—with a phaser, with a grenade, I could've gotten him out!"

"The hell you could," Sisko said. Despite his words, his tone was fairly calm, and Kira gave him an incredulous look. "Major, I don't have time for this. There is a Cardassian fleet less than two hours from the station, and we have to free O'Brien before it gets within battle range."

Kira blinked. "Cardassian fleet? What the hell are they doing in Bajoran space?"

"In hot pursuit, apparently," Odo said.

"That's ridiculous," Kira snapped.

"I quite agree," Sisko said. "Unfortunately, I'm not in a position to do anything about it until O'Brien is safe aboard. So, Major, if you'd be so kind—?" He gestured to the console at the back of the compartment, where the long-haired smuggler was already bending over a new set of controls.

Kira frowned. "I'm—sorry, sir. But I don't see what I can do?"

"The pirates used a Trojan horse to lower our shields so that they could beam you and Chief O'Brien off the station," Bashir said. He pulled an optical chip from the transporter's data storage block. "Dax thinks that Tama there can return the favor."

"If that meets with your approval, Major," Sisko said.

Kira bit back her angry response, aware that she had deserved the reprimand. "Sir," she said, and moved to join Tama. The smuggler edged sideways without glancing up, and she stared at the complicated image spread out on his double screen. In the left-hand screen, *Helios* hung at the center of a web that she recognized as a schematic representation of its shields and sensor pattern; the right hand screen showed the same image, but in this one a blue triangle appeared and disappeared apparently at random in the spherical web.

"That's the scan window," Tama said. "I've been trying to come up with a pattern, but it seems to be genuinely random."

"What about your Trojan horse?" Odo asked.

"I'm still looking for an opening," Tama answered.

"Commander," Bashir broke in. "Transmission from the station."

"Put in on my viewer." Sisko swung to face the communications screen as it unfolded. Kira glanced over her shoulder to see Dax's face taking shape in the little display.

"I'm afraid it's bad news, Ben," Dax said without preamble.

Kira couldn't see Sisko's face, but the commander's voice was even more expressionless when he answered. "Go ahead."

"The Cardassian fleet has gone to its top speed," Dax said. "They'll be in battle range in one hour."

"All right," Sisko said, after a barely perceptible pause. "Keep tracking them, Dax, and inform me the minute they enter this system. Sisko out." He turned back to face the others, his face smoothing to something like his usual expression, but not before Kira had caught a glimpse of the anger and determination that was hidden below the surface calm. "Now. Let's get that program installed."

O'Brien hauled himself out of the tube that gave access to the interior of the cloaking device, and stood, brushing shards of glass-like fused fiber from his gloves and uniform. Jarriel did the same, and stood picking pieces of bloodied fiber out of a rip in his left glove. O'Brien watched him without sympathy, and said, "That's beyond repair, and I think you know it."

For a moment, he thought Jarriel wasn't going to answer, but then the other engineer said, "The projector took serious damage, and we couldn't risk shutting it down. When it finally blew, the explosion flashed back into the main compartment. Two of my techs were killed."

That would explain it, O'Brien thought, and swallowed hard, tasting bile. He looked back over his shoulder at the access tube. The air smelled faintly of burned components, and other, less pleasant things; the smell had been worse in the crawl space, and the thick walls still held the heat of the flash fire. The circuits were mostly gone, or so charred as to be useless. It would take a fully equipped dry dock a month and a few dozen square meters of the millimetrically calibrated replacement boards even to begin to repair the damage. The floorplates below the mouth of the tube glittered with shards of fused fiber, like a rain of rainbow-colored ice.

"Well, Jarriel?"

That was Kolovzon's voice, and O'Brien turned slowly, hiding his hatred of the Trehanna. The captain was flanked by a phaser-wielding guard, and O'Brien made himself relax. This was not the time, not yet. . . .

"How are the repairs going?"

Jarriel shrugged, his thin face for once unguarded, revealing his exhaustion.

"We need the cloaking device," Kolovzon said. "And we need it now." He waved his escort away, out of earshot, and O'Brien tensed, judging distances and angles. *No, not yet,* he told himself, *wait for it.* . . . Kolovzon went on, in a lowered voice, "Gul Dukat's fleet is moving in. He'll be in range to open fire in an hour."

O'Brien laughed in spite of himself, and Jarriel gave him a quick, warning glance. O'Brien ignored him, said, "You should've expected that, Captain." He gave the title an unpleasant emphasis, and was glad to see Kolovzon frown. "You didn't think they were just going to let you walk away, did you? Not the Cardassians. And by God I think I've finally met people who deserve what the Cardassians will do to them."

"Let me remind you," Kolovzon said, through clenched teeth, "that your precious *Deep Space Nine* is in the middle of the battle zone." He took a deep breath, and continued in his usual tone, "So, the sooner you and Jarriel get these repairs done—particularly the cloaking device—the sooner all danger to your station and your family will be ended."

"That piece of junk won't be fixed short of dry dock," O'Brien said, and gestured to the access tube. "If then. So if I were you, Kolovzon, I'd start running now. That's your only chance."

"You will fix it," Kolovzon said, and O'Brien laughed.

"Not me, Kolovzon. And not anybody on this ship."

Kolovzon reached beneath his tunic, came up with a small and vicious-looking phaser. He pointed it at O'Brien's head, then, slowly and deliberately, lowered his aim until it was centered on the engineer's gut. "This is a very adjustable weapon," he said, almost conversationally. "And even these days, a belly wound can be a slow and very painful way to die. Particularly if you don't get medical attention quickly, or at all. It would be a shame, with so many miracles being worked by the Federation's doctors, to die this way barely a stone's throw from help."

O'Brien held his ground, suddenly aware that he'd gone too far. He took a slow breath, searching for words that might help him out of this situation, and Kolovzon gestured with the phaser to the mouth of the access tube. "Now, get to work."

"I can't fix it," O'Brien said. "It can't be fixed."

Kolovzon's hand tightened on the phaser, and O'Brien braced himself for the searing pain. Then Jarriel stepped between them, blocking Kolovzon's shot. The Trehanna snarled wordlessly, and Jarriel said, "Demaree. I told you myself it could not be repaired."

There was a little silence, O'Brien holding his breath, and then Kolovzon relaxed slightly. Jarriel said, "We'll concentrate on the things that can be mended."

Kolovzon nodded, reluctantly, his great eyes still fixed on O'Brien. "All right," he said, through clenched teeth. "All right. For now."

O'Brien watched him walk away, aware that his own hands were shaking. He folded his arms to hide the trembling, said, in a voice that he barely recognized as his own, "So, is it true about the Cardassians?"

"Oh, it's true," Jarriel said, grimly. "But that's the least of your worries, *kurin.*"

O'Brien ignored him, mind racing. If the Cardassians were on their way in force—and Gul Dukat would do nothing less—then DS9 was in mortal danger. Dukat would like nothing better than an excuse to destroy the station, the only Federation presence in the area, and even if Kolovzon kept his word and moved away from his current position, it was more than likely that Dukat would take the excuse to fire on the poorly defended station. O'Brien sighed. He had no illusions about his own chances, had known from the minute he'd awakened in *Helios*'s cells that his chances of survival were small indeed. But the station—and Keiko and Molly . . . It would be worth the loss of his own life if he could somehow save them. And if that meant helping Jarriel repair this ship, so that it could meet the Cardassians on a more even footing . . . so be it. O'Brien nodded to himself, mind made up at last. "All right, Jarriel," he said. "Let's see what we can do with your engines."

Bashir frowned at the chains of numbers filling his screen, flickering past in an ever-changing sequence. They came tantalizingly close to forming a recognizable pattern, something that he had seen before, in training . . . Kira leaned close above him, but he was barely aware of her presence, so caught up was he in the evolving sequence. He *had* seen this pattern before, at the Academy, on one of the older machines, and in that instant he was sure he knew where the break would come.

"I've got it," he said aloud, and stabbed at the membrane, freezing the pattern at its most vulnerable point. "There."

Tama grunted agreement, hunched over his own keyboard, his fingers flying as he adjusted *Carabas*'s computers to transmit the Trojan horse to *Helios*'s sensors. If he had calculated right, Bashir knew, the pirate would accept the program as one more piece of data, brought in through the constantly shifting sensor windows that pierced the deflectors. If he was wrong— It didn't bear thinking about.

"We're queued," Tama said.

"Stand by," Bashir said, his full attention fixed on the screen in front of him. "The window will open—now."

"Transmitting," Tama said.

Bashir held his breath. His memory was good, and this particular pattern had nearly beaten him, back at the Academy, it should have been burned into his memory as a result—but he could have gotten it wrong. He pushed aside that unworthy thought—he knew how good his memory was, just short of eidetic—but it took all his strength of will not to drum his fingers on the edge of the console.

"Well?" Kira demanded.

"Still transmitting," Tama answered. "No, they've taken it. They've accepted the program."

Bashir grinned, and Sisko said, "Well done, Doctor. You have unexpected talents."

"Yes," Kira said, and tapped him on the shoulder. "I thought you were a doctor, not a hacker."

Bashir nodded, but his pleasure faded quickly. "So what do we do now, Commander?"

"We wait for them to try to use their shields," Sisko said. "Assuming the program works, you and Tama will find O'Brien and transport him aboard. Then we return to the station."

"Always assuming *Helios* doesn't decide to stop us," Möhrlein muttered.

Sisko glanced at him. "I think they'll have other things to worry about, Möhrlein."

"As may we," Odo said. He sounded, Bashir thought, almost as though he relished the prospect.

"The Cardassians," Sisko began, and a tone sounded from his console. The communications screen unfolded, and Dax's face appeared in its center.

"Dax to *Carabas*."

Sisko swung back to face the screen. "Sisko here."

"Sir, the Cardassian fleet is coming into phaser range now."

"Damn." Sisko glared at the screen. "Warn them off, Dax. Remind them that this is Bajoran space, under Federation protection, and they've no right to interfere."

"Shall I tell them we still have people on board *Helios?*" the Trill asked.

"Try it," Sisko said. "If Dukat doesn't respond, take DS9 to battle stations and put up all the deflectors. Don't fire unless you're attacked first, but if you're fired on, you have my full permission to retaliate as you see fit."

"Yes, sir," Dax said reluctantly. "Benjamin, if we raise the shields, there's nothing we can do to protect *Carabas*— we won't even be able to take her into the docking rings once the outer deflectors are in place."

"I know that, Dax," Sisko said. For an instant, Bashir thought, it was as though there were no other people in *Carabas*'s cabin, or in Ops, as though the two old friends spoke only to each other. "But the station comes first. *Deep Space Nine* and the people aboard are to be protected at any cost—and that includes *Carabas*, Dax. You know that."

"I do," Dax said, quite softly. She held Sisko's gaze for a moment longer, then dipped her head in acknowledgment. "Very good, Commander. I'll attempt to warn off the Cardassian fleet, and go to red alert if Dukat doesn't respond."

"Thank you, Dax," Sisko said. *"Carabas* out." He looked around the crowded cabin, gathering his people with his eyes. "All right. If everything goes to plan, *Helios* should be trying to raise her shields at any moment. And that is our only chance to rescue O'Brien. Kira, man the transporter. Beam him away the second you lock on. Bashir, Tama, keep scanning the pirate—try the cells and the engineering sections first, but keep looking. Bashir, you know what to look for."

Bashir nodded, his mouth suddenly, embarrassingly, dry. He had brought O'Brien's latest medical scan, had already set the sensors to scan for that pattern, but now at the moment of truth he was abruptly uncertain of himself. Suppose he'd gotten it wrong—suppose he'd set *Carabas*'s sensors badly, or failed to produce a workable dataset out of the incredible detail of the medical scan? For God's sake, he was a doctor—and a Starfleet officer, he reminded himself firmly, and touched his communicator lightly for the reassurance. He was a Starfleet officer, and he had done his best. That was all he could do. He saw Tama looking at him, a wry smile twisting his wide mouth, and somehow summoned a smile of his own in response.

"The Cardassian fleet is in range of the station," Möhrlein reported. "The station is hailing them."

"Can you pick it up?" Sisko asked.

"No, it's tight-beamed," the smuggler answered. "There's no response from the flagship."

"Keep me informed," Sisko said.

CHAPTER
12

"THE CARDASSIANS are still moving in," Möhrlein reported. "I count three, no, four, ships. Two frigates and a heavy cruiser; the fourth's a scout, and she's falling behind."

"Range?" Sisko asked.

"Coming up on phaser range," Möhrlein answered.

Sisko nodded, watching the viewscreen. The Cardassian ships were just visible at standard magnification, sleek bright shapes moving fast against the stars. By comparison, *Helios* looked battered and ungainly, Leviathan turning at bay to face a pack of wolves.

"The lead frigate is in phaser range now," Möhrlein reported.

"*Helios* is trying to boost its shields," Tama announced, and gave a whoop of glee. "And the deflectors are down. It worked, damn it."

"Get on it, Bashir," Sisko ordered. "Find O'Brien and lock on."

The young man didn't answer, bent close over his console,

his face drawn in fierce concentration. Patterns and symbols flickered in his screen, but he ignored them, searching for a single life-form among the pirate's crew. "Nothing in the cells," he said, after a moment.

"Try engineering," Sisko said.

"Sir." Bashir touched his controls, adjusting the scanners' focus. "Nothing so far—and I'm getting interference."

"They're trying to raise their deflectors," Tama said.

"How long?" Sisko asked.

"Maybe another two minutes, maybe three," Tama answered.

"The lead frigate has gone to battle status," Möhrlein said. "I don't think we've got three minutes."

"Bashir?" Sisko asked.

"Still nothing," the doctor answered. "No, wait, I'm picking up something, it might be him—" His voice trailed off as he bent over the controls, as though he could feel O'Brien's presence in the warmth of the membrane board beneath his fingers.

"Open a channel to the flagship," Sisko ordered. "Try the cruiser first."

"The channel's open," Möhrlein answered, "but I'm not getting an acknowledgment."

Sisko ignored him, fixed his eyes on the communications screen as it unfolded for him. There was almost no chance that Gul Dukat would pay attention to his protest, or even respond, but anything that could delay their attack, even by seconds, might give them a chance to save O'Brien. "Gul Dukat," he said aloud, and did his best to project a threat he could not easily muster, a sense of the Federation's power waiting to back up his words. "This is Commander Sisko. I warn you, you are trespassing in Bajoran space. I suggest that you turn back at once to Cardassian territory." He paused, waiting for a response or for some further inspiration to strike, but the screen remained obstinately blank, as though he were talking to a mirror. "Sisko out."

"No answer," Möhrlein said, softly.

Bashir swept the sensors across the ship once again, beams probing for the one particular pattern that would be O'Brien. For a long moment there was nothing, just the wavering multicolored static, and then the screen strobed, the numbers leaping out at him. "I think I've got him," Bashir said, and touched keys to lock the fix. "Yes, I'm sure of it." He swung in his couch, eyes wild. "Kira, I'm passing the coordinates—"

"Got them," Kira answered. Her hands danced over the pad. "Damn it, Bashir, I'm losing him, can't you give me anything more?"

"I'm trying—" Bashir broke off, stabbed at the console as the lines wavered and began to fade. "I'm at maximum now. . . ."

"Helios is underway," Möhrlein said.

"She'll have shields up in less than a minute," Tama said.

In the main screen and in his own smaller readout, the massive ship swung on its long axis, turning its torn side away from the oncoming Cardassians. The solar face turned toward the invisible wormhole, as though searching for its source.

"Dukat," Sisko said, "I warn you—" He broke off. "Transport him now, Major."

"I don't have him," Kira protested. "I'm not sure—"

"Do it, Kira," Sisko said. "There's no more time."

The Bajoran took a deep breath, and slapped her hand over the light bars, drawing them down into the energize position. The beam flared briefly, empty. Kira's mobile face contorted, and she touched more keys, slaving the transporter signal to the main sensors, then tried again. It was a risky maneuver, Bashir knew, even with Starfleet equipment, and he reached for his controls to try to help. The sensors were designed to provide a different input, and using them to direct the transporter beam risked scrambling its signal, but there was no choice, no other chance of rescuing O'Brien. . . . The transporter hummed, its beam thickening to a brilliant swirl of light, far brighter than the new systems aboard DS9. A shadow appeared, a kneeling man, and Kira gave a little cry of satisfaction. Then it flickered out again, and Bashir swore, numbed by the sudden sense of failure.

"Bashir!" Kira cried.

"Reverse the field," he said, and held his breath. That was even more dangerous than slaving the transporter to the sensors, a last resort, used only when there was no other chance of retrieving the pattern.

"Reversing," Kira said, and her voice betrayed the same fear and incipient despair.

The transporter hum deepened, the light seeming to thicken momentarily, and then the kneeling man reappeared. The shape hung for a second between solidity and translucence, and then, with shocking suddenness, took full form. O'Brien knelt on the pad, hands outstretched as though to something on the platform in front of him. He looked around, visibly taking in his surroundings, and Bashir saw him draw a deep breath.

"Bloody rough ride," he said at last, and his tone was less certain than his words. "You left that to the last minute, sir."

Sisko smiled, his own relief an almost painful lightness in his chest. "We'll try to do better next time, Chief." He turned back to the main console. "Möhrlein, get us out of here."

"Sir," the smuggler acknowledged. "Returning to the station."

"Whatever your top speed is," Sisko said. "Use it."

Out of the corner of his eye, he saw Möhrlein nod, but his own attention was fixed on the scene unrolling in the main viewscreen. *Helios* had turned fully, presenting its least damaged flank to the oncoming Cardassians; even as Sisko watched, the lead Cardassian ship fired, and he saw the phaser bolts blaze against the stars before dissipating in a blue flash of Cherenkov radiation.

"They've got their shields back," Tama said, unnecessarily.

Sisko touched his controls, throwing a tactical grid and projected-course lines across the onscreen images. "They're running for the wormhole," he said, as much to himself as to the others. Gul Dukat had seen it, too: in the screen, the Cardassian ships fanned out, trying to drive the bigger ship away from the approach to the wormhole—and back toward the station. "Möhrlein, how long to get to DS9?"

"Forty minutes," the smuggler answered, and Sisko could hear the strain in his voice. "And I'm at maximum now."

"Let me see what I can do," O'Brien said. Sisko glanced at him, and somehow the engineer achieved a grin. "Hell, sir, I've been practicing on stranger equipment all day."

"Do it, Chief," Sisko ordered.

Bashir relinquished his place at the technical console, and O'Brien stooped over the controls, his hands working even before he sat down.

"The Cardassians are firing again," Möhrlein said.

Sisko saw the lights flare in the viewer, saw the answering blue flash as the bolts struck *Helios*'s shields. The big ship seemed to ignore them, plunging on as though nothing had happened—but the shields had to be feeling the strain, Sisko thought. Not even Helios could take that kind of punishment for very long—and why didn't Kolovzon return fire? Had his phasers been out of service all along, and all his threats nothing but a bluff? Light flared suddenly on the screen, bright enough to make him blink: *Helios* had finally returned fire. The lead Cardassian ship seemed to stagger briefly, yawing away from the bolts before returning to its original course.

"Their shields are holding," Tama reported. "But they're at forty percent over the starboard quarter."

Helios swept on, ignoring its enemy's vulnerability, fired at the second ship without effect, and kept going. *Why?* Sisko demanded silently. *Why not finish them off—* The tactical grid held the answer, and he swore under his breath. *Helios* was driving for the wormhole, but the Cardassians were pushing her inexorably off the direct course.

"I've got it," O'Brien said, from the technician's station. "I can bypass the transformer, that'll double our power output. It'll be a rough ride, but we'll be back at DS9 in twenty minutes—or maybe less."

"If it doesn't blow the entire system," Möhrlein protested. "And my internal compensators, not to mention destabilize every control surface I've got."

"You mean you can't handle it?" O'Brien asked, and Möhrlein's lips thinned.

"Anything you can rig, I can fly—engineer."

"Do it," Sisko said.

"Strap in," Möhrlein said. He looked at Sisko then, mouth curving into a gambler's smile. "Like the man said, it's going to be rough."

Sisko reached for his own safety webbing, the heavy, archaic grey synthistel, and drew it tight across his body. Behind him, he heard the rustling as the others did the same, and then O'Brien said, "The bypass is ready, sir."

"Ready here," Möhrlein said, and sounded grim.

Sisko glanced for a final time at the tactical grids, at the warships sliding smoothly across the stars, and nodded. "Do it, Chief."

The lurch of acceleration flung him back in his couch, tugged painfully at heart and guts before the gravitics reasserted control. He risked a glance sideways, and saw Möhrlein's teeth bared in a grin that was more like the snarl of a corpse. O'Brien braced himself against his console, pushing himself away from the panel with one strong arm while he adjusted the controls with his free hand. At his side, Tama pushed himself back into his chair, tightening his safety web with shaking hands. Blood showed at the corner of his mouth where his head had hit the console. Bashir started to go to him, loosening his own webbing, but the smuggler waved him back as *Carabas* lurched again.

It was a ride Sisko would never forget. The ship lurched and seemed to skid as the gravitic compensators tried and failed fully to match the increased acceleration, and the ship's controls alternately held and slewed wildly. It was like being on a roller coaster, Sisko thought, clinging to the sides of his console, but a roller coaster that moved in three dimensions, not two. He heard Kira whoop wordlessly— she seemed almost to be enjoying the mad ride—and Odo snarled something in answer.

"And will we be able to dock under these conditions?"

Sisko looked at Möhrlein, who shrugged, his hands never moving from his controls. "If we get there in one piece, they can tractor us in. If the deflectors are down."

Sisko looked at the tactical display, at the ships now locked in roiling battle, and at DS9 still out of the worst of the danger zone. If everything held, he thought, if it all held together, they would survive—*if.*

"Come on," Möhrlein muttered, under his breath, hands white-knuckled on his console, "Come on, don't fall apart on me now."

Sisko reached for the communications console, his grasp

uncertain in the shifting gravity, but on the second try opened the channel to DS9. *"Carabas* to *Deep Space Nine.* Come in, Dax."

"Benjamin!" Dax's voice was sharp with alarm. "Commander, your course is very erratic—"

"I know," Sisko answered, and was shaken with the desire to laugh aloud. Erratic was hardly strong enough a word for what he was feeling. "We're coming up on the station. Can you take us aboard?"

There was a brief pause before Dax answered. "We're at red alert, Commander. Can you give me a definite approach vector? And velocity?"

"No. You'll have to bring us in by tractor," Sisko said.

"Very well," Dax said, and her voice sounded momentarily less certain than her words. "Stand by."

"Standing by," Sisko answered, and relaxed, letting the uncertain gravity pull him back against the couch's padding. He had done everything he could; the rest was up to Dax.

Dax frowned at the readouts streaming across her screen, looked up a final time at the display filling the main viewer. *Carabas*'s course was a red line—a broad red line, compensating for the unstable progress—aimed at the station; beyond it, a tangle of gold lines tipped by wedges marked the ongoing pursuit. She spared that only the slightest glance—*Helios* was slowly gaining on her pursuers, struggling toward the wormhole—and turned her attention to *Carabas*. The little ship was coming in at too high a velocity, and under imperfect control: hard to catch effectively in the clumsy tractor, even harder to catch safely, so that the shock of mismatched velocities didn't override the already stressed compensators and turn her passengers to jelly. And yet, if they slowed down, the shields would have to be lowered for an even longer period—and that was an unacceptable risk to the station.

She scowled at the uncompromising numbers, her mind racing. Keep the same velocity, but somehow make sure that the shock of the tractor's "catch" didn't override *Carabas*'s compensators . . . *All right,* she thought, *if* Carabas's *relative velocity has to remain the same, can I make the tractor relatively "quicker," closer to* Carabas's *apparent speed— make it somehow elastic, so that it gives with the ship's pull, countering its velocity that way?* There was something she had read before, years before, in another lifetime, another host . . . Her frown cleared, and she keyed in the name, the references, praying that the station's library computer would have the article she had so suddenly remembered. She held her breath as the screen went blank, and then cleared. The equations lay before her, the solution in black and white. She suppressed the desire to shout her elation, and turned to the communications screen.

"Dax to *Carabas.*"

"Sisko here."

"We can take you aboard by tractor," Dax said, and this time didn't bother to hide her smile.

In the screen, Sisko frowned. "What about the deflectors? The station's safety—"

"Is my first priority, Benjamin," Dax cut in. "The screens will be down for the minimum possible time, well within acceptable limits. We're going to use Ballanca's equations."

Sisko frowned. "I don't think I'm familiar with that, Dax."

"Bloody hell," O'Brien whispered, behind him, and Sisko felt a sudden twinge of uncertainty.

"It's a way of making the tractor beam behave as though it were elastic," Dax said. "In effect, it will 'stretch' a little as it takes you in tow, damping out the shock of matching velocities."

"I hope you've worked this out right, Dax," Sisko said.

There was no other choice, and he knew it, but it wasn't a particularly pleasant prospect.

"So do I," Dax answered, with a little smile. "My calculations show you'll reach the optimum point for pick-up in two minutes. Please confirm."

Sisko looked at Möhrlein, who nodded.

"I confirm that, Dax," Sisko said.

"Then stand by for pickup in two minutes," Dax said. *"Deep Space Nine* out."

Sisko took a deep breath. "All right, people, check your safety webbing now. This is likely to be very rough."

He heard the murmur of acknowledgment, and then the rustle of movement, barely audible over the moan of the engines, as the others obeyed his order. He dragged his own webbing tight again, grateful for its firm embrace, and a set of numbers flared in his screen: Möhrlein had set a count-down running. He made himself take slow, deep breaths as the numbers clicked down, and, as the last second ticked away, lifted his voice to carry to the full compartment. "All right, people, hang on—"

His last word was snatched away in the sudden impact as the tractor beam struck the ship. *Carabas*'s engines whined, and the ship yawed against the beam, threatening to tumble out of control as the tractor momentarily overrode the control surfaces. Möhrlein, white-faced, white-knuckled, struggled to bring the ship back into its proper alignment, and Sisko lunged forward and sideways against the safety netting, adding his input to the system. *Carabas* lurched again, the gravity surged and dropped sickeningly, and then, quite suddenly, the ship steadied.

"Carabas," Dax's deceptively placid voice said from the main screen, "we have you in tow. Stand by to come aboard."

It took less than three minutes to bring the ship the rest of the way into the docking port, but Sisko did not relax until the airlock had closed over the ship. He wrestled himself free of the safety netting, calling, "Dax, raise the deflectors. I'm on my way to Ops."

"What about shutdown?" O'Brien protested, and Sisko shook his head.

"Leave it—let Möhrlein handle it, it's his ship. We're needed in Ops, all of you."

The hatch was already open, and he charged through, his officers close on his heels. They made it to Ops in record time—ever afterward, Sisko wished they had recorded their progress—and he burst from the turbolift to see his crew staring openmouthed at the viewscreen. In its darkness, *Helios* hung at bay, slewed round at last to face the pursuing Cardassians, the solar face, now stained with the scoring of a direct, shield-piercing phaser blast, glaring down at them.

"Benjamin—" Dax exclaimed, and stopped, biting off her instinctive cry of relief and welcome, replacing it with the practical response of a Starfleet officer. "They're right at the wormhole, sir, but they're losing power."

"Helios?" Sisko asked, and the Trill nodded.

"Our sensors report they've lost aft shields, and forward deflectors are down by thirty percent."

Light flared in the screen, brilliant, blinding, a light Sisko had seen only in training, the killing glare of a full phaser barrage, every battery on *Helios* firing in a single massed pattern. Sisko lifted his hand to his eyes, and the screen went momentarily white as the visible-light sensors struggled to compensate. The brilliance faded slightly, and Sisko, blinking through the clouds that blurred his vision, saw the first of the Cardassians swinging out of control, away from its proper course. Its hull was dark, only the emergency lights flickering across its hull.

"We're picking up a distress signal from *Vindicator*," a technician said.

Sisko grinned. "She's swinging across the cruiser's course

—oh, that was nice shooting." He remembered then who he was praising, and was silent, but the unregenerate starship commander in him cheered at the Cardassians' defeat.

And then the wormhole opened, blue disk roiling out into space, the shaft of light at its center beckoning *Helios* onward. The ship swung again, accelerating into that brilliance. The remaining Cardassians fired again, but the cruiser's fire fell short, blocked by the need to avoid the damaged frigate. The second frigate scored one, perhaps two hits, and then *Helios* had vanished, absorbed into the light, and the wormhole had started to close, spiraling back in to cover and conceal its course.

"The Cardassians have lost their sensor suite," Dax reported. "They're not going to be able to pursue."

Obviously Kolovzon's intention, with that last barrage, Sisko thought. *A clever move, maybe even brilliant.* He said, "Could *Helios* have survived the passage through the wormhole?"

Dax shook her head, and turned away from her console. "They'd taken a lot of damage, Benjamin. And they weren't in good shape to start. The stresses—they were starting to break up as they went into the wormhole, but there's no way to tell for certain."

Sisko nodded slowly. "Stand down from red alert."

"Sir," Kira said, and Sisko rejoiced inwardly to hear her familiar voice. "Sir, the Cardassian cruiser is hailing us."

"Put it on the main viewer," Sisko said.

Gul Dukat's face glared down at him, technicians scuttling back and forth in the background, and Sisko hid another grin. Clearly, *Helios* had done her fair share of damage.

"Commander Sisko," Dukat said. "I warn you, my government will consider your behavior an act of direct aggression—"

"Hold it, Dukat," Sisko said. "You were warned that I had staff being held prisoner on that ship, and that I would do whatever was necessary to get my people off in one piece." He allowed his real anger to show for the first time. "And you did nothing whatever to protect them, or this station— and yet you were still unable to carry out your government's orders."

"Your interference," Dukat began, and Sisko's temper finally broke.

"We did not interfere with anything, Dukat. The only interference here has been yours—your egregious violation of Bajoran sovereignty, not to mention your callous disregard for the safety of the people aboard this space station. I suggest that you and your fleet depart Federation space immediately—or as soon as you're able to get under way— before your presence causes further diplomatic repercussions." In the screen, Dukat's mouth opened and closed twice without sound, like a fish feeding, but Sisko swept on without waiting for an answer. "Now, Dukat. Sisko out."

He gestured for Kira to cut the connection, and the picture vanished, to be replaced with the image of the three ships hanging against the starscape and the invisible wormhole. The lead frigate—*Vindicator*—was still drifting, distress lights now flaring along her sides.

"The cruiser is changing course," Dax reported, after a moment. "She's heading for the border, Commander. And the other frigate is taking *Vindicator* in tow."

Sisko nodded. "Good. After all that, I'd've hated to have to offer assistance."

Dax smiled back at him, and he heard a chuckle, quickly suppressed, from Kira. Sisko squelched his own feeling of triumph—it was too soon, there was still too much to do, to indulge himself yet—and turned to Dax. "What's our general status, Lieutenant?"

Dax bent over her console. "Running diagnostics now, sir. Everything seems to be in order—" She broke off abruptly, fingers stabbing at her controls. "Sir, docking port five is open, and *Carabas* is no longer in the bay."

"Find it," Sisko ordered.

"Scanning now," Dax answered. A moment later, she looked up again, unsuccessfully struggling to hide a smile. "Commander, I have the ship on sensors. It's heading out of the Bajor system at top impulse power."

Sisko heard a soft noise behind him, and turned to see Odo glaring at the screen. "Constable?"

"They were under arrest, Commander," Odo said, through clenched teeth. "Sir, I must put myself on report for carelessness. I should have stayed behind, made sure they did not escape."

Sisko shook his head. "There were other things going on, Odo. You had other concerns."

"Nevertheless," Odo began, and Sisko held up his hand.

"Don't worry about it, Constable. Considering all the help they gave us, getting Kira and O'Brien back, it would have been a little awkward to see them go to jail—I would have felt obliged to act as a character witness, which might have been embarrassing."

Odo gave him an odd look, disapproval and agreement mingled. "Indeed it might."

Sisko grinned, and looked around the operations center as though he were seeing it for the first time. The station was safe, his people, his family and crew, all safely restored to their proper places. He took a deep breath, savoring his victory, and then his eye fell on a datapadd abandoned on the operations table. He picked it up, scanned it idly, and then more carefully as its import sank in. It was a list of minor systems failures and necessary repairs that had been reported since the crisis began. Over a dozen items, Sisko thought, and it was almost certainly still growing.

"O'Brien," he said, "I think you'd better get onto these."
He held out the datapadd, and O'Brien took it, a look of
resignation settling onto his round features.

"Aye, sir."

"But do it tomorrow," Sisko said, and headed up the
stairs to his office. "It's good to be home."

About the Author

Melissa Scott was born and raised in Arkansas, and holds degrees from Harvard College and Brandeis University. She is also the author of *Trouble and Her Friends, Burning Bright, Dreamships,* and eight other science fiction novels, as well as the forthcoming fantasy *Point of Hopes,* written with Lisa A. Barnett.